THE TRIO OF NEWCOMERS CAME OUT FIRING.
BUT NOT AT THE *ENTERPRISE.*

Flattened dull gray hulls with scalloped flanks featured triple-engine nacelles mounted underneath the convex main body of each starship. Varying only a little in size from one another, each massed slightly less than the watching Federation vessel. It was impossible to tell from looking at them if the simple, unnecessarily streamlined design was the result of a different engineering approach or alien aesthetics. At first glance, the basic shape and construction implied a lower grade of technology than that possessed by the Federation.

There was nothing primitive about the weaponry they unleashed on the Perenorean colony ship, though. Loosed from three different sources, energy weapons and explosive projectiles clawed at the larger alien vessel's shields, filling empty space with fire, disruption, and an unbridled eagerness to destroy.

"This is an uneven fight if I ever saw one!" Stepping forward, McCoy placed a hand on the back of the command chair and leaned close to Kirk. "Jim, you've got to do something! *We've* got to do something!"

STAR TREK®

THE UNSETTLING STARS

ALAN DEAN FOSTER

BASED ON *STAR TREK*
CREATED BY GENE RODDENBERRY

GALLERY BOOKS
NEW YORK   LONDON   TORONTO   SYDNEY   NEW DELHI

Gallery Books
An Imprint of Simon & Schuster, Inc.
1230 Avenue of the Americas
New York, NY 10020

First Gallery Books trade paperback edition April 2020

GALLERY BOOKS and colophon are registered trademarks of Simon & Schuster, Inc.

For information about special discounts for bulk purchases, please contact Simon & Schuster Special Sales at 1-866-506-1949 or business@simonandschuster.com.

The Simon & Schuster Speakers Bureau can bring authors to your live event. For more information or to book an event, contact the Simon & Schuster Speakers Bureau at 1-866-248-3049 or visit our website at www.simonspeakers.com.

Manufactured in the United States of America

10 9 8 7 6 5 4 3 2 1

Library of Congress Cataloging-in-Publication Data

Names: Foster, Alan Dean, 1946– author. | Roddenberry, Gene, other.
Title: The unsettling stars / Alan Dean Foster ; based on Star Trek created
    by Gene Roddenberry.
Other titles: At head of title: Star Trek
Description: First Gallery Books trade paperback edition. | New York :
    Gallery Books, 2020. | Series: Star trek
Identifiers: LCCN 2019054440 (print) | LCCN 2019054441 (ebook) | ISBN
    9781982140601 (trade paperback) | ISBN 9781982140618 (ebook)
Subjects: GSAFD: Science fiction.
Classification: LCC PS3556.O756 U57 2020 (print) | LCC PS3556.O756
    (ebook) | DDC 813/.54—dc23
LC record available at https://lccn.loc.gov/2019054440
LC ebook record available at https://lccn.loc.gov/2019054441

ISBN 978-1-9821-4060-1
ISBN 978-1-9821-4061-8 (ebook)

HISTORIAN'S NOTE

This story takes place in an alternate timeline created in 2233, when the *Starship Kelvin* was destroyed by a Romulan invader from the future (as seen in the 2009 film *Star Trek*). The main events in this story take place after Stardate 2258.42, when a new captain and an inexperienced crew took a repaired *U.S.S. Enterprise* out of spacedock for a simple shakedown cruise.

STAR TREK®

THE UNSETTLING STARS

1

'm having some difficulty decoding the content precisely, Captain," Lieutenant Nyota Uhura said. "It's being broadcast in dozens of different languages and codes. Some of it is pretty amateurish—but it's definitely a distress call."

From his position at the science console on the wall to the left of the commander's station, First Officer Spock turned his slender frame to where a very young and still comparatively untried Captain James T. Kirk sat in the command chair. "I concur, Captain. The parameters are new but the basics unmistakable. A distress signal."

Restraining her emotions, Uhura continued her report without turning from her console on the opposite side of the bridge from Spock. "As near as I can make out, it's a universal appeal, Captain. Whoever is doing the sending, they're asking for help from anybody."

"And very loudly." Spock lingered over one particular read-out. "The signal is remarkably strong and consistent."

Slightly slumped in the command seat, Kirk absorbed the information provided by his crew and silently pondered. Seated at the helm and navigation in front of him, Sulu and Chekov awaited orders. The *Enterprise* was still on her shakedown cruise, a routine exploration of a little-visited corner of the Federation. Or at least as routine as it could be considering that the majority of the crew had been promoted into their current positions in haste, handmaidens of circumstance. He knew perfectly well that, despite their recent achievement in dealing with the threat posed by a certain renegade time-traveling Romulan, there was ongoing discussion at the upper levels of Starfleet as to whether or not their battlefield promotions should be made permanent or rescinded. As a result of the successful resolution to the Nero confrontation, more than a few members of the *Enterprise* had jumped the promotional queue. As had been true throughout history, the dogs of envy and resentment were forever nipping at the heels of the successful.

That was the nature of battlefield promotions, he knew. As far as he was concerned, everyone on the ship who had re-ceived one deserved it. There was no false pride in feeling that he certainly deserved *his own*. Sitting up straighter in the chair, Kirk sighed heavily. You could destroy an enemy with an array of phasers. You could overwhelm his shields with a barrage of precisely placed photon torpedoes. Neither weapon was effec-tive against envy.

Everyone on board was aware of this state of affairs. Despite their accomplishments, their individual positions and ranks were precarious. One serious mistake, one collective slipup, and the whole range of promotions could be withdrawn as swiftly as they had been bestowed. There was even the possibility of field-demoted officers being sent back to the Academy for additional training. Kirk shivered at the prospect.

While he enjoyed the ancillary social benefits of the Academy, Kirk considered himself finished with studies. *This* was where he belonged. Not in a classroom but out in deep space, in command of a starship and its crew. Having survived everything Nero had thrown at them, every member of the crew had looked forward to what Christopher Pike referred to as their "delayed shakedown." This voyage offered an opportunity for everyone to settle into their respective assignments, to familiarize themselves with the intricacies and eccentricities of the ship, to get to know their shipmates, to work hard at and continue to master their specialties, and to do so without interruption or interference. Except . . .

Now this.

Spock could not read Kirk's thoughts, but he could see that the captain was vacillating. He did not believe that Kirk was afraid of making a wrong decision. Left to his own devices, the inexperienced captain would immediately have acknowledged the distress call and ordered the relevant course change. Except now that Kirk was responsible for an entire ship, its crew, and everyone's professional future, he was hesitating.

The science officer felt that this was an encouraging development.

Pavel Chekov spoke up from his seat at navigation. "Captain, utilizing the communications data, I have traced the source of the signal to the Marr-i-nul system."

"Uninhabited, Captain." Spock provided the information without having to be asked. "And unclaimed. It lies just outside Federation boundaries and distant from even the usual extravagant Klingon maps. Neutral territory."

Kirk muttered something unintelligible before commenting. "It's also near enough that we could get there quickly and size the situation up without deviating radically from our course."

Spock raised an eyebrow. "I am compelled to point out, Captain, that insofar as Lieutenant Uhura has been able to determine, the distress signal is not typically issued of a Federation or allied vessel. As we are engaged in what originally was intended to be our shakedown cruise, Starfleet could see it as presumptuous of us to intervene—however altruistic the motive."

A new voice sounded on the bridge. "How did I know you were going to say that?"

The science officer glanced in the direction of the oncoming sarcasm. "I do not know, Doctor. Perhaps in the considerable leisure time you have enjoyed since our departure from Earth, you have finally mastered the ability to predict the future."

Leonard McCoy eyed him sourly, mumbling to the captain, "If I *was* going to probe another sentient's mind, it wouldn't be . . ."

"I predict you're both going to be quiet for a moment," Kirk declared, just forcefully enough that both officers looked embarrassed. It went silent on the bridge while he ruminated a moment longer. Then he looked to his right and spoke firmly. "Mister Chekov, set a course for the Marr-i-nul system. Stand by to go to warp factor eight. Mister Sulu, when we drop out of warp, I want shields up and phasers on standby."

"Aye, sir." The lieutenants hurried to make the requested preparations.

Doctor McCoy had moved over to stand behind and to one side of the command chair. "You sure you know what you're doing, Jim?"

Kirk turned to frown at his friend. "I had the impression you wanted us to check out this signal."

"I do." The doctor smiled affably. "I'm just practicing the query because I 'predict' that I'm going to have opportunities to use it a lot."

Having risen from his seat at the science station, Spock walked over to join them. "Captain, I must point out that given the specifics of our mission, we are not authorized to intervene in a distress situation that does not involve Federation citizens or property. This is plainly a hastily composed distress call, and one that is being propagated from outside Federation boundaries." He eyed McCoy, who glared back but said nothing. "In my ongoing and apparently never-ending research into the arcane dimensions of human metaphor, it might be called 'sticking one's nose into someone else's business.'"

Kirk inclined his head slightly. "Mister Spock, I bow to your growing familiarity with human language. However, we're still going to try and find out what's going on in the Marr-i-nul system."

For a second time in the past few moments, an eyebrow rose slightly. "Rationale—for the record, sir?"

Kirk nodded. "For the record, as captain I consider sticking my nose into someone else's business part of my job description." Returning his gaze forward, he raised his voice. "Mister Sulu, warp factor eight."

The *Enterprise* immediately leaped forward at many multiples of the speed of light.

Behind Kirk, McCoy repressed a grin as he murmured, "A captain is allowed to use his discretion, isn't he, Mister Spock?"

"That is so, Doctor. Unfortunately, in my limited experience 'discretion' is a term I have yet to learn how to apply to James Kirk."

The massive alien ship sat in a high orbit around the second of three large moons that traveled in majestic procession around a gas giant twice the size of Jupiter. Its design was functional and unlovely. From the base of six joined spheres arrayed around a central locus, half a dozen huge conduits tapered to the point where the enormous warp engines were located.

Appearances, however, proved deceiving.

"Science, report." Kirk stared intently at the image

hovering forward of his position. While notably larger than the *Enterprise*, the appearance and design of the peculiar alien vessel seemed to hold none of the *Narada*'s menace. Externally it was almost featureless.

"Type unknown, Captain." Spock's full attention was directed to the science station's readouts. "Origin unknown. While presently putting forth a minimal amount of power, there are indications that the vessel is capable of generating a good deal more energy than it is presently deploying. As alien aesthetics are of course unpredictable, at first glance the design would appear to be an interesting amalgamation of the advanced and the purely utilitarian."

Kirk indicated his agreement. "Straightforward and functional." He looked to his right. "Mister Sulu?"

The lieutenant was assiduously scrutinizing his readouts. "They have shields up, Captain. The energy signature of their defenses is unique. Ever since our arrival I've been trying to get an analytical handle on the subatomic structure of their defensive deployment, and so far it defies the norms. The vessel appears to be maintaining considerably more powerful shields than the *Enterprise* while utilizing a good deal less energy to do so."

"Fascinating," was the single responding observation.

Kirk did not have to look around to identify the source of the one-word commentary.

"Never mind the shields," muttered McCoy. "What about their weapons? And if they have them, where are they pointed?"

"Not at us." Sulu's fingers manipulated the controls in front of him swiftly and assuredly. "Other than the fact that they have shields raised, I can detect no hint of antagonism." He calmly added, "We also have our shields raised, and phasers on standby."

"So everyone's being careful. Fair enough." Kirk turned his head slightly. "Lieutenant Uhura, are we certain this is the source of the distress signal you picked up?"

"It's not just the distress signal any longer, Captain. They started hailing us the moment we arrived. I've been running through thousands of possible variations on record, but as yet it's a mess of unidentified codecs. I just about have it narrowed down." She fingered several contacts. "I think I've got it now." Together with everyone else on the bridge, she gazed expectantly in the direction of the main forward viewer.

Tension gripped each member of the young crew. The last time they had dealt with an unpredictable and unknown communication, it had originated from a ship whose commander had declared his intent to destroy the entire Federation. Though like the now-destroyed *Narada* this strange vessel was also of unknown origin, unlike the Romulan craft it had made no hostile gestures in their direction. That did not lead to a lessening of caution on board the *Enterprise*. Everyone was well aware that a distress signal could be a ploy, a lure to coax unsuspecting good Samaritans to a waiting doom. Hence the captain's well-considered decision to energize phasers and approach the unknown supplicant with shields up.

A human from an earlier, more naïve age would have been disarmed and reassured by the first sight of the creature that finally appeared on the viewscreen. Present-day explorers, however, did not suffer from the distractions proffered by seemingly innocent visuals. The old saying that appearances could be deceiving held true as much in deep space as it had when humanity had been confined to a single planet. What a sentient looked like had nothing to do with how it might act, nor what the social and cultural underpinnings of its civilization were, or its potential reactions to the presence of others different from its own kind. Something that looked benign could hail from a society founded on periodic orgies of communal homicide, whereas a giant fanged arthropod might be interested only in the peaceful advancement of mutually beneficial commerce and cultural exchange.

The being that gazed back at Kirk was comfortingly bipedal and bisymmetrical; it appeared to stand a good head shorter than the average human. It was slight and smooth of build, with double-jointed arms and legs that doubtless allowed for great flexibility of movement. There were seven similarly double-jointed fingers on each hand. Instead of keratinous claws or nails, each digit terminated in a soft spatulate pad lined with close-set parallel ridges. The face was angular, with large rectangular ears that swept backward and flexed perpendicular to the side of the skull when listening intently. There were no visible nostrils, though Spock theorized that a slightly prehensile fleshy organ dangling from each ear might possibly perform a similar function. The mouth was small, round, and lipless. Opposing horny plates took the place of teeth. Oversized eyes that peered out of the flat face featured slitted gold-hued pupils set in startlingly bright-yellow sclera.

The alien was clad in a single spiraling strip of muted material tinted shades of brown and ochre that appeared to have been wound around its body rather than slipped on. Where it was not covered by clothing, there was revealed thick beige centimeter-long fur that had been trimmed and shaved into intricate patterns. When the creature shifted its stance, iridescent highlights shimmered within its pelt.

It was not exactly cute, Uhura decided as she joined the others on the bridge in contemplating this newly contacted species. The angular skull mitigated against that. But its outward appearance was certainly anything but threatening.

It was left to McCoy to voice what everyone was thinking. "Goo-goo eyes or not, whatever that thing is, it represents a species capable of building a mighty impressive starship protected by powerful shields of an unknown type. Maybe they have equally powerful weapons."

"I find myself in agreement, Doctor." As he spoke, Spock was directing his attention to the captain. "Distress signal and unthreatening physical appearance notwithstanding, we should proceed with caution."

"When have you ever known me to do otherwise?" Kirk replied without irony. Leaning forward, he addressed himself to the alien on the viewscreen. "I am Captain James T. Kirk commanding the United Federation of Planets *Starship Enterprise*. We received your distress signal." He glanced over at Spock, then back at the alien. "Have we interpreted the context of your transmission correctly, and if so, what is the nature of your emergency?"

There was a pause as relevant instrumentation on both the *Enterprise* and the alien vessel strove to analyze and organize the linguistics necessary to allow for face-to-face, as opposed to machine-to-machine, conversation. Chekov leaned toward Sulu and lowered his voice. "Is it just me or does there seem to be a great deal of activity taking place on their bridge?"

"I've noticed it too." The helmsman was trying to divide his attention between his readouts and the fascinating alien. "The background blurring suggests additional figures moving rapidly. It would be nice to know what they're in such a hurry about."

"Hopefully not arming weapons," Chekov commented darkly.

Sulu was openly doubtful. "Sensors indicate that they're not doing anything other than maintaining their present position. There's no change in energy output. I have a feeling that this species doesn't pose any danger."

"Yes, tell the captain that you have a 'feeling' about it. I'm sure he'll order you to drop our shields."

The alien's response seemed as hurried as the movements of his fellow beings behind him. That it was indeed a "him" who was responding was confirmed by Uhura's semantics algorithms.

"*I am Taell, Leaderesque of the colony ship* Eparthaa *of the Perenorean Outreach. On a journey to settle a new and uninhabited world that was revealed by one of our deep-space probes, we were thrown off course by an unprecedented combination of mechanical problems and navigation errors. Damage was sufficiently extensive that we were unable to resume our original intended flow. Fuel and engineering limitations prevent us from returning home.*

"While striving to find a suitable world on which to settle within the much-reduced range of our ship, we subsequently found ourselves brutally attacked and without warning. Our assailants gave us no opportunity to elaborate upon our wholly peaceful intentions. As a result, we have been fleeing and defending ourselves ever since."

As the biped suddenly muted the sound, he glanced behind himself without turning his body. McCoy carefully whispered, "He's like an owl." Everyone on the bridge of the *Enterprise* had noticed that this new species was able to rotate their heads almost a full hundred and eighty degrees on their short necks.

The alien resumed communications. *"Though it may at first appear otherwise, our ship has been seriously damaged and we have suffered casualties. We are transporting a full colonial compliment of several thousand individuals, including reproductive females and subadults. Though we possess some limited defensive capability, the* Eparthaa *is not a warship and repeated assaults have left us hard-pressed to maintain its structural integrity. Hence the desperate broadcasting of our omnidirectional distress call. We do not know you and you do not know us, but we appeal to you as fellow peaceful sentients. Will you help us, Captain Kirk of the Federation?"*

Down in engineering, where the crew had been following the transmission, the chief engineer summarized the unexpected situation in his usual pithy fashion.

"By Wallace's bleedin' underwear!" Montgomery Scott turned to his first assistant. "Just what we need on a supposed shakedown mission—a request for help from a colony ship full of wee, sleekit, cowerin', timorous beasties!"

Assistant Engineer Lieutenant Arif Ben-Haim was gazing in fascination at the image on the screen. "They may be wee, and I don't have a clue what 'sleekit' is, but they don't look very cowering or timorous to me, Mister Scott." He gestured at a nearby readout. "I've seen their shields. Minimum power, maximum shields."

Scott harrumphed. "Well, if I know anything about our captain, we'll bloody well find out soon enough. Be ready for any sudden demands for power." As Ben-Haim turned to pass the word, the chief engineer continued to study the screen. "And somebody see if they can find where I left the last half of my sandwich!"

"Captain, these people have suffered damage and incurred injuries," said Spock. "You do have it within your purview to render assistance. However, if they have been attacked and may be again, then by offering assistance, you will place us in the position of appearing to be their allies. At the moment, we have only Leaderesque Taell's version of what may have transpired. We know nothing of his species or of his claimed assailants, nor what may have provoked conflict between them. He may be telling us the truth, or some version of it. It is imperative that we ascertain which he is telling us before we proceed. We should not place ourselves in a position where our actions might lead to a misinterpretation of the Federation's official position with regard to the Perenoreans or whoever may have assaulted them. For all we know, the Perenoreans may very well be the aggressors."

McCoy considered this before replying. "Maybe a visit to their vessel to see for ourselves the condition of wounded females and offspring might preempt the need for excessive diplomatic caution, Mister Spock."

Inured by now to the doctor's characteristic sarcasm, the science officer replied without rancor. "I agree that it would be a useful first step, Doctor. Visible evidence of aggression against palpable noncombatants could certainly serve to underscore the veracity of this Taell's narrative."

Sulu's eyes widened and his hands suddenly flew over his instrumentation as he leaned forward. "I think something else is going to take precedent over a ship-to-ship visit, Mister Spock." He looked back at Kirk. "We have incoming, Captain!"

2

"Shields on full!" Kirk shouted. "Red alert, arm photon torpedoes!"

Throughout the ship, meals were abandoned unfinished, conversations terminated in midsentence, and casual activities cast aside as the crew scrambled for battle stations. On the bridge, all attention remained focused on the forward viewscreen. The last image they had of the Perenorean leaderesque Taell showed him turning away from his own bridge's visual pickup, his fluid multijointed gestures increasingly rapid, an inescapable manifestation of panic spreading across his flattened, furry face.

His likeness was replaced by a far larger field of view supplied by Chekov, which revealed first one, then two, and finally three new vessels emerging from warp. Considerably smaller than the *Eparthaa*, they were equally alien in appearance, as different from the Perenorean vessel as the large craft was from the Starfleet ship.

The trio of newcomers came out firing. But not at the *Enterprise*.

Flattened dull gray hulls with scalloped flanks featured triple-engine nacelles mounted underneath the convex main body of each starship. Varying only a little in size from one another, each massed slightly less than the watching Federation vessel. It was impossible to tell from looking at them if the simple, unnecessarily streamlined design was the result of a different engineering approach or alien aesthetics. At first glance, the basic shape and construction implied a lower grade of technology than that possessed by the Federation.

There was nothing primitive about the weaponry they unleashed on the Perenorean colony ship, though. Loosed from three different sources, energy weapons and explosive projectiles clawed at the larger alien vessel's shields, filling empty space with fire, disruption, and an unbridled eagerness to destroy.

"This is an uneven fight if I ever saw one!" Stepping forward, McCoy placed a hand on the back of the command chair and leaned close to Kirk. "Jim, you've got to do something! *We've* got to do something!"

Spock ignored the fiery mayhem that now filled the viewscreen in favor of studying his readouts. "Despite the apparently overwhelming firepower being directed against them, the Perenorean shields appear to be holding." He glanced querulously in Sulu's direction. "Interesting that a self-declared colony ship would travel equipped with such extensive and advanced defensive capability."

"The Perenoreans are returning fire." Sulu's sensor read-outs confirmed what was sometimes difficult to discern on the viewscreen. "They're not just sitting and taking it. But their weapons capability doesn't appear to come close to matching their defensive technology."

"Or else they are diverting the majority of ship's power to their shields," Chekov reasonably pointed out. "In any case, based on what I am seeing here"—he indicated his instrumentation—"despite their initial achievement in resist-ing the attack, I do not see them holding out against such a concerted multipronged assault for very long."

"*Jim!*" McCoy was unrelenting.

Kirk ground his teeth. Instinct told him to open fire on behalf of the seemingly inoffensive alien colonists. Doing so would likely put the Perenoreans, and by inference their spe-cies and society, forever in the Federation's debt. Conversely, it would also make enemies of their present assailants. Experi-ence, as limited as it was, cautioned him against taking sides too impetuously in a conflict of whose origin and causation he was still ignorant.

The trouble was that, as usual, ongoing battlefield condi-tions did not allow for extended contemplation of alternatives.

"Captain, we're being hailed again." If not her words, Uhura's tone indicated that her sympathies lay wholly with Doctor McCoy. Kirk refused to be swayed.

"On-screen," he tensely ordered.

The face and upper body of Leaderesque Taell reappeared before them. Though his admirable surplus of facial expressions were alien and as yet uninterpretable, he communicated his anxiety efficiently via translation.

"Captain Kirk, I beg you—on behalf of our younglings if no other—please help us! We are not a warship. Our engines are nearing overload. We cannot withstand the concerted assault of the Dre'kalak for much longer! They will kill us all!"

Chekov looked askance toward the science station. "Dre'kalak?"

"Another unknown species." Searching swiftly through available information, Spock found nothing.

A moment later his search was rendered superfluous.

"Captain," Uhura announced, "we are being hailed by the nearest of the attacking vessels. Establishing communication will require a moment to sort and analyze syntax and verbalizations."

"Get it right, Lieutenant," Kirk told her. "We want to be sure everyone understands each other. In a situation like this, we don't have any room for misperception. Take your time."

"We have time, Jim," McCoy put in, "but I'm not so sure about the Perenoreans."

Once more confirming the multiplicity of honors she had received at the Academy, Uhura's response came sooner than anyone on the bridge dared hope. "Full comprehension is not perfect, Captain. Not as good as with the Perenoreans. The language of the Dre'kalak is rougher on enunciation, and their fundamental grammar is more complex. But I think we'll be able to understand each other."

"Then go ahead and acknowledge their hail, Lieutenant."

Once more the forward viewscreen cleared and an image formed. It was decidedly less attractive than those previously viewed.

Several other representatives of the speaker could be seen behind it. "It" because unlike with the Perenoreans, Uhura could not ascertain the sex of the individual communicating—or even if it was of a particular gender. For all she had been able to construe, its species might reproduce asexually.

From a rippling lump of gray-green flesh a trio of tentacles waved erratically. Three round lime-green eyes, each a different size (and perhaps evolved for individual and dissimilar functions), seemed to float untethered in the middle of the upper portion of the roughly cone-shaped body. There was no visible nose or ears, though a distinct cavity located near the crest of the body might have provided either function—or neither. The mouth was wide, narrow, and surrounded by a single contiguous rubbery lip. The creature's speech sounded like a series of painful groans, with which the *Enterprise*'s translation software and instrumentation struggled mightily.

"*Unknown vessel,*" the Dre'kalak rumbled. "*I am Podleader Ul-tond, squadron commanding! We of the Ultimate Circle are on critical hunt-and-destroy mission. Do not interfere with ongoing action! Repeat, do not interfere! Such actions will be regarded by the Circle as allying self with hated Perenoreans and kindle angry responding by full might of the squadron!*"

McCoy could barely contain his outrage. " 'Hunt and destroy'? Hunt and destroy what? Harmless colonists? Jim . . . ?"

Kirk addressed himself to the chair's pickup. "This is Captain James T. Kirk of the *Starship Enterprise*. Until now, both the Dre'kalak and the Perenoreans were unknown to us. As such, we are patently not a party to any disagreements that exist between your two species. However . . ."

Hearing that word, Spock braced himself.

The science officer was needlessly worrying. Kirk continued formally enough to make his Academy instructors in interspecies diplomacy proud. "It would serve to expand our knowledge of the situation and understanding of your apparent grievances if you could enlighten us as to why three ships of the Dre'kalak are attacking a single Perenorean ship, when the latter appears to be a vessel carrying colonists."

Responding immediately, the Dre'kalak podleader abruptly terminated the transmission. Kirk sharply swiveled around.

"Uhura? I didn't get a translation of that last part."

"Neither did I, Captain." The communications officer checked her displays. "Much of it was apparently too colloquial for the linguistics core upon which our initial exchange of verbalizations is based to interpret correctly."

"I can tell you what it consisted of." McCoy voiced confidence. "He—it—was saying 'Mind your own damn business.'" The doctor held resolutely to his position. "Well, Jim? What about it? *Are* we going to mind our own business?"

Kirk had less than a minute to think it over when his already churning thoughts were interrupted by another communication from the Perenorean ship. It was Taell again, bruised and unsteady this time, with extraordinarily dark blood trick-

ling from a gash on his forehead just above one of those luminescent slitted eyes.

*"Captain Kirk! Our shields are on the verge of failing! I plead
with you one last time, can you not . . . ?"*

The desperate transmission dissolved into static. Forward
of the command chair, Sulu looked back at his commander.
"Captain, sensors indicate that the Perenorean ship is losing
power. It is reasonable to assume that when it reaches a critical
point, they will lose their shielding entirely." He paused. "They
will be completely defenseless."

This time Kirk didn't hesitate. "Uhura, hail the leading
Dre'kalak vessel."

She complied. To those on the bridge, it seemed to take
forever before the image of the alien commander reappeared
on the main viewer. Kirk framed his communiqué carefully
even as he wondered if the inadequate translation algorithms
Uhura was employing would convey his mood and intent correctly and with sufficient force.

"Podleader Ul-tond! It is not the policy of the United Federation of Planets to interfere in disputes between nonallied
species."

"We of the Circle are glad to hear that," the Dre'kalak replied.

"However," Kirk continued as Spock winced ever so slightly,
"it *is* the policy of the Federation to step in when its assistance
is requested by those in clearly identifiable distress. The fact that
your people are apparently the source of that distress creates what
I must politely refer to as an awkward set of circumstances."

"I understand, though I do not sympathize with your rea-

soning, Captain Kirk." No doubt the Dre'kalak commander's viscous upper body allowed for a considerable range of expression, but if so, Kirk remained ignorant of what the alien movement signified. *"I restate the position of the Circle: This not your fight. Remain neutral, and all will be well."* The transmission cut off again.

Kirk turned. "Spock? Opinion?" The attention of everyone on the bridge shifted in the direction of the science officer.

For one of the few times in their admittedly brief time together, Spock appeared to hesitate. Though not for long.

"You have stated the formal Federation position clearly and concisely, Captain, to which stance I have nothing to add."

"Spock . . . ," an anxious McCoy began.

"However," the science officer continued, drawing a hint of a smile from his commanding officer, "as a member of a refugee race, I find that I am sufficiently conflicted to the point where I cannot say what I might do if our present positions were reversed."

Don't you wish, Kirk said, but only to himself. "Mister Sulu, Mister Chekov, stay sharp and be ready for anything. We want these Dre'kalak to see and understand that we're making preparations for more than just talk."

"Aye, Captain." Sulu's hands darted over his instrumentation as the *Enterprise* crew completed the shift to battle stations.

"Show of force without showing any force," said Chekov. "Little is risked with the possibility of much being gained. A knight's move."

"Forward or sideways?" Sulu commented. "A hundred

years before the establishment of the Shogunate, there was a battle three hundred clicks south of Edo that—"

"Please, no samurai stories now, Hikaru. Or I'll have to tell you how my great-great-great-great-grandfather Boris ended up as a model for one of the crowd in Repin's *Reply of the Zaporozhian Cossacks.*"

"Not *that* again." Sulu's attention was immediately diverted by other, more immediate concerns. "Captain, one of the Dre'kalak vessels is disengaging from the attack and heading for the *Enterprise.*"

"A hostile gesture." McCoy's voice dropped to a whisper. "Jim, we could open fire. Clearly you'd be in the right."

This time Kirk didn't look back at his friend. "Bones, don't you have work to do in sickbay? If we're going into a fight, there are liable to be casualties."

"Yes, you're right, Jim." Whirling, McCoy exited the bridge.

After tracking the doctor's departure, Uhura's attention shifted to Spock seated ready and ramrod straight at his station. She peered harder. Was that a hint of satisfaction on his face—or just a shift in the light? Her own instrumentation commanded her attention and she turned back to her console.

"The Dre'kalak are hailing us, Captain."

"Mister Sulu, Mister Chekov, be ready. Put them on, Lieutenant—after our detectable power-up they may still want to talk."

"They don't strike me as a particularly conversational species," Sulu muttered. At the captain's command, the *Enterprise* was ready to unleash destruction. The helmsman was tense but not nervous. Alongside him, the same resolve could be seen writ plain on Chekov's face.

The ship's shakedown cruise had morphed—they were being tested once again.

The alien's tone was as bellicose as before. But this time, there was something previously unheard underlying Ul-tond's anger. Kirk couldn't put his finger on it and Uhura's translation program offered no hint.

"*You appear to have prepared your ship for battle.*" The podleader framed his observation as a threat.

Kirk's expression remained neutral as he replied, "I compliment you on the sensitivity of your sensors."

"*You are unaware of the complexity of circumstances you have encountered,*" Ul-tond continued. "*Yet you are prepared to fight on behalf of those of whom you know nothing. You are ignorant of the danger posed by Perenoreans!*"

Spock could not contain himself. Or more likely, chose not to. Time and additional knowledge had brought a shift in his hitherto cautious thinking. "What danger does a single off-course and low-on-fuel ship full of colonists, including reproductive females and young offspring, pose to the Dre'kalak? Or for that matter, to anyone else?"

Plainly more comfortable with combat than conversation, Ul-tond struggled to formulate a reply. As he did so, a thin line of glistening white fluid dribbled from the lowest corner of his wide mouth. A consistent physiological phenomenon,

Spock wondered, or the Dre'kalak equivalent of a human sputtering?

"You do not understand! Perenoreans are dangerous species, fatally dangerous! Not knowing them, you cannot envision threat that they represent! Is beyond your imagining!"

Kirk allowed himself a small comfortable smile. "Try me."

"Are the Perenoreans an inherently hostile species?" Spock inquired of the Dre'kalak commander.

"No, but . . ."

Having already interrupted his captain, the science officer barreled forward. "Are they a people that has demonstrated a proclivity for war? For attacking others without provocation?"

"No." Ul-tond was beside himself. Almost literally, Kirk thought as he observed the alien commander's highly fluid physical contortions. *"The danger they present is— You do not understand!"*

"Can you enlighten us, then?" Kirk's calm tone was backed by an inviting grin. "Why don't we all stand down? Get together somewhere that's mutually agreeable. If the Dre'kalak have some long-standing grievance against the Perenoreans, we offer our services as mediators. We might be able to resolve the differences between you without any further hostilities."

Having made his offer, Kirk glanced toward the science station. *Why not?* Spock did not smile back, of course, but by way of response he did appear to nod ever so slightly.

As carefully and courteously as Kirk had framed the suggestion, it was just as swiftly rejected.

"You still do not understand, Captain Kirk of the Federation!

You cannot negotiate with Perenoreans. You cannot talk to them. Just talking with them can destroy you. You cannot 'resolve differences between' with only words. They must be obliterated!"

"Agreeable species, aren't they?" Chekov's expression was grim. Sulu did not respond. He suspected what was coming next.

And he was right.

The Dre'kalak commander's ship opened fire with every weapon in its arsenal. Waves of energy accompanied by ominous projectiles were dispatched simultaneously on an intercept course toward the *Enterprise*.

"Evasive action!" Kirk snapped. Sulu's and Chekov's fingers were already in motion before their captain's order had finished ringing in their ears.

The *Enterprise* lurched sharply as a rush of pallid amber light enveloped the ship. It was accompanied by a brief but unmistakable shuddering. This passed rapidly, followed by a series of detonations.

"An unknown energy weapon." Spock's attention was locked to the science console. "Powerful—but no match for our shields. It is the same for their equivalent of photon torpedoes."

"No reduction in shields' strength, Captain," Chekov reported.

Kirk's expression was set. "Let's see if the same holds true for theirs. Fire photon torpedoes, Mister Sulu. Standard spread."

Sulu complied. While both vessels remained in constant

motion and the Perenorean colony ship continued its desperate defense against the three Dre'kalak craft, a brace of torpedoes rocketed from the *Enterprise* to impact against the shields of its own assailant. The resulting blasts and brief flare momentarily obscured the target.

"Sensors detect a diminution in the protective energy field surrounding the Dre'kalak vessel." As he made the observation, Chekov expressed quiet satisfaction. "I would estimate a reduction in the neighborhood of one-third to one-half." He glanced back at the captain. "They are firing at us again."

"Respond in kind, Sulu," Kirk ordered. "Photon torpedoes and phasers this time."

Two more waves of amber energy flowed over the *Enterprise*. Some concussive damage was reported amidships, but her shields held and full hull integrity was maintained.

"Initial exchanges of fire and counterfire would seem to indicate that we are stronger than the Dre'kalak vessel is, Captain." Left to himself, Chekov would have unleashed everything in the *Enterprise*'s considerable armory. He awaited Kirk's order. Most significantly, at any moment the Dre'kalak commander might request aid from his flanking craft. Doing so, however, would leave one or more of them exposed to a counterattack from the Perenoreans. Given such a scenario, Chekov wondered, would the Perenoreans attack? Or provided with a temporary respite, would they take the opportunity to flee? That would leave the *Enterprise* to battle the trio of Dre'kalak warships alone. He voiced his concerns to Sulu.

"I believe I have an idea of what the captain is thinking, Hikaru."

"Do you, now? Your accelerated matriculation must have crammed in a lot of subjects. Command psychology as well as navigation?"

"It is not difficult to see. If you are correct in your battle-field assessment that the *Enterprise* is more powerful than the Dre'kalak flagship, then in a one-on-one fight we are likely to defeat it. If its commander requests assistance from the rest of his battle squadron, then it opens the possibility that the Pere-noreans may be able to retreat into warp space. Or in a con-sequent one-on-one fight, even defeat a Dre'kalak ship. Either way, if the Dre'kalak turn the majority of their attention to us, then they risk allowing those they really wish to destroy a chance to get away."

Chekov found one particular aspect of the battle puzzling: the inability of even one Dre'kalak warship, much less all three attacking in concert, to defeat the Perenorean colony ship.

"They are much better defended than a Federation colony ship would be," the ensign pointed out. "Based on what we have seen of Dre'kalak battle technology, it is surprising that the Perenorean shields have held up. And they continue to fight back with their limited weapons."

"They'd better." Sulu was studying his sensors. "Captain, a second Dre'kalak vessel has broken off the attack on the *Epar-thaa* and is opening fire on the *Enterprise*."

Having aced Interstellar Battle Theory and Practice, not to mention having engaged in a real and near-fatal combat with a ship from the future, Kirk was concerned but far from impressed by this new information.

"Mister Chekov, maintain our present position relative to the *Eparthaa*. I'm sure the Dre'kalak's tactical personnel are intelligent and they won't hit one of their own. Keep their flagship between us and their second craft—it'll mitigate against the latter's use of their own weapons. Mister Sulu, continue to direct all phaser fire against the Dre'kalak flagship and send a double salvo of photon torpedoes to skim it. Engulfing pattern."

"Very clever, Captain." There was muted admiration in Spock's voice. "They won't be sure who we're firing at, and the resultant confusion can only be to our benefit."

Kirk nodded. "Just like in a bar fight. Pretend to hit the guy in front when you're really aiming at the one behind him. He ducks your punch and the load who's second in line never sees it coming."

"I wouldn't know, Captain. But from what I have heard, it is evident that your knowledge of such tactics is extensive."

Kirk only grinned. And not just because he was mildly flattered to learn that the ship's science officer had taken the time to peruse his captain's personal history all the way back to Iowa.

Rattled by the ferocious counterattack, the enemy vessel slipped sharply to port. In doing so, it avoided every one of the photon torpedoes that had been launched from the *Enterprise*. What the Dre'kalak failed to realize was that none of them had been aimed at the flagship in the first place.

The majority of them found their intended target—the second Dre'kalak warship, which was accelerating in its haste to come to the aid of its commander's vessel.

Overwhelmed by the concentrated release of energy from the tightly grouped salvo of torpedoes, the Dre'kalak ship's shields briefly collapsed. This allowed the remaining torpedoes to make proximate contact with the alien hull. Though only two of them got through before shields were restored, the resultant detonations were enough to seriously cripple the ship. Incapacitated and therefore unable to continue fighting, it withdrew from the battle.

Kirk offered: "That ought to even the odds a little. While maintaining contact with our opponent, Mister Chekov, see if you can't maneuver us closer to the *Eparthaa*."

"I'll try, Captain."

The *Enterprise* and the Dre'kalak flagship continued to dance around each other and exchange furious fire. Spock's thoughts were focused on his readouts, while the science officer continued searching for openings in the enemy's defenses. A part of him was silently contemplating the circumstances in which they and their determined adversaries presently found themselves.

Were Vulcans the only species in the galaxy that chose logic and reason over emotion and conflict? Were all disagreements between space-going sentients destined to be resolved at the end of a phaser? It was not logical. As a youth, he had often engaged in long discussions with his instructors and his father over the nature of humans, as well as that of other intelligent species. Sarek had repeatedly pointed out to him it was not necessary to participate in bloodletting to master the art of warfare. Humans who engaged in simulated combat never concluded the exercises by killing the loser.

So why then were they and other similar species predisposed to slaughter? Calm, reasoned discussion invariably produced similar conclusions. Today, the Federation had made contact with not one but two entirely new intelligent species, and true to form, one was seeking the extermination of the other. While he was unwilling to accept the Dre'kalak commander's slightly hysterical insistence that the Perenoreans posed a threat, neither was he ready to grant the Perenoreans claim to be harmless and lost. Entirely benign races did not display the kind of weapons mastery that was displayed via the *Eparthaa*.

Phasers, torpedoes, plasma beams, disruptors—why did so many sentients choose to resort to them? Clearly it was going to take some time to try and make sense of it all, to clarify that which continued to remain opaque to him. If time and circumstances permitted, perhaps he could seek the wisdom of his elder self, since no one else could elucidate what appeared to be a galaxy-wide conundrum.

A cry from Lieutenant Sulu interrupted Spock's reverie.

"A hit! One of our torpedoes got through to their flagship, sir!"

Logic and reason would have to wait, Spock told himself. There was a battle to be won. "Lieutenant Sulu is correct, Captain. The Dre'kalak flagship is showing every indication of losing power. Its shields are on the verge of failing."

"They're hailing us again." Uhura fought to restrain her excitement.

"Why am I not surprised?" In contrast to his mildly sardonic words, Kirk's expression was somber. "On-screen, Mister Chekov."

The face—or at least the region of the dark green conical upper body that one presupposed was the face—of the Dre'kalak commander appeared before them. A dark patch or bandage of some sort covered his left side and one of his three eyes appeared to have slid several centimeters southward. Behind him could be seen several Dre'kalak moving about in considerable haste, their conical shapes occasionally obscured by flowing streaks of smoke like gray alien ghosts.

"Captain Kirk. We are withdrawing."

His scientific precocity did not prevent Chekov from betraying his age by letting out a cheer. When he realized that he was alone on the bridge in loudly punctuating the Dre'kalak commander's concession, he tried to shrink into his seat. Kirk ignored the youthful outburst.

"You admit defeat." Kirk was watching the alien closely, trying to read meaning into the rippling of soft skin and the flexing of powerful tentacles.

"Yes, we have lost. But we do not surrender. We will depart under fire, if you insist on persisting."

Kirk did not directly respond. Let the Dre'kalak think the *Enterprise* was eager to continue the fight when in fact only good tactics and slightly superior armaments had prevented disaster. Furthermore, he was not about to pursue three alien warships without backup. And even had they been so inclined, the badly battered Perenoreans were in no condition to assist.

Besides, the *Enterprise* had achieved their aim, which was to prevent the Dre'kalak from destroying the Perenorean colony ship.

A quiet Spock was mentally reviewing exactly the same scenario. It would be interesting to see if the Perenoreans argued for pursuing and annihilating their assailants. That would suggest that they were far more aggressive and more dangerous than they had presented themselves. It was reassuring when no such call to continue the battle reached the *Enterprise* from the *Eparthaa*.

This time, Kirk did not consult with anyone on the bridge. "I would say go in peace, but it's a little late for that. So, just go."

The image on screen was breaking up, possibly from damage to the enemy flagship's communications systems, perhaps from making preparations to initiate the jump to warp space. *"We have lost, Captain Kirk—but so have you."*

The image crackled once more, then vanished entirely. As the bridge complement looked on, first the Dre'kalak flagship and then its two flanking vessels went to warp speed. In their wake, they left a gas giant, several huge moons, and two starships: one lightly impacted, the other severely damaged.

"Receiving a hail from the *Eparthaa*, Captain," Uhura informed him.

It was Leaderesque Taell. The bandage he had been sporting was gone. *"You have saved us, Captain Kirk. I and everyone on our ship owe you our lives, for however much longer we may continue to exist in this plenum."*

Kirk coughed into his closed fist. Normally, excessive praise made him swell up like a balloon, but this was a bit much. It was left to Spock to proportionately reply.

"Federation laws explicitly allow for the providing of assistance to refugees. Whatever the nature of the disagreement between your kind and the Dre'kalak, we are certain it could and would have been better resolved through rational discussion. As the Dre'kalak declined, rather brusquely, to participate in such a prudent dialogue, we were compelled to persuade them by other means."

"As you certainly have done." Taell's voice was soft but emphatic. *"Though we can never properly repay you, we would beg the privilege of thanking you in person. Will you do us the honor of visiting our ship so that we may present proper homage?"*

"We would be honored. *Enterprise* out."

To the captain's surprise, Spock was immediately agreeable. When he asked why, the science officer responded without hesitation.

"Were the intentions of these people hostile, they could have fired on us now, Captain. Insofar as I have had time to study it, their initial psychological profile does not suggest a species inclined to treachery or violence. Given the present condition of their vessel, I do not think they could mount a serious threat to the *Enterprise* even if they were so inclined."

Kirk considered, then smiled slightly. "Is that the sum of your reasoning in this matter, Mister Spock?"

"No, Captain. I admit that I am curious to meet them in person. Not only as representatives of a new species, but as someone who is also a refugee."

Rising from the command chair, Kirk walked over to stand beside his science officer. "You know, Spock, while it's not explicitly forbidden by regulation for a captain and his first officer to be off ship at the same time, it *is* frowned upon."

"Yes, Captain. I will file a formal report on the inadvisability of taking such action—as soon as we return."

"All right, Spock. I understand. I'm more than a little curious to meet these people myself." He looked to his right. "Lieutenant Sulu. Mister Spock and I will be paying a formal visit to the Perenorean colony ship. Until conditions on board the *Eparthaa* can be properly evaluated, we will conduct such transfers via shuttle. You are in command."

"Aye, aye, Captain." Rising from his station, Sulu moved to assume the captain's chair. Settling into it, he instinctively felt that if given the chance, he could get used to the position.

"And," Spock continued, "I believe that Doctor McCoy should accompany us."

Kirk did not try to hide his surprise. "Mister Spock, I wasn't aware that you so earnestly desired his company."

The science officer visibly stiffened. "If Leaderesque Taell has been telling the truth, then there are likely to be wounded on the Perenorean vessel. Doctor McCoy's presence in a professional capacity would be appreciated by the Perenoreans, and therefore stands to accrue additional goodwill toward the Federation."

"Yes, of course. I should have thought of it myself."

"Captain." It was Uhura again. "Lieutenant Ben-Haim for you." She frowned uncertainly.

Puzzled, Kirk leaned into Uhura's station. "Mister Ben-Haim, what is it? Mister Spock and I are about to go across to the Perenorean ship."

"I'm sorry to interrupt diplomatic efforts, Captain, but we have a problem in engineering."

Kirk let out a heavy sigh. "On my way."

"If you prefer, Captain, I can . . ." Spock began.

Kirk cut him off. "No, I'll take care of it." He smiled. "Inform Doctor McCoy that he'll be joining us. I'm sure he'll enjoy hearing it from you personally."

"Captain." The first officer's dry tone was even more than usually pronounced.

3

Confident he could deal with the situation in engineering whatever its cause, Kirk moved purposefully to that section of the *Enterprise*. As he entered the area where the chief engineer was usually found, the first inkling of the nature of the predicament manifested itself, though not in any of the several forms he had anticipated. Surrounded by the immense tangle of silvery conduits, processing cylinders, sealed wiring, and photonic connectors, he descended the access walkway until he was intercepted by an engineering officer, Lieutenant Ben-Haim.

A rousingly loud bellow resounded from somewhere behind and below Ben-Haim.

"Oohhh, there was a young lady from Inverness,

"I stopped to ask her about her dress . . . !"

While casually following the words, Kirk looked sideways at the ship's second engineer. "Is that singing?"

The continuing lyrics were rapidly approaching warp nine on the bawdiness scale. Ben-Haim looked uncomfortable. "I believe so, Captain."

Kirk's expression hardened. "Is that Chief Engineer Scott singing?"

The engineer looked as if he would rather be anywhere else. "Yes, Captain."

"Thank you, Mister Ben-Haim." Kirk started past the other man. "I'll deal with it. Go about your business."

"Yes, sir." The engineer moved past the captain.

One did not have to have a bat's sonar to locate Montgomery Scott. The chief engineer's bellowing burr reverberated loudly between the walls and conduits, tubes and instrumentation. Kirk found Scott by himself, noting the information being displayed on a panel.

"Scotty?"

The chief engineer's less than profound and decidedly off-key chorale stopped. "Ah, Jim! That little dustup was one for the ages, it was! We have done a good thing. Rescued some lost and kindly souls from an evil slug with one too many eyes, we have." He wagged a knowing finger in Kirk's direction. "First rule of interstellar contact: Never trust anyone with more than two eyes. You never can tell what the others might be looking at."

"Not my first rule." Kirk regarded his chief engineer. "I was told there was a problem here."

Scott looked away. "Nothing mechanical, Captain."

"So what's troubling you, Scotty?"

The chief engineer hesitated, then turned from the panel. "I heard that you're making the first visit to the alien craft via shuttle."

"And . . . ?"

"Captain, I put you and Mister Spock inside the *Narada* under considerably more stressful circumstances. Suddenly you feel you have to use a shuttle when both ships are practically within caber toss of each other." His eyes searched Kirk's face. "Have you lost confidence in me and my abilities, Captain?"

"Is *that* what's bothering you?" The suddenly serious Scott nodded. Kirk smiled and put a hand on the older man's shoulder. "Scotty, I am convinced beyond a shadow of a doubt that you are not only the finest chief engineer in all of Starfleet, but the most inventive and adaptive one as well."

"Captain, the words are profoundly gratifying, but it still doesn't explain why you're not usin' the transporter."

"We are unfamiliar with the interior of the Perenorean vessel, Scotty. You know that." When the chief engineer appeared ready to protest anew, Kirk raised a forestalling hand. "Yes, I know, we were also relatively unfamiliar with the layout of the *Narada*. In contrast, we know absolutely nothing about Perenorean design."

Scott was only partially mollified. "I still think that given the opportunity I could put the three of you right on their bridge."

"We have barely an inkling of what their 'bridge' may be like, Scotty. It would be bad for interspecies relations if, purely by accident of course, we were to materialize inside, say, one of their hydrology conduits."

Scott eyed him sharply, seemed about to say something equally cutting, and then slumped. "I cannot argue with that, Captain. Shuttle it is, then. And—I appreciate you explaining the decision to me in person."

"Just as long as you understand that the choice of transportation is in no way a reflection on you or your competency, Scotty. I'm just proceeding cautiously."

The chief engineer hesitated, then broke out in a wide grin. "James T. Kirk proceeding 'cautiously'? For sure, the galaxy is full of surprises."

"There's a time and a place for everything, Mister Scott. Even caution. Especially when working to establish a relationship with a newly contacted species." There was a twinkle in his eye. "There's even a place for song."

Scott blinked. "Captain?"

Drawing himself up, Kirk replied in as officious a voice as he could muster. "You'll kindly oblige me by finishing the song you were singing when I arrived here. I have always had a secret interest in regional terrestrial poetry."

"What?" A broad smile spread across the chief engineer's face and he winked. "Oh, aye, aye! 'Tis an old sailors' chantey from Glasgow. It sounds better in its original dialect, but if it's sung that way, then no one but another Glaswegian can understand it."

For the next few minutes, the metal and composite–ribbed jungle of engineering echoed to the sound of something more boisterous and considerably more warming than the unfeeling machines that were its permanent occupants.

"I'm looking forward to making some new friends." McCoy's tone soured. "Though not to the trip across, of course."

Kirk's exasperation was plain. "I swear, Bones, for someone with such a visceral dislike of space travel, I don't understand why you didn't just ask for a permanent posting on a Federation world."

McCoy looked away. "I would have, but it's important for me to keep moving. If you want to know why, ask my ex-wife."

"Physician, heal thyself," Spock offered, though not a glimmer of a smile cracked the Vulcan's face.

The doctor responded immediately. "Oh, so now you presume to know the intricacies of human personal relationships? I didn't realize that your studies of our culture had progressed to that point."

"I am merely an interested observer, Doctor. I confess that I find such particulars highly illogical. In contrast to human males and females, the relationships between subatomic particles and waveforms act in a logical manner."

"You need to do more work in chaos theory, Spock," said Kirk. "You'd be surprised at the analogies that crop up."

They entered the shuttlebay. Positioned in the stern, a pair of the unlovely but functional craft were lined up within yellow and black launch lines, facing the airlock doors. Storage and equipment bays lined both walls. Two techs were concluding a final inspection of one of the shuttles. At the approach of the trio of senior officers, they straightened up. Kirk returned their acknowledgment with a casual wave. He was still getting used to being a senior officer.

Not that he didn't enjoy the perks.

The colony vessel loomed larger. It was not overwhelmingly vast—it looked like the living quarters, work areas, and supply sections formed by the six interconnected globes were spacious.

I must remember to ask exactly how many colonists there are, Kirk reminded himself as Spock maneuvered the shuttle into the welcoming open bay of the *Eparthaa*.

As the science officer set the shuttle down and the bay doors closed behind them, the three visitors had their first opportunity to examine aspects of Perenorean engineering. It was, Kirk decided as he peered out the shuttle's forward port, oddly indistinct. In place of the usual highly visible conduits and instrumentation one would expect to find on any other starship, there were only a few ivory-hued bumps and ridges. *Perhaps for aesthetic reasons*, he thought. The Perenoreans might prefer to conceal their engineering works. The absence of in-your-face material did not necessarily mean a lack of skill.

Leaderesque Taell was there to greet them. As the three Starfleet visitors made fine adjustments to their translation earbuds and the translator systems woven into their uniforms, the Leaderesque alternated speaking with a pair of dignitaries who accompanied him in spilling a stream of embarrassingly effusive praise on the Starfleet officers. By the time the last of the formal welcome speeches had concluded, the translator algorithms had both the guests and their hosts conversing without difficulty.

Their grammar is pretty straightforward and simple, the *Enterprise*'s communications officer had explained earlier, *but their vocabulary will take some time to process. It's quirky.*

Essential communication would not be a problem, Uhura had assured them. She was confident in the ability of the ship's science officer to make any necessary on-the-spot corrections.

They were led through a corridor and onto an internal conveyor. Unlike the turbolifts aboard the *Enterprise*, the Perenorean lift seemed to follow a variety of curves. *Was this too a decision driven by aesthetics?* Kirk wondered.

Expecting to be transported to the *Eparthaa*'s bridge, or its engineering section, or perhaps a conference chamber of some kind, the visitors were surprised to find themselves in a sickbay.

Not a sickbay, McCoy thought. *A triage area.*

In line with the Perenoreans' slightly smaller stature, the ceiling was low, though not claustrophobically so. The large room, the original purpose of which remained obscure, was filled with what appeared to be a variety of inflatable pads or cushions. Administering medication or treatment as needed, Perenorean medical technicians moved among the dozens of wounded. Interrupted by the occasional soft, whistling cries of injured younglings, the dominant sound in the chamber was a persistent collective mewling around the visitors.

Taell's multijointed arm rose and fell like a dancer's as he pointed out individual survivors. "You see before you the consequences of relentless Dre'kalak pursuit and attack. If not for your timely intervention, my friends, all you see receiving treatment here would likely be dead."

McCoy looked to Kirk. "Jim, if you and our hosts don't mind, I'd like to help. Certainly I can learn something."

Taell's ears folded forward and down in the doctor's direction: the Perenorean equivalent of a polite bow. "As you wish, noble physician. Any assistance you can render will be welcomed, even if it is no more than a thought or a suggestion. We are always eager to learn from our betters."

McCoy flushed. "Hey now, nobody said anything about anyone being better than anyone else. I'm just hoping to learn a little about your physical makeup." He held up the tricorder he had brought with him. "I'd like your permission to take some readings."

"Do as you wish, physician." Taell's remarkably flexible ears folded forward a second time. "We will provide you with an escort suitable to your expertise. You will be welcomed wherever you go and may ask whatever questions you wish." The small mouth pooched slightly forward, like a human blowing a kiss. "But be warned. You will likely have to suffer many questions in return."

McCoy smiled. "I'm not shy. Happy to share information."

The *Enterprise*'s science officer was less enthused. "Stay within visual range, Doctor."

"Relax, Spock." McCoy was already wading in among the closely packed patients and their solicitous attendants. "If an unforeseen problem should develop, Mister Scott has a transporter lock."

While McCoy immersed himself in the rudiments of Perenorean medicine as they waited for his special guide to arrive, Kirk and Spock were given a more formal tour of the expanded hospital sector. Just as in the shuttlebay, there was a notable paucity of visible instrumentation: only a great deal of what appeared to be white-clad conduits and apparatus buried in the walls, deck, and overhead. When queried, Taell was quick to explain.

"The equipment and mechanisms are present; it is just that we prefer to keep such things out of sight."

"Is it a matter of aesthetics?" Spock asked, precisely echoing Kirk's previous thoughts.

Once again, Taell gestured with his ears. "Yes, that, and also of practicality. The smooth surfaces that you seem to find so remarkable everywhere exist because they are difficult to bump into or trip over."

Kirk nodded thoughtfully. "Makes sense. Can't trip over a pipe or cable that's been subsumed into the body of the ship."

A new Perenorean approached, halted, and ear-bowed. His face was the narrowest of any they had seen thus far. It was matched by the solemnity of his attitude and voice. There was about him the suggestion of great age.

"Most honored guests, I am Founoh. As masteresque physician in charge of colony well-being, I have been asked to solicit the advice of your own ship's doctor."

"That'd be me." Stepping forward, McCoy extended a hand. Founoh studiously regarded it.

"Thank you for your kind offer, but I already have a sufficiency of my own."

"Excuse me?" McCoy did a double take, then chuckled. "Well, well; right off we learn that the Perenoreans have a highly developed sense of humor."

"Your pardon, Doctor," commented Spock, "but the reply struck me as a perfectly logical response to your straightforward offer."

"Yeah, it would." Smiling, McCoy gently reached out to take the elderly Perenorean's more delicate seven-fingered, double-jointed hand in his own and carefully moved it up and down. "Among my species, this is a common method of extending a friendly greeting. We call it a handshake. Do you have an equivalent?"

Founoh acquiesced to the contact. "One might lick the ear of another."

McCoy flinched slightly. "Why don't we stick to the human method for a while? I can always try yours later."

"Perfectly satisfactory." Turning, Founoh gestured into the interior of the vast chamber. "If you would care to accompany me, I will try, in my wholly inadequate way, to acquaint you with some details of Perenorean physiology. It may be that our internal systems are not so different, and you may be able to offer some assistance. At the moment, we are a bit overwhelmed with the number of injuries. Any suggestions you might have will be greatly appreciated."

"I'll do what I can and learn as I go." In the face of broken bodies and crushed bones, too many of them belonging to younglings, McCoy activated his tricorder, eager to start.

Spock leaned over to whisper to Kirk. "Captain, while I am not personally averse to Doctor McCoy embarking on a medical mission, do you think it wise for him to be on his own?"

"He has his communicator, Mister Spock." Kirk similarly kept his voice low. "If these people wanted to hurt us, they've had ample opportunity to do so already. I have a feeling they're far too grateful to us for helping them escape destruction at the hands of the Dre'kalak to consider any such kind of treachery."

Spock straightened. "Ah. That 'feeling' again."

"That's right, Spock," Kirk replied cheerfully. "Might as well get used to it."

"I am not sure that I ever will, Captain. But for now, at least, we have other matters to focus on."

"Why do you lower your voices?" Taell sounded honestly bemused. "I cannot hear what you are saying."

"Private matter," Kirk informed the Perenorean captain. He then took out his communicator. "I'll have our chemists analyze some of your food and medicines. I doubt that we can supply everything you need, but if our synthesizers can reproduce what you've lost, we can certainly help make up the shortfall until you can make it to . . ." A new thought gave him pause. "Where are you going to, anyway?"

"That is just it, Captain Kirk." Taell's ears flared as wide as possible. "We don't know. We have come too far, burned too much fuel, and used too many of our supplies to be able to get anywhere near the planet that was recommended to us as a potential colony. And the Dre'kalak may be waiting. We cannot go back, yet it seems we cannot go forward." Huge golden eyes met Kirk's own, pleading. "For us, it is no longer a question of wanting to settle somewhere. We *have* to settle somewhere, before the last of our supplies run out. We were hoping that you or your Federation might have some ideas."

Kirk was taken aback. He had hoped to be able to provide the battered colonists with additional food, medicine, and other supplies. He had not expected them to ask him to provide an entire world.

"Taell, I don't see how we can—"

Once again Spock interrupted. "Captain, I am sure the Federation Council would want us to help the Perenoreans."

"That's all very well and good, Mister Spock," Kirk grumbled, "but I don't happen to have a spare habitable planet in my pocket."

"I may, Captain." Without further explanation, the science officer pulled out his communicator, and connected with Uhura, who went to work researching the problem.

Taell proceeded to show the two officers around the *Eparthaa*. It was impossible in a couple of hours to get a complete overview of the huge colony vessel—the two officers were given a good look, not only at the sickbay adjunct, but also at the ship's bridge and engine room. Both sectors featured the same bland, oddly featureless design and construction as the vessel's shuttlebay. Nor did it escape the two Starfleet officers that in addition to their requests to see certain parts of the alien vessel being immediately granted, these comprised even the most strategic portions of any starship.

"They are being awfully accommodating." Kirk looked on with interest as a pair of passing Perenoreans engaged in what appeared to be a brief exchange of ideas simply by manipulating their swept-back ears. "Bridge, engineering—I wonder if they'd be willing to show us their weapons systems as well?"

"People in desperate need cannot afford the luxury of secrecy, Captain." Spock continued to alternate his attention between their constantly changing surroundings and checking his communicator. "If, as they say, they are running desperately low on energy and supplies, there is little for them to gain by hiding anything from us."

Kirk nodded toward the floating holo that accompanied them while providing multiple views of the rest of the six-part ship. Taell had explained that unless dismissed, the projection followed him wherever he went so that as leaderesque he could keep constant tabs on the vessel under his command no matter where he happened to find himself.

"If they are hiding something, they're mighty good at it. Everything we've asked to see they've shown us. Every question has been answered. As far as I can tell, we're being granted access." Kirk pulled out his communicator. "Bones? We're seeing everything and it's all interesting, but I'm starting to feel like we're overstaying our welcome. It's time we got back to the ship. How are you coming?"

McCoy sounded tired but exhilarated. *"Learning a lot*

about Perenorean physiology, Jim. It's unavoidable when they open someone up right in front of you."

Kirk glanced at Spock, who frowned. "Excuse me? Say again, Bones?"

"Right under your nose, Jim. It's remarkable. They have only one surgery on this whole enormous vessel, and it's used only for the most serious cases. According to my guide Masteresque Founoh, most of the time they use what they call a 'hermetical orb.' It's a little difficult to describe. They blow a multifunction bubble around the patient. It exudes a special kind of moisture that filters the air inside the bubble so there's no need to sanitize an entire room. You can stick your hand and whole arm in it, and everything you're holding is sterilized by the intrusion. Then you go to work with whatever portable instruments you choose. It's like operating in an antiseptic fog. And Jim—they don't use anesthetic! When I asked, Founoh told me that every Perenorean learns from an early age how to control their pain. The young and badly wounded remain conscious through the entire operation—and sometimes they offer advice to the surgeons who are working on them!" There was a pause. *"Spock would understand."*

Kirk turned to his first officer. "Sounds like very accomplished mind control."

"Or very accomplished minds. I am beginning to wonder, Captain, if we are not seeing something important that is right in front of us."

Kirk studied his friend. "What are you getting at, Spock?"

"Nothing specific, Captain. Leastwise, not yet."

A moment's hesitation, and then Kirk addressed his communicator once more. "Have your colleague bring you back to the shuttlebay, Bones. I presume you've gathered sufficient material to keep you busy back on the ship?"

"That's putting it mildly, Jim. I've recorded enough data to keep half the research staff at the College of Xenomedicine active for a year! Why, there are potential applications that—"

"See you in a few minutes, Bones." Kirk hastily closed his communicator. In a very short time, he had learned that while McCoy would discourse happily and without end on virtually any subject, it was medicine and its potential advancement through newly acquired knowledge that could keep him chattering enthusiastically for hours. And while all of it was fascinating, a great deal was highly technical and obscure. McCoy would keep rambling, unless he was courteously cut off.

With Taell's guidance, they found their way back to an airlock outside the *Eparthaa*'s shuttlebay and waited for McCoy to rejoin them. As his first officer was putting away his communicator, Kirk asked, "Well, Spock? You said you might have a planet or two in your pocket. Did you ever find them?"

"No planets, Captain," the science officer replied, "but Lieutenant Uhura did manage to track down another possibility. More modest than what I'd hoped to find, but perhaps adequate for the situation at hand."

Kirk was instantly attentive. "And?"

The science officer checked to make sure they were alone. Alone as they could be, that is, on an alien vessel whose total population was still an unknown. Their guide Taell stood off to one side conversing with several subordinates. None of the Perenoreans appeared to be paying them the slightest attention.

"Not far from our present coordinates at modest warp speed and on the edge of this quadrant of the Federation lies a world called SiBor."

Kirk strained his memory. "Can't say that I've heard of it."

"That is not surprising, Captain, as it is not a member of the Federation. SiBor is a low-level inhabited world with which commercial, social, and political contact was made by Federation envoys only thirty years ago. The SiBoronaans are by all accounts a peaceful, nonexpansive species interested in further contact with the galaxy, and most especially hands-on assistance in developing their sluggish single-world economy."

Kirk flashed a wry grin. "Sounds like the best thing we could do for them is stay far away."

Though he recognized the irony, Spock did not respond in kind. "As you are amply aware, Captain, for better or worse, once a sentient species has experienced the satisfactions to be gained from advanced technology, they are most reluctant to regress. The SiBoronaans would appear to be no different from any other sentient species that has undergone such contact. No species chooses to forgo the opportunities for advancement in favor of establishing themselves as a permanent tourist attraction. Or to put it another way, one individual's quaint traditional community is another's backward nation. Consequently, the SiBoronaans seek outside help to more rapidly advance their civilization."

Kirk had turned thoughtful. "Are you suggesting that the Perenoreans might be that help?"

"SiBor is orbited by several moons. All are small save one, DiBor, which is roughly the size of Mercury. Most scientists would refer to SiBor-DiBor as a dual planetary system, with the smaller sphere orbiting the larger. Astronomers often refer to Earth-Moon in the same way. As is not uncommon in such twinned-world systems, DiBor boasts an environment virtually identical to that of SiBor: atmosphere, water, temperate weather, and a vibrant native ecosystem. But, it is and always has been uninhabited. It has not been colonized or otherwise developed by the SiBoronaans because they have not mastered the necessary technology and skills required. Nor have they felt any urgency to do so because their own world is far from being exploited and their population density is modest."

Kirk pondered the implications. "You're suggesting that the Perenoreans settle on the SiBoronaans' moon."

The first officer diffidently shrugged. "I believe it to be an option worth pursuing. Before presenting the idea to the Perenoreans, we must naturally first explore it with the SiBoronaans. I propose it as a possible solution, since it could potentially be of as much benefit to them as to the Perenoreans. The latter would gain a new home while the SiBoronaans would benefit from the immediate proximity of the advanced Perenoreans. The fact that the Perenoreans are a species that is not politically allied to the Federation should render the situation even more appealing to the inherently cautious SiBoronaans."

Kirk smiled at his first officer. "I see the potential. What about the possibility that the SiBoronaans might be over-whelmed by their new neighbors?"

"While not densely populated or in possession of a technology equal to the Federation median, SiBor is a mature world with a fully developed culture. According to the available information, there are just over a billion SiBoronaans." Spock indicated their surroundings. "Extrapolating from the size of their ship, the number of Perenorean colonists cannot number more than a few thousand at most. And in the event of any conflict, the Federation can stand ready to step in and settle any unforeseen disputes."

Kirk exhaled deeply. "Mister Spock, you realize that Starfleet and the Federation government will want to examine all the possible ramifications."

"They will have to come to a decision more swiftly than usual, Captain, as the Perenorean supply limitations indicate that they do not have much time left. I think the process will go more quickly, since the intention is to place the refugees in a new home that is not part of the Federation."

"I suppose it's possible that there are one or two government bureaucrats who are capable of moving faster than particles chilled to near absolute zero." Kirk's jauntiness returned. "It's a *fine* idea, Spock."

He glanced around. Their Perenorean hosts were still conversing animatedly among themselves and continuing to ignore the two visitors.

"We'll explain the situation to Starfleet. If we can get a

preliminary go-ahead, we'll contact the government on SiBor. Provided they agree, even if it's only on a provisional basis, I suspect the Perenoreans will jump at the offer."

Spock nodded, clearly pleased. "Starfleet can agree to supervise and perhaps, to a limited extent, underwrite the establishment of the settlement. Provided everything proceeds as hoped for, the Federation stands to gain the gratitude of not one but two sentient species."

On the shuttle back to the *Enterprise*, upon learning the details of Spock's initiative, McCoy was even less restrained.

"This isn't just a 'good and useful' thing you've come up with, Spock. It's much, much more than that."

The science officer found McCoy's unstinting praise more disconcerting than the doctor's usual sarcasm. "I am only seeking to find a way to aid refugees whose situation is not unlike the Vulcans'. I have lost an old world, and we both seek a new one." He spoke as he guided the shuttle the short distance back to the *Enterprise*. Knowing McCoy, he braced himself. "If not 'good and useful,' what would you call it, Doctor?"

McCoy's expression turned uncharacteristically solemn. "I'd say it qualified as downright noble, Spock."

4

Locating Uhura in the mess, Spock sat down opposite the *Enterprise*'s chief communications officer and regarded the remaining portion of her midday meal with a mixture of curiosity and distaste. None of this was visible on his face, of course, but Uhura knew him well enough to know when he was feeling ill at ease. She prodded the central portion of her plate with a fork.

"It would look worse if the artificial gravity was off."

"I confess I find the general appearance of your meal unsettling." He studied the alien conglomeration with as much scientific detachment as he could muster. "What is it?"

"Nyama choma, ugali, and curried mung beans. The synthesizer doesn't do mung beans very well, but it makes an excellent curry."

"I see. You will not take offense if I prefer not to try it?"

Spearing a piece of roast, she placed it delicately between her lips and chewed slowly. Very slowly. "Spock, I wouldn't take offense at anything you prefer not to try. Or to try. You should know that by now."

He looked around. Their table was isolated from the other diners. "I would like to think that I do, but I find personal relationships between humans and Vulcans frequently bewildering."

She laughed softly. "Well, that beats 'incomprehensible,' which is the descriptive term you used to use."

"I like to think that, in the last year, my knowledge of human ways has progressed."

She eyed him. "Oh, it has, Spock, it *has*. Nice of you to keep me company for the rest of my lunch, though."

"Actually, I did come with a serious question to ask."

"Would I ever have thought otherwise?" She sighed. "What is it?"

"Captain Kirk, Doctor McCoy, and I have just concluded an extensive visit to the Perenorean ship. While we utilized standard Federation translation equipment equipped with your program, I noticed no similar apparatus in use among the Perenoreans. Yet they were able to understand and to communicate with us with varying degrees of fluency and without hesitation." He leaned toward her, his tone intense. "While we were on the *Eparthaa*, did your Perenorean counterpart or anyone else from their vessel contact you or anyone in your section for information on Federation language, its vocabulary, or its rules of grammar?"

She put her fork down. "No."

He considered: "Most interesting. It suggests that Pere-norean translation equipment is highly miniaturized and extremely efficient—or else the Perenoreans are extremely proficient linguists."

Uhura was shaking her head in disagreement. "Spock, no known species is capable of mastering an alien language without intensive preparation—much less in a day. Your first guess must be correct: they just have very good and very small translation gear."

"Yes, of course. That must be it. To imagine otherwise would be foolish. Unprecedented, even."

Seeing that he was puzzled, she knew from experience that he was likely to be up all night pondering every potential ramification, however negligible they might be.

"They might be exceptionally skilled linguists and fast learners. Or just good mimics. There are higher-functioning animals on Earth who have that skill. Tell them something once and they can repeat it back to you perfectly. Combine that with an array of miniaturized concealed instrumentation, and it might look as if they actually were learning the language on the fly when in reality they're just relying on clever mimicry."

"Yes, appearances can be deceiving. Such a theory has merit." He sounded unaccountably relieved. "I appreciate your insight, Lieutenant."

She smiled back at him. "Anything else in sight you appreciate, Commander?"

"You are playing with words. They are, of course, your specialty." He sounded as confident as he looked. "My studies have allowed me to comprehend a good deal more of such human games."

"Uh-huh. So what do you get from *this*?"

Seated directly across from her, he straightened sharply. "I comprehend that the toes of your right foot are advancing vertically up my leg."

"Very good," she replied. "And what do you foresee as the final result of this lazy podiatric wandering?"

He rose rather quickly. "We are about to initiate contact with the SiBoronaans so that we may present them with our proposal. I must be present when that occurs." He started to leave, hesitated, and looked back. "Though I am not reluctant to confess that I would much prefer to remain and follow your attempted podal misdirection to its logical conclusion."

"All in good time." She dismissed him with a diffident wave of her hand as she resumed eating. "Go and have your meeting. What matter the wishes of one woman when the fate of two species is at hand?"

He paused, started to say something, thought better of it, and hurried to exit the dining area. *Yet more proof*, he told himself. As if any additional was needed.

Bewildering, indeed.

McCoy's enthusiasm as he paced the bridge was so boundless that Kirk half expected his friend to rise off the deck.

"I'm telling you, Jim, these people, these Perenoreans, while not as advanced as us when it comes to weaponry and other technical stuff, have access to other knowledge that is going to be of enormous benefit to the Federation. Just talking with Masteresque Founoh for a few hours made me feel that, if we could do research alongside them, we might in a few years produce the kinds of results Federation biologists have been working toward for centuries!" His voice fell to an intense whisper.

"Do you know, Jim, that they've developed something that I can only describe as a self-morphing antibiotic? When applied to an infection, it doesn't just adapt to kill the threat, it *evolves* to kill it! It's a be-all that really is an end-all. They have a couple of different varieties, but basically one application kills everything and anything intrusive because it continuously adapts and alters itself once it has been introduced into the patient's body. It's like a drug with its own brain. That's how we finally beat cancer, with a hunter that adapts once in the system to kill whatever kind of cancer it happened to encounter. Like that, this Perenorean infection killer is wonderfully egalitarian: it just mutates to wipe out whatever the infection happens to be." He paused to catch his breath.

"And that's not the least of it, Jim. Their discoveries are aesthetically sensitive as well as scientifically groundbreaking. They're constantly striving to improve their own physical morphology. I'll mention just one example that they gave me. You've noticed that they're completely covered with body hair, or fur? Well," he added triumphantly, "they've synthesized a simple application that can grow hair! Anywhere on the body, in any color, in any density."

Kirk was less than overwhelmed. "That's great, Bones. I suppose it provides one more point of mutual reference to learn that there's still another species that worries about matters of individual appearance." He glanced back as Spock entered the bridge. "We can talk about what you've learned later. Right now, we have to prepare for some potentially ticklish diplomatic negotiations."

McCoy was contrite. "Sorry, Jim. I just couldn't contain myself. These people are so full of surprises. You want me to leave?"

"No. Everyone will know soon enough whether we've achieved our aims. Stay. And the SiBoronaans might have some questions relevant to your specialty about the Perenoreans. Whether our contingent of refugees are subject to occasional outbreaks of disease that might have cross-species potential, plagues—that sort of thing."

"You mean plagues besides our human failings, Jim?"

"I am Four Amek. It is a pleasure and an honor to greet representatives of the great United Federation of Planets. It has been too long since we have done so."

On the bridge, Kirk and his crew listened politely to the formal speech. No one explained that the reason for the extended interval between visits by Starfleet vessels was because there was no compelling reason to make the journey to SiBor. Neither its people nor the world itself held much of interest to the faster-moving culture of the Federation. Kirk carefully studied the image on the viewscreen. The SiBoronaans were a species that was new to him and he used the opportunity to examine the droning diplomat in detail.

Identical to the majority of its kind, the SiBoronaan envoy was tall and slender, almost reed thin. Any suggestion of suppleness was an illusion. The SiBoronaans scuttled along on a flaring mass of thick, strong pseudopods that spread outward in all directions from the base of their bodies like roots from a tree. Though slow moving, they were possessed of great endurance. A race between a SiBoronaan and a human would be a genuine tortoise-and-hare affair, with the human leaving his alien counterpart in the dust only to exhaust himself days later while the patient, indomitable SiBoronaan, whose pace never tired, crept placidly and inexorably past the human's worn-out and overheated mammalian body.

The diplomat's eyes were situated on opposite sides of its head. Able to see in two directions at once like a terrestrial chameleon, a SiBoronaan could create binocular vision by extruding and then folding forward the highly flexible sides of its upper body. Each protruding flap held an eye that could then cross-check its line of sight with that of its companion. There was no need to identify the speaker by gender since the species had none: SiBoronaans reproduced by asexual budding.

The envoy was clad in a single long, flowing, intricately embroidered purple cloak of some unknown fabric, yet of luxurious consistency and exquisite workmanship. The single flexible tentacle that emerged from a reinforced hole in the center of this material and from the cylindrical body beneath split into four smaller limbs that in turn divided themselves into four still smaller prehensile digits. As the diplomat stood facing its own translator pickup, these multiple limbs were incessantly twisting and writhing among themselves like a quartet of serpentine gymnasts. Finding the pythonic ballet more than a little mesmerizing, Kirk had to remind himself to respond.

"I am Captain James T. Kirk commanding the *Starship Enterprise*." From his seat in the command chair, he gestured to his left. "Standing next to me is my chief science officer, Commander Spock, and next to him is my chief medical officer, Doctor McCoy." He turned back to his right. "This is Leaderesque Taell of the Perenorean colony vessel *Eparthaa*."

Two of the SiBoronaan's sub-limbs rose. *"Your indulgence a moment while I consult."* Looking off-screen, his eye-holding face folding sideways like the wingtips of a manta, the diplomat went quiet as he studied something out of the officers' view. His remarkably flexible face shifted while the rest of his body except for the continuously contorting limb remained ramrod straight.

Perhaps he was communicating through gestures with others of his kind, Kirk thought. While he had taken the time to study up on the SiBor system, the captain was painfully aware not of what he had learned but of what he still did not know. Spock might have been able to find purpose in the SiBoronaan's movements, but Kirk was hesitant to expose his own ignorance.

Four Amek turned to face them once more. *"We are famil-*

iar with many species that claim allegiance to the Federation and also with many who lie outside its boundaries, but the designation 'Perenorean' is new to us." The eyes shifted again. *"As is the physical appearance of the one you call Taell. It/he/she appears to be undergoing a process of dawdling disintegration."*

Kirk had to smile. "As a result of stress, Leaderesque Taell has lost some of his fur, Four Amek. Fur, or hair, is a soft material that is produced in individual strands by the Perenorean body as well as by humans, Vulcans, and other species that are related through long-recognized convergent evolution arising from a panspermic diaspora. Your people, who evolved independently of that diaspora and do not possess this body covering, might find its variability somewhat alarming."

The diplomat lowered all four sub-limbs. *"I apologize for my ignorance, and if I have given any offense."*

"Not at all." A cheerful Taell was relying on the humans' translation technology to make sure he was understood by the SiBoronaan.

Gratefully excused from the minor diplomatic faux pas, Four Amek continued. *"To what do the people of SiBor owe this welcome but unannounced and unexpected visitation from the Federation?"*

Spock leaned over to Kirk, whispering, "Captain, we represent the Federation but we do not speak for it. Any agreement we come to with the SiBoronaans will have to be formally confirmed through Starfleet."

"I understand, Spock." Addressing himself to the image on the forward viewer, Kirk cleared his throat and raised his voice.

"In the course of what had been a routine mission, we picked up a distress signal. It turned out to be coming from Leaderesque Taell's vessel, the *Eparthaa*, which was being attacked by ships of another species, the Dre'kalak. Tracing the signal led us to encounter a . . . divergence of opinion between the two. Until then, both species were unknown to us."

"As they are to us, Captain Kirk." It was impossible to read the SiBoronaan's expression since the diplomat had very little to express with. Kirk suspected there were subtleties he was missing, but he had no time to linger and hypothesize.

"Leaderesque Taell is in command of a colony ship that, because of the ongoing attacks by the Dre'kalak, has now traveled much too far and expended too many of their supplies to have any chance of reaching its original objective."

"The Perenoreans are refugees," Spock put in. "As are my people, the Vulcans. Humans have permitted survivors of the disaster that has overtaken my people to live among them. We would ask the same of the SiBoronaans."

Kirk continued. "The Perenoreans asked us—as representatives of the Federation—if there was some way we might be able to help. Examination of our charts indicates that there are no options lying within remaining range of their ship." He kept his voice as even as possible. "The only option is the habitable SiBoronaan moon DiBor.

"Allowing this small group of Perenoreans, who number only in the thousands, to establish themselves there would not only save them, but it would be of great benefit to the SiBoronaans. The Perenoreans have valuable expertise in many areas of technology that exceeds your own"—he glanced at Spock as he said this—"and in certain specific areas may even equal or exceed that of the Federation."

The tips of Four Amek's single manipulative limb swept to the right. *"I continue to listen."*

Taell took a step forward. His long ears were pressed straight back against the sides of his head and he had extended his double-jointed arms so that they were parallel to the deck. All fourteen fingers pointed downward.

"All that we have, all that we are, all the knowledge of the Perenoreans that we carry with us, we will gladly share with you if you will allow us to settle on this moon of yours. We will be the best of neighbors! The SiBoronaans will never regret permitting us to live near them as friends—*never*. No matter what we are doing, no matter how important our needs of the moment, yours will always take precedence!"

Four Amek did not immediately reply, though his multiple limbs resumed their air dance.

"This is not for me to decide. On a matter of such import, I must consult the Others. Five Kend, Six Jol, and Twelve Covot must be given the opportunity to render their opinion. Only when that has been done can a prudent reply be given to so momentous a request." All digits dropped to the front of the magnificent cloak. *"We will give you our answer in one hundred and thirty qualums."* The diplomat's image was replaced with a starfield.

Kirk had risen halfway out of his chair. "Wait! The Perenoreans—they don't have enough supplies left to . . . !"

Spock took a step toward him. "Captain, one hundred and

thirty SiBoronaan *qualums* do not constitute a long waiting period."

"Really?" McCoy had been quiet, watching and absorbing details. "Exactly how long *is* that, Spock?"

The science officer regarded the doctor evenly. "Two days and six hours, Doctor. Ship time. Exactly."

"Oh." McCoy let out a muted grunt and looked slightly abashed.

Taell remained uncertain. "We will use two days of our remaining supplies just waiting for an answer from the Si-Boronaans. Are there no other options for us?"

"None that you could reach in time." Having walked around the back of the captain's chair, Spock towered over the shorter and more lightly built Perenorean. "There are worlds that would accept you as refugees, but far beyond your range. Whereas yours still exists somewhere in the far reaches of the galaxy." A sudden, chilling thought made him hesitate. "It does still exist, doesn't it?"

"As far as we know, yes," said Taell. "We have come so far, ducking in and out of so many star systems in our attempts to throw the Dre'kalak off our track, that I am not certain even our redoubtable Finderesque Ornean could find the way back—even if we had fuel and supplies enough to allow us to try." Taell hesitated. "We wouldn't want to impose ourselves on those not inclined to help us." The fingers of one hand flexed but the joints did not crack. "We will wait the two days." He made a complex gesture with the seven fingers of his other hand. "If at that time the SiBoronaans turn us down, we will have no choice but to look for other possibilities."

Spock was clearly pleased by the leaderesque's response. "The Perenoreans are a most logical and rational people. I think you would get along well with Vulcans."

"I do not believe I could dispute that." Taell's slitted gold pupils expanded.

Spock saw no reason to linger. "I am off duty. I will leave you with a traditional parting of Vulcans." Raising his hand, he parted his fingers; two to the left, two to the right. "Live long and prosper, Leaderesque Taell."

The Perenorean commander duplicated the Vulcan gesture on his very first attempt. "Live long and prosper, Commander Spock."

Observing the exchange, Uhura decided that the familiar gesture was even more impressive when executed with seven fingers.

While instinctively wary, Four Amek declared on behalf of the Others that as civilized beings, they could not ignore the plea of helpless sentients who had nowhere else to go. Therefore, the government of SiBor would be pleased to allow the inhabitants of the colony ship *Eparthaa* to found a settlement on the SiBoronaan moon DiBor. They would assist the Perenoreans in establishing themselves, insofar as it was possible for the SiBoronaans with their limited resources to do so.

One did not have to know a word of Taell's language to recognize the unbounded joy that this response produced on board the Perenorean vessel.

Coordinates were consulted, details elaborated, and timings exchanged, whereupon the two vessels entered warp space at an agreed-upon speed that was intended to see both craft emerge simultaneously in the SiBoronaan system.

The crew of the *Enterprise* returned to sharpening their specialties and polishing their skills prior to arrival at SiBor. In other words, they reverted to shakedown status—though everyone was aware of the serious nature of the mediation role they had entered into.

"It must be hard for you," Uhura remarked to Spock.

"What must be hard for me? And why do you keep bumping into me? Are you suffering from an illness that is affecting your balance?" There was a hint of concern in Spock's voice.

Glancing back down the corridor and seeing other members of the crew trailing behind them, Uhura reluctantly put a little more space between her and the ship's science officer as she sighed. "I can see that this is going to take some time. There's nothing wrong with my *physical* stability, Spock. You should know that by now."

"I was referring to your present walking and—"

She impatiently cut him off. "There's nothing wrong with *me*. Let's change the subject. Isn't it hard for you to encounter representatives of another people who find themselves in a situation similar to that of your own? How can you be sure your decisions concerning them are objective? It's got to be hard to suddenly find yourself having to deal with refugees."

They turned down another corridor. "On the contrary, Lieutenant." Spock looked around. "Nyota. I believe that the desperate situation in which the Perenoreans find themselves only redoubles my resolve to help resettle my own people. Though we still know very little about them, based on our preliminary contacts and our ongoing exchanges, I find the Perenoreans to be like Vulcans."

She smiled. "Only fuzzier."

"An irrelevant epidermal characteristic. Those with whom we have had interchange—"

She bumped him again. "What did you say?"

"Your irreverence is truly charming, Nyota, but I am being serious."

Her sigh was deeper this time. "What a shock. All right, what about 'those with whom we have had interchange'?"

"They have shown that they will invariably proceed logically and sensibly, with concern for those around them and with an ingrained courtesy that I find refreshing after having to live and work entirely among humans."

"So, you're saying that we're lacking in courtesy?"

"Present company and certain other individuals excepted, of course." They paused outside the entrance to her cabin. "It is not your fault. Occasional rudeness appears to be a congenital defect of the human condition."

"And that is a trait unknown among Vulcans?"

"Not unknown. I could cite you certain examples from my

own childhood that would differ only in general content from the sufferings human children normally inflict on one another. But rudeness is not common between adult Vulcans."

"Really?" She was meaningfully eyeing him.

One eyebrow went up. "Do you mean to imply, however obliquely, that I have been rude to you?"

"I wouldn't think of *implying* such a thing." She indicated the sealed doorway. "But let's put it to the test. There are some aspects of Perenorean dialect that I am having trouble mastering. I could use the help of someone else qualified in advanced linguistics to help me resolve the finer differences." She pressed the door control and the cabin opened. "As a science officer, you're the most qualified to provide the kind of assistance I need. It might take a little while."

Spock hesitated. "Such studies might be better pursued in the ship's research center."

Her eyes twinkled. "Why, Mister Spock, are you turning down a request from a fellow officer? Others might construe that as being downright *rude*." She stepped into the doorway.

This time he didn't waver. "You are quite correct, Lieutenant. I have no choice but to accede to your request. It is the logical thing to do."

She nodded as she stepped aside to let him enter. "I promise you it'll be a damn sight more than logical, Spock."

"Inverness Gold."

Lieutenant Arif Ben-Haim shook his head violently as

he gazed across the deck at his superior. "Loch Kilarney, aged *sixty-two years*."

"The magic is in the barley, Arif." Scott refused to give ground. "The Inverness distillery owns their own farm. They grow their own so they can control every ingredient that goes into the final product."

Punching in a series of commands, Ben-Haim carefully studied the screen in front of him until the rapidly scrolling sequence of figures on the left matched those on the right. A follow-up series of commands fixed them at the level he sought.

"Loch Kilarney has been using the water for its whiskey from the same spring for five hundred years. Its quality has never varied and they bought all the land for kilometers around just to ensure its continued purity."

Attending to his own instrumentation, Scott remained defiant. "There *has* to be a way to settle this!"

"The ship's food synthesizers are state-of-the-art, but they can't work miracles." Putting his data tablet down, Ben-Haim walked over to stand beside the chief engineer. The other members of engineering were attending to their own business and none were looking in their direction. "I just happen to have a couple of small flasks of Loch Kilarney in my cabin."

"And I have a fine bottle with *me*—give me traditional glass over self-chilling metal any day. But . . ." Scott's voice reflected his disappointment as he lowered his gaze. "But I've made a promise to the captain."

Ben-Haim was taken aback. "Are you telling me that Captain Kirk extracted a promise from a Scotsman to forbear from drinking whiskey?"

An increasingly glum Scott responded slowly. "Aye. I've vowed not to drink while on duty. And since the chief engineer is *always* on duty, I'm afraid there'll be no imbibin' for me while I'm aboard this ship."

Ben-Haim considered this. "Suppose you manage to get yourself appointed to the delegation that's going down to SiBor?"

"First of all, me lad, there's no indication that anyone from this vessel is even going to get the chance to set foot on this planet of perambulatin' tent poles. For all I know, the final negotiations will take place from ship to ground. Second, if there is a landing party, and if I were to somehow manage to wangle me way along, I do not think the captain would look kindly on his chief engineer smellin' of spirits while the formalities were bein' conducted. And lastly"—he eyed Ben-Haim unblinkingly—"while the captain extracted no similar promise from you, I'm doin' so here and now. No drinking while on duty. Which means no drinking at all."

Ben-Haim's eyes widened. "Mister Scott! Has our friendly little debate offended you in some way? If so, I'm truly sorry that I—"

Raising a hand, Scott forestalled any further apology. "Easy, Arif. No, you haven't offended me. I'm only holdin' you to the same standard that the captain expects of me."

"But he didn't catch *me* drunk on station. Are you penalizing me because of what he's requiring of you?"

While it was decidedly disrespectful of his fellow engineer to bring up the earlier incident, Scott let the remark go.

"Nay, Arif, I'm not penalizin' ye. I've got another reason."

"What's that?"

Chief Engineer Scott said without hesitation: "I'm doing it because it's right."

5

Buoyed by the unbridled enthusiasm and rapturous applause from the assembled officers and administrators, Admiral James T. Kirk strode to the podium. Resplendent in his dress uniform, a modest selection of only his most important decorations gleaming on his chest, he smiled paternally at the raucous crowd as he waited for the clapping and cheering to die down. This was not the pinnacle of his career, he knew, but only one more step in his inexorable rise to the top. Appointment as commander of Starfleet was virtually a certainty, a mere formality. As the youngest officer to ascend to that rarefied position, there would inevitably be some minor carping about his meteoric rise, but it would be drowned out by the universal acclaim that had greeted his innumerable achievements. Beginning with the defeat of the time-traveling Romulan renegade Nero, it had been followed by the peaceful and successful settling of the lost colonists of the Perenorean Outreach on the SiBoronaan moon of DiBor and the consequent allying of both species with the Federation.

A diplomatic triumph on all counts, the latter had boosted his astonishing ascent within the ranks of Starfleet. None could match his accomplishments, nothing could compare with his mastery of everything from interspecies diplomacy to interstellar battle tactics. The treatises he had composed and the books he had written were eagerly devoured by classes of hopeful cadets as well as the general public. He was feted throughout the Federation for his wisdom, his experience, his foresight, his . . .

Something was wrong. The cheers had morphed, shifted, their tone had changed to . . . laughter. The whole audience of his peers, glittering and attentive in their dress uniforms, was laughing and pointing. He looked down at himself.

He was wearing nothing below the waist.

With a moan, he shot up in bed and looked around wildly. His cabin was nearly dark; the pale blue luminescent lighting automatically responded, coming up to one-quarter. Through the bed, he could feel the faintest, barely perceptible vibration: the *Enterprise* at warp speed. As he turned slightly to his left, the dream was already fading.

Good riddance, he told himself.

"Computer, status report."

A cool feminine voice replied immediately. *"Speed warp factor eight. We are two days out from the SiBor system. All systems are functioning normally. Ensign M'parl is in sickbay with a mod-*

erate intestinal flare-up—something to do with hairballs. Ensign Nanduparvi is being treated for a minor skin irritation. All other members of the crew are healthy. Do you wish elaboration of ship's status?"

"No." Reaching up with both hands, Kirk rubbed at his eyes. "No, that'll be sufficient."

The synthesized voice went silent. It was dead quiet in the captain's cabin. Involuntarily pondering the remnants of the dream as he climbed out of bed, the lights brightened around him when he started to dress. While slipping into his duty uniform, he reflected on the events of the past several days.

The meaning of the dream was simple enough. He had been getting ahead of himself. Anticipating accomplishments before they had been achieved. Counting on promotions prior to being recommended. The confrontation with Nero had ended victoriously—but it had been a near thing. He had gained ample credit for that, but as significant as it was, it was still only one achievement.

He had time, he told himself. He was young . . . and impetuous. Two character traits that did not sit well with Starfleet brass. In order to reach the heights of which he had just dreamed, he would have to demonstrate that he had earned them. That meant reining in his tendency to leap and then look. There were many equally adept, well-qualified, and more-experienced officers in Starfleet.

Admiral, he told himself. His expression twisted. He would never make admiral. He would be lucky to keep command of the *Enterprise*. It was interesting, however, to note the instructional value of an inadvertent dream. No doubt Spock would be able to discourse at length on its virtues.

Kirk had no intention of telling him about it, of course.

Irouth was slight of build even for a Perenorean. As a representative of his kind invited to make the voyage to SiBor aboard the *Enterprise,* he had taken to not only observing Sulu at his work, but to following the helmsman around when he was off duty. This did not trouble Sulu, who found the attention flattering, and the Perenorean was a font of polite and often unintentionally amusing questions.

Take their present location in the ship's gymnasium, for example. While watching Sulu preparing to engage in his daily fencing exercises, Irouth had observed the helmsman flexing his épée and had innocently inquired, "What are you going to do with that cooking utensil?"

When Sulu had finished chuckling, he proceeded to explain the épée's history and purpose. Irouth closely examined the practice version of the ancient blade.

"A very primitive weapon. Surely your kind do not use it in battle now?"

The helmsman's smile widened. "I agree that a phaser is more useful in modern combat. But there's an elegance pertaining to certain antique human fighting techniques that's lost when energy or projectile weapons are employed. I feel that by continuing to work with it, I not only challenge myself physically and mentally, but that I'm also helping to maintain an ancient tradition. It offers excellent exercise that's far more interesting than simply struggling with resistance machines or performing simple calisthenics."

Irouth stepped back out of the way. "May I watch?"

"Of course." Turning away from the Perenorean, the shirtless Sulu slid his left leg back, extending his right arm holding the épée, raised his left hand, and barked a command.

"Alexandre Dumas, *Three Musketeers*—Richelieu's men! On my mark—now!"

In front of him, a brace of swordsmen dressed in seventeenth-century French military costumes were materialized by the exercise room's holo-projector. They came for him one at a time. And one at a time he dispatched them, in the process suffering only a single stab wound to his left thigh. Like the soldiers of the ancient regime and the blade that had inflicted his "wound," the injury to his leg consisted of nothing more intrusive than a concatenation of coherent light.

After half an hour of such exertions involving combat with holos of swordsmen from ancient France to Austria, Sulu was perspiring profusely as he turned to check on his guest. As he had from the very beginning of the exercise period, Irouth was staring keenly at him, having missed nothing.

"What wonderfully controlled movements!" The Perenorean was gesturing expansively with his multijointed hands. "Such a refined combination of grace and strength! In a similar situation, I fear that my people would be reduced to clumsily throwing rocks." He stepped forward, having to tilt back his head to look up at Sulu as he drew closer. "I know that I am presuming unworthily on a friendship in its earliest stages, but—would you teach me?"

Sulu blinked. "What? Teach you fencing?" He studied the smaller and lighter alien. "I don't see why not. Except for all the extra joints, the basic movements should be similar." He gestured at the alien's narrow skull. "You'll just have to be careful to keep your ears out of the way."

Both of the Perenorean's unusual and oversized hearing organs immediately flattened themselves against the sides of his gaunt head.

"I will be very careful to do so! Thank you, Lieutenant Sulu, thank you! I know that I will struggle, but I promise to do my best to absorb whatever lessons you can spare the time to impart to me."

"Don't worry. We'll take it slow and easy." He walked over to the arms rack and began to thoughtfully study its contents. "Let's see if we can find you a slightly shorter weapon. As you see, they all have tips blunted with the necessary integrated electronics, but we'll still have to work up some kind of makeshift protection for you if I'm going to give proper instruction. I think we can modify one of the smaller competition suits."

They were halfway through the second lesson when after a quick and unexpected thrust by Irouth, a thumbnail-sized red orb appeared above and in front of Sulu's forehead. A dozen such orbs already occupied the equivalent space in front of his opponent's body, but the unexpected appearance of the red sphere proximate to his hairline still gave the helmsman pause.

"What did you just do?"

Irouth lowered his practice épée as he straightened. A touch on the side of his modified mask caused the transparent faceplate to fold up and out of the way. "Parry, retreat, parry, feint low, go high. Just as you taught me, Mister Sulu."

The helmsman slowly shook his head. "I didn't teach you that. What you just did was . . . different."

Golden eyes met Sulu's own. "I may have varied my final thrust somewhat. I thought it might have a better chance of slipping past your guard."

Raising his eyes, Sulu spared a glance for the accusatory red orb floating before him. It moved when he did. "Obviously you were right." He smiled anew. "Very clever move. I'll be on the lookout for it from now on." Lowering his own mask, he slid back into a fighting stance. "*En garde!*"

"*En garde,*" echoed the Perenorean as he mimicked both the human's words and posture.

An hour later, Sulu pulled off his mask and wiped at the sweat that was streaming from his brow and cheeks. The time was approaching when he would be required to report to the bridge to begin his shift. Exercise and schooling were over. Thirty-two red orbs drifted above and in front of Irouth.

Twenty-two drifted above and in front of the helmsman.

"You have a facility for this, Irouth." Walking up to the alien, Sulu stuck out a gloved hand. "Congratulations. I've never seen anyone pick up the skill so fast."

The Perenorean gestured dismissively with both hands and ears. "I have tried very hard, but any success I have had today is due entirely to the fact that I have been working with the most excellent instructor! It is certainly a more enjoyable form of primitive defense than throwing rocks!"

Sulu had to laugh as he picked up a towel and dried his face. "Maybe tomorrow we'll try some work with the wakizashi. You should do even better with something that length. Right now I'm due on the bridge, and if I don't shower first, you can bet Mister Spock will have something to say about ship's officers setting an example in personal hygiene." Lowering the cloth, he saw that Irouth was gazing intently at another of the racked exercise weapons. "Most of those are sabers. Fighting with them demands a completely different set of techniques."

Irouth picked up one of the lightweight practice swords and examined it as carefully as if he was absorbing its substance, its heft, and its design into his very being. His tone was appropriately deferential.

"Will you teach me?"

To Chekov, Nathtal looked very much like a Perenorean male. Any secondary sex characteristics were concealed beneath the elaborate wrapping that was wound around her body. The only outward sign that she was other than male was the fact that her ears were noticeably larger and longer.

"What is that?" She indicated the object that was sitting on the table in front of the navigator.

"It's the setting for a game called tridimensional chess." Leaning forward, Chekov moved a rook from one level to another. "I'm competing against a trio of my shipmates." He smiled pridefully. "Back home, I am considered a pretty good player."

One seven-fingered hand twisted in a gracile gesture. "Can you show me how to play?"

A youthful grin creased Chekov's face. "It is not so simple. Being of another species, you have no cultural references."

Gliding into the chair opposite, she reached out to lightly finger several of the hand-carved wooden pieces. What she discovered surprised her. "The components are solid and organic, not electronic."

"That is a tradition with this game, though it can be played electronically. The pieces can be made of any material. There are many older variants among my people. It began as a two-dimensional game that is still played and enjoyed as such. This version has evolved subsequently."

"My people enjoy competition. We enjoy anything that is mentally stimulating. You would call it a form of exercise."

"Certainly. But one has to be careful. Too much physical exercise can sprain the body." He tapped the queen. "Too much mental exercise can sprain the brain."

Reaching out, her other hand came to rest on the back of his wrist. The soft fur was gently ticklish against his bare skin.

"I will be careful, but I want to learn. I want to learn as

much as I can about those who saved me and my fellow colonists." Huge yellow-gold eyes gazed back into Chekov's own. "Even to understanding what you do for amusement and entertainment."

He checked a chronometer and sighed. "Wery—very well. We'll start with the names of the pieces. Once you know those, I'll explain the moves; what each piece can and cannot do. If you're comfortable with that and we have any time left, we'll move on to basic game play."

She eagerly pulled her chair forward. Despite their smaller stature, their multiple joints allowed the Perenoreans to make passable use of furniture designed for humans and other larger bipeds.

When Chekov ended his shift and returned later in the day to where the game was set up, he was surprised to see how the pieces on the boards had been moved. The longer he studied the new arrangement, the more puzzled he became.

"You shifted the pieces. Half of them are gone." Anger mixed with curiosity as he looked over at the alien. "What did you do?"

She was instantly apologetic. "I have been studying. After you left, some of your friends, the ones you have been playing against, came around. They were as interested to converse with me as I was with them. Discussion evolved toward the game. I allowed as how you were teaching me to play, and they responded with suggestions of their own." Her head turned away and her ears, remarkably, folded forward to cover her eyes. *Is that a Perenorean indication of embarrassment?* Chekov wondered.

"I ventured to make one move on your behalf. This occasioned much comment among your shipmates and fellow game players. They seemed surprised. After discussing it among themselves, they offered a countering move. I immediately answered." Her ears slowly drew back to expose her eyes. "As many competitions do, this one proceeded to take on a life of its own." She indicated the board and her tone reflected happiness. "See? You were losing the game before, but now you are winning, yes?"

Chekov sat down in the chair he had occupied earlier that day. He studied the tripartite setting closely, his eyes shifting from one piece to the next, from position to position.

"You have cleaned out half of their major pieces." His eyes rose. "How in Gogol's name did you *do* it?"

She brightened. "A variation on the Khalinkov strategy about which you spoke briefly." Dancing in the air, her remarkably agile fingers traced the history of each move. "Top board to bottom with only feinting action between. You see?"

"No," he muttered. "I don't see. What I do see is that this morning you had never seen or heard of tridimensional chess, and now you are beating opponents in a three-on-one." His gaze narrowed as he fought to fathom what might lie hidden beyond those alien pupils. "You must be incredibly smart, Nathtal. Or an accomplished game player among your own kind." Sitting back, he gestured at the vertically linked game boards. "Still, to achieve something like this in so short a time is—it's nothing short of amazing!"

She looked down and her ears folded backward. "I was

fortunate to do as well as I did. But it was only because I had such a patient and empathetic teacher . . ."

The signal was incredibly weak. It was sheer luck that the *Enterprise* and the *Eparthaa*, traveling together through warp space, picked it up. Even so, both vessels had sped well past the point of origination when the ship's computer system alerted Spock to what it had detected.

The science officer studied it carefully, did some rapid cross-checking, analyzed the signal again, and finally turned toward the center of the bridge.

"Captain, our sensors just picked up and recorded an unusual signal in free deep space."

Uhura had been chatting quietly with McCoy. Now both turned curiously toward the science station as Spock continued.

"It was so weak as to be barely perceptible, but the signature identification is positive. It is quite ancient."

Kirk frowned. "Is that all you've been able to learn about it, Mister Spock?"

"No, Captain. I have processed the signal, enhanced and clarified it, and there is a surprising match. It would appear that on our way to SiBor, we have crossed the path of one of humankind's first interstellar probes."

McCoy looked immediately to Kirk. "Jim, this is wonderful! A historic moment! If this object can still send out a detectable signal, then it's likely to be relatively functional. We have to go back and pick it up."

Kirk drew back slightly in the chair. "Go back? Bones, we're on a vital diplomatic mission. We can't go back. The Si-Boronaans are expecting us and . . ."

The doctor moved toward him. "Come on, Jim. This is important too. It won't take very long to check it out." When Kirk didn't reply, the doctor turned hopefully toward the science station. "Spock, given the present circumstances, you wouldn't pass up the chance to recover an important artifact from Vulcan history, would you?"

The science officer's expression never wavered. "I would have to say no, Doctor, I would not." He turned to Kirk. "Doctor McCoy is correct when he points out that retracing our course to the point where the signal was encountered will take very little time. The Perenoreans are intensely curious. I believe they would not object to the detour."

"So I'm outnumbered," Kirk said. "*Can* we find the signal again, Mister Spock? After all, we're traveling at warp eight. I'm presuming that the signal source in question was also moving."

Spock paused a moment to check one of his readouts. "It is, Captain. But at a velocity so minimal compared to ours that it would appear to be virtually standing still. Were we to backtrack, we would easily find it."

"An important artifact from human history." Kirk mulled his options. The delay in reaching their intended destination would hardly register on the SiBoronaans, and if the Perenoreans raised no objection, so be it.

"Very well, Mister Spock. Let's have a look at whatever's generating this signal the ship insists it picked up. Inform the Perenoreans, and make certain they understand that this will be a minor delay."

"Great, Jim!" McCoy's enthusiasm was almost sufficient to make someone believe he was enjoying being in deep space.

With the *Eparthaa* and its compliant colonists following, the *Enterprise* emerged from warp into the great void between the stars. Kirk was frowning as soon as Uhura activated the main viewscreen. All that was visible were stars like sequins cast against filaments of glowing nebulae.

"There's nothing here." He glanced sharply to his right. "Mister Chekov?"

The navigator was studying his instrumentation. "These are the coordinates. We should be right on top of . . . whatever it is."

The science officer swiveled around. "Indeed we are, Mister Chekov. Almost literally. I have locked in the signal and its source." Without looking at his instruments, his left hand made a fine adjustment. "The viewscreen's magnification is too high. This should be better."

"There!" An excited McCoy unnecessarily pointed at a portion of the viewscreen.

The source of the signal that had both intrigued and puzzled them was so minuscule that it would hardly be noticed if it was sitting in any of the starship's cargo bays. A simple circular antenna mounted atop a crude collection of sealed instruments from which protruded, insect-like, an assortment of cameras, linear antennae, and struts.

"Primitive, all right," Sulu murmured as he stared at it.

Spock had turned back to his station. "Research should only take a— I have it." He turned back to the rest of the bridge. "We are looking at one of humanity's earliest attempts to reach beyond its own solar system." With one hand he indicated the object now clearly visible on the forward viewer. "A probe from the Voyager series."

Though entranced by the sight, McCoy found himself frowning. "Never heard of it."

"I have." Kirk was staring at the ungainly little spacecraft before them. "Ancient history course. There were more than one of them." Gazing at the crude conglomeration of metal and spindly antennae, he felt disappointed. "I'd hoped it might be something more impressive." He looked toward the science station. "Mister Sulu, prepare to resume our previous heading. Warp eight."

"Aye, Captain."

"Uhura . . ."

Taken aback, McCoy moved up alongside the captain's chair. "Jim, we can't just leave it here!"

"We're not just leaving it, Bones." Kirk spoke quietly. "We're going to let it continue on its course, as its makers intended."

"A course to nowhere. It'll keep going forever, until its power source gives out completely and it falls into the gravity well of a sun or trickles out of the galaxy."

"Oh, I don't know about that, Doctor." A mischievous smile creased Chekov's face. "Maybe someone else will pick up its signal and take it home."

"Oh, right, that's likely," McCoy shot back. "Jim, this is a piece of Earth's history. There are people who will want to study this ancient machine, people who'll want to admire it, even in some small way venerate it."

Kirk sighed. "You're not going to let me alone until I agree to take it back with us, are you, Bones?"

The doctor straightened. "I'm just saying that we should value our history." He gestured at the unimposing image on the viewer. "There's no harm in letting it continue on its way, but wouldn't it be better to bring it back so that it can be properly examined, and placed in a museum?"

"All right, all right." Kirk turned. "Mister Spock, assign a detail to bring this Voyager on board. I'm sure an empty corner can be found for it in a cargo bay. Have a force field put around it." He glanced back over at McCoy. "Just in case."

"Thanks, Jim." McCoy returned his gaze to the view forward. "Amazing how far something so small and primitive has managed to travel."

"I suppose. In any case, I guess it's a kind of poetic justice that its journey ends here in the middle of nowhere."

6

As a grand meeting hall hastily decked out in order to host a gathering of great consequence, the Pillarz of AruSiBor was not especially impressive. At least not to citizens of the Federation who had spent time in comparable structures on other worlds. While the small group of humans, Perenoreans, and one ever-curious half-Vulcan were escorted down the length of the smooth-floored vestibule, Kirk reflected that the entire hall would have fit easily into one of the starship final assembly blocks he had often passed while riding his bike back in Iowa, or inside any number of Starfleet's administration buildings in greater San Francisco. Not to mention truly grandiose indoor spaces like roofed-over south Manhattan or the preserved Colosseum in Rome.

Knowing that the hall was considered a vaunted architectural achievement of the SiBoronaans, he and his companions took pains to admire the showy if shallow decorations that had been placed on walls and walkways to mark the solemn occasion. McCoy was especially fulsome in his praise, to the point where one of their native escorts requested and received permission to remove a particularly detailed piece of indigenous embroidery from a wall, roll it tightly between manipulative digits, and press it on the visitor as a present.

A disapproving Spock was quick to comment. "As you are an official member of a formal diplomatic representation, Doctor, you must realize that the accepting of gifts on an individual basis is strictly forbidden by Starfleet regulation one-one-six-eight, section twenty."

Carrying the exquisite if slightly odiferous roll of fabric under his left arm, McCoy eyed the science officer sourly. "I wasn't going to keep it, Spock. It'll go back to Earth to find its proper place among hundreds of similar gifts to the Federation." Lifting one end of the roll, he sniffed as inconspicuously as possible. It was likely their anxious hosts would be unable to correctly interpret his action anyway, since their olfactory organs were of a different design and located elsewhere on their bodies. "After it has been properly disinfected and sterilized, of course. Not that you or I are likely to be affected by any local organisms whether dangerous or benign, but as a doctor I've always been a strong believer in preventing disease wherever possible."

Spock put a little more space between them as they continued to follow Kirk and Taell down the polished cut stone walkway. "I did not mean to criticize, Doctor. I was merely voicing a reminder of a regulation of which I am sure you were already aware."

"Uh-huh. Just like I'm aware that a good portion of your attention since we set down here has been on Lieutenant Uhura instead of your duties." McCoy's expression and tone turned impish. "Correct me if I'm wrong, but I don't believe you're paying quite as much attention to Leaderesque Taell or Masteresque Founoh."

Spock's reply was stiff and formal. "As you should know by now, Doctor, my concern for Lieutenant Uhura is that as communications officer she will be in the forefront of these negotiations should our translation equipment require adjustment, and that ultimately she will be the one relied upon to clarify any misunderstandings."

McCoy smiled and shook his head. "Spock, do you think everyone on the ship is blind?"

"Since that is patently not the case, I fail to follow your line of reasoning, Doctor."

McCoy tried another tack. "There's an old saying: The only thing in Einsteinian space that can travel faster than light is gossip."

"I'm not sure I . . ." The science officer paused. "Oh. Your commentary is unnecessarily convoluted, Doctor, but I understand now. Lieutenant Uhura and I are good friends. That is all."

"Riiight." They were approaching a very low dais crowded with SiBoronaan officialdom, and his voice dropped to a whisper. "And before leaving spacedock, the *Enterprise* wasn't afflicted with dribbles."

Spock's gaze narrowed. "Afflicted with what, Doctor?"

"Dribbles," McCoy repeated. "You know—persistent leaks in the ship's hydrologic structure."

The science officer turned his attention to the indigenous diplomatic assembly directly ahead of them. "From your sarcastic tone, it is plain that you doubt my assertion concerning the relationship between myself and Lieutenant Uhura."

McCoy's reply was a disbelieving whisper. "Spock, everyone on the *Enterprise* would doubt your assertion."

For once, the Vulcan was not allowed a rebuttal. Kirk, Uhura, and Taell had come to a halt before the dais. Ascent was via a sloping ramp of gentle gradient. Given their multiple pseudopodal means of locomotion, it was self-evident that even the most athletic SiBoronaan could not manage a step up of more than a dozen centimeters or so.

As hidden speakers blared forth a mildly disagreeable dissonance that reminded Kirk of energetic children mindlessly smashing snails with rocks, one lavishly draped individual slightly taller and broader than the others stepped forward and managed to shake hands, or at least momentarily lock manipulative digits, with him and then Taell. Absent any fleshy folding, each relaxed eye was able to independently regard the two visitors.

"I am Twelve Covot." Releasing the visitors' hands, the multiple branchings of the single limb curved around to identify the august presences standing behind the speaker. Kirk recognized the name Six Jol, but the rest were new to him. Both Uhura and Spock were preserving the moment on their tricorders.

"You are welcome to SiBor, representatives of the Federation. You are welcome to SiBor, representatives of the Perenoreans."

Before Kirk could offer the formal reply—Uhura's program had chosen the appropriate one—Taell astonished him and every other non-Perenorean in the delegation by dropping to his knees (easy enough to do when one is double-jointed) and spreading both his arms and his ears as wide as possible. In this unexpected gesture, he was joined by every other Perenorean present, including the aged Masteresque Founoh.

"We freely and gratefully abase ourselves before our saviors," Taell declared softly. "If not for the kindness and generosity of the SiBoronaans, all on board the *Eparthaa* would be lost. We would have wandered helplessly in search of a place to settle, orphaned between the stars in search of a home that was not to be, until eventually our meager remaining supplies were exhausted. Now, thanks to your people, we look forward to a new home, a new life, a new beginning. We of the Perenorean Outreach promise to be the very best of neighbors to our new friends, to extend our help whenever possible and to give of ourselves all that we have. We owe everything to you, the SiBoronaans, and we will not forget!"

Having thus expressed his gratitude, the leaderesque of the Perenoreans arched his back and bent forward from his kneeling position until the tips of his ears were touching the floor. For a second time, his actions were copied by his fellows.

It was dead silent in the lavishly ornamented receiving hall save for the grinding, crackling music. An unseen SiBoronaan technician finally had the presence of mind to turn it off.

Twelve Covot continued to face the diplomatic delegation, but his eye flaps folded backward so that he could see behind him. Anxious chittering came from his colleagues as they commenced to converse in low, excited tones among themselves.

An astonished Kirk gathered his own crew around him. With a jerk of his head he indicated the still supplicant Taell and his fellow refugees. Surprises at diplomatic meetings were not to be applauded.

"What the hell is this? Bones, you've spent time alone among them. What does this mean?"

McCoy sounded contemplative. "Maybe it's nothing more than what it appears to be, Jim. Refugees showing their thanks to strangers who have agreed to take them in. I admit that no Federation delegation would act this way, but at this point we know more about Perenorean science than their culture. You know how they're almost apologetically grateful for the smallest kindness. They may engage in this sort of demonstration all the time. It may be perfectly normal for them."

Kirk nodded tersely and turned to his science officer. "Mister Spock?"

"The reason for the display may be exactly as the doctor says, Captain. Or it may be a clever ploy by the Perenoreans to draw all attention directly to themselves."

"And away from us?" As he spoke, Kirk was studying the arching, floor-kissing shapes of the refugees.

"Perhaps. In any event, it is now a fact with which we must

deal. I see no great harm, and from the very first contact the Perenoreans have given us no reason to suspect them of harboring ulterior motives toward the Federation."

"They didn't bow down before us," Kirk was quick to point out.

A note of irritation crept into the science officer's voice. "Do you feel that you have been deprived by the omission, Captain?"

"No, but I . . ." Kirk stopped, realizing that he was looking for trouble where none might exist. Of course, that was part of his job. "When this ceremony is over, I think I'll have a word with Taell. Politely, of course. Just to let him know that we'd prefer not to be hit with any last-minute cultural revelations at sensitive moments."

"Jim," McCoy observed, "I say again that this may constitute typical behavior for the Perenoreans. In fact, right now they may be wondering why we don't join them in genuflecting."

"Then if that's the case, I'll explain it to them in such a way that there's no mistaking our attitude toward such displays. Will that be adequate, do you think, Mister Spock?"

"Quite, Captain. However, it is not their surprise actions that particularly intrigue me." His gaze traveled around the small group of humans. "Leaderesque's effusive expression of gratitude was delivered not in his own language via a translator but directly and in quite passable SiBoronaan."

There was a brief pause following which everyone turned to Uhura. She looked momentarily defensive.

"As soon as the SiBoronaan agreement was struck, the Perenorean communications specialist, my counterpart, asked if we had any examples of or instructional materials in the Si-Boronaan language. I shared what we have."

"No harm, Lieutenant," said Spock, quick to reassure her. "Does anyone here speak SiBoronaan? Doctor McCoy? Captain?" He looked to his left. "Lieutenant Uhura?"

"Just a few phrases," she said. "There's no need for it. When communication is required, translators do a perfectly good job of rendering SiBoronaan into our language."

"I was not criticizing your, or anyone else's, lack of fluency in an obscure alien tongue." Raising his gaze, Spock focused once more on the still inclining Perenoreans. "I was pointing out the remarkable, even unprecedented speed with which Leaderesque Taell—and perhaps others of his kind—has managed to learn sufficient SiBoronaan to deliver such impassioned speech in their own language."

McCoy shrugged, unmoved. "Taell's words came from the heart. I can see him wanting to establish good relations right from the start. The fate of their colony depends on it. What better way than to show your saviors, as he put it, how much you appreciate what they've done than to thank them in their own language?"

Spock's concern was not allayed by the doctor's eminently sensible rationalization. "It is not the motivation that interests me, Doctor, so much as the seeming ease with which it has been accomplished."

"Who said it was easy?" McCoy replied. "For all we know,

Taell has gone without sleep these past couple of days just so he could memorize that one short speech. He may not be able to say another sentence in SiBoronaan or to understand a word of the local lingo."

"That is so, Doctor. Still . . ." Staring past McCoy, the science officer affected an air of intense interest in the paused procedure.

"So they have an aptitude for language." McCoy shrugged off the science officer's concern. "They've already shown that much in the time they've spent on board the *Enterprise*." His attention shifted to the ship's communications officer. "Isn't that so, Uhura?"

"They certainly have given every indication of being exceptionally adept linguists."

The doctor felt vindicated. "Hardly a *dangerous* talent—wouldn't you agree, Mister Spock?"

"Any talent can be put to inimical use, Doctor. Even medicine." He slumped slightly. "I suppose I worry too much. It may be that the difference between Vulcan expressions of gratitude and those of the Perenoreans are extreme enough to provoke unwarranted wariness on my part. I imagine that unless hard evidence emerges to indicate otherwise, I should, as you would surely insist, 'give them the benefit of the doubt.'"

"Damn right," McCoy snorted. "See? They're getting up already, without waiting to be told. I reckon it's just their way of expressing extreme thanks, that's all."

The slightly off-putting alien music resumed as the Perenoreans regained their feet. In response, Twelve Covot retreated. He did not turn; he simply reversed direction, like a ground vehicle. With podal digits like translucent flexible tree roots extending nearly a meter in all directions from the base of their bodies, the SiBoronaans could move freely without twisting or turning their torsos. As a means of locomotion, it was slow but extremely effective.

It was impossible to tell the age of the smaller individual who replaced Covot, but from the attitude of those behind the SiBoronaan, Kirk had the impression that this individual was one regarded by the others with exceptional respect. Unlike any of its slender pole-like brethren, the new speaker clutched a tall, engraved metal staff in half of its coiling manipulative digits. Whether its purpose was ceremonial or served as an aid in staying upright, Kirk could not tell from looking at it. Like Covot, the newcomer used one eye to keep watch on the humans and the other to monitor the anxious Perenoreans.

When the distinguished representative spoke, the voice that emerged sounded more or less the same as Covot's, though it was impossible to be certain since Kirk had to rely on the speaker's words as they were conveyed via his own translator. Able to understand at least some of the local language, a linguistically talented Perenorean might be able to pick up greater subtleties in their speech.

The ability for someone else to comprehend another's language when one could not might prove dangerous, especially in something as fraught with multiple meanings as diplomacy. Fortunately, neither the SiBoronaans nor the Perenoreans had shown the slightest hint of enmity toward the crew of the *Enterprise*. Kirk told himself that, much like Spock, he was worrying too much.

The senior staff-carrying SiBoronaan who had come forth was speaking to Taell and not to the representatives from the *Enterprise*.

"I am Two Wuvemm. Your gratitude is appreciated but overstated. Understand that we are allowing you to settle on our moon as much from hope and expectation as from philanthropy. We are fully aware of DiBor's potential for development and have been for hundreds of cycles. But we do not yet possess the technology necessary to make use of its resources, and we do not yet need the moon. Our population is modest and kept properly under control." Raising the staff he gestured upward, toward the arched ceiling that was decorated with colorfully inscribed geometric patterns.

"It is our hope that in return for this gift not only will your people prove to be good neighbors, but that you will show us how to develop such resources and to improve our own technologies. We have the numbers, you have the knowledge." Now the eye flaps moved so that both oculars were focused on Kirk and his companions.

"We did receive some instructions from the Federation, and for this we are grateful. But the distances between SiBor and the nearest Federation worlds are considerable, and even at the warp speeds of which vessels such as the *Enterprise* are capable, it takes time. Having even a few representatives of a more advanced species so close to SiBor will allow for an easier and speedier exchange of materials and instruction." Once again the staff moved.

"So you see, Taell of the Perenoreans, we of SiBor are not entirely altruistic in this matter. We have selfish reasons for allowing your people to settle here."

"We will do our best to satisfy them," Taell assured his taller host. "Besides the acquisition of new knowledge, the Perenoreans like nothing better than freely sharing what we know with others." He bent forward again. It was not quite a bow. The gesture was far more fluid and relaxed than any human could have managed.

Two Wuvemm did not bow in return. Restrained by its species' equivalent of what in a human would be a fused spine, a forward-inclining SiBoronaan would simply fall over on its face. Instead, clutching the ceremonial staff tightly with every digit, Wuvemm held it parallel to the floor as his eye flaps tilted upward. Gazing at the ceiling, he recited something swift, brusque, and unintelligible, a kind of musical cackle. Whether prayer, resolution, request to the gods, or formal diplomatic language Kirk could not tell because his translator was unable to untangle the syntactic intricacies of the swiftly paced declamation.

Noting the captain's confusion, Uhura edged closer. "The representative is speaking in an elaborate departure from the common contemporary SiBoronaan tongue, sir. Possibly an archaic variant. The linguistic logarithms necessary to process a proper translation are not in my database."

"We'll request a proper translation later." Pulling out his communicator, Kirk whispered into it while trying not to appear too obvious about what he was doing. "Mister Scott, we're recording the proceedings down here but are you getting all of this?"

The engineer's voice whispered back at him. *"Aye, Captain. The channels you've ordered held open are picking up auditory loud and clear."*

"Thank you, Mister Scott. Kirk out."

Though the meeting between the Starfleet delegation, the Perenoreans, and the SiBoronaans was nonbelligerent, it was always good to know that everything was being filed away in the *Enterprise*'s library computer as well as by the tricorders on the ground. That way, if any kind of disagreement about what had been said should arise, there would be a record of everything. With all recording being duplicated directly aboard the ship, there would be no uncomfortable surprises awaiting future diplomats.

Not that Kirk anticipated any difficulties. If anything, the negotiations and exchanges of greetings were going exceptionally well.

"All are in agreement, then," Wuvemm declared when the unintelligible invocation had been concluded. "The ill-fated refugees on board the *Eparthaa* will be allowed to settle wherever they wish on DiBor, and in return they will assist the people of SiBor in advancing their technology and base of knowledge. It is done!"

A sound like a million crickets all complaining at once filled the great hall. A questioning look on his face, Kirk leaned slightly in Uhura's direction.

"They're cheering, Captain."

He nodded. That was a relief.

Wuvemm was not quite finished, however. "I say here and now that there will be peace and friendship forever between our new neighbors and the people of SiBor. Any future disagreements will be mediated as between friends. And should we be unable to reach agreement on a matter of disputation, the Federation will assure the integrity and well-being of SiBor."

Uh-oh, Kirk thought, remembering what Spock had told him. They could represent the Federation in these negotiations, but they could not offer ultimate guarantees. That authority rested with the government back on Earth. As captain of a starship he could oversee treaties and agreements, but he could not offer the full weight of the Federation behind them until they were ratified by the government.

Spock stepped forward.

"While sympathetic to the plight of all refugees, the United Federation of Planets must review each situation in order to be able to respond accordingly. As a member of a refugee race, I am familiar with the accord that has been reached. I can therefore assure the government of SiBor that all necessary steps will be taken to ensure that the peace and tranquillity that exists will be maintained."

Kirk marveled at the science officer's ability to handle the situation without actually promising anything. What was important was that his translated words appeared to satisfy the SiBoronaan delegation. It took the ability of a natural diplomat to speak logically and clearly while saying nothing. Sarek would have been proud.

At a gesture from Wuvemm, two more SiBoronaans scuttled forward. "These are Nine Omurt and Twenty-five Yelerik. They will accompany you to DiBor, both to formally record the presentation of whatever territory will be selected for the purposes of settlement and to offer what assistance they can. Although we have not colonized DiBor or any of our moons, we have studied them for many hundreds of cycles." The diplomat pivoted to face Taell. "If you will provide details as to your physiology and its needs, they can recommend the most efficacious places for you to settle. Once you have chosen a site, both our people will assist in the setting up of your new home."

Taell's right hand flexed in what Kirk had come to recognize as a gesture of understanding. "As a proper colonial expedition, we are prepared to establish ourselves on our own and through utilization of the resources we bring with us, but we welcome any additional help from our new benefactors, the SiBoronaans. We give thanks in advance for even the slightest assistance."

McCoy leaned toward Kirk. "Thanking-est people I ever saw. You'd almost think they were from the South."

"South what, Doctor?" inquired a curious science officer.

McCoy sighed. "It's a human geocultural reference, Spock. I was just saying that the Perenoreans are an exceptionally grateful and polite species."

"Indeed they are," Spock agreed. "One would almost think

them excessively so, if not for the numerous indications that their gratitude is entirely genuine."

"Then we've done a good thing here." Kirk looked on as Two Wuvemm and Leaderesque Taell exchanged quiet conversation. "We've helped refugees representing a previously unknown sentient species, and in turn we've brought a steady stream of advanced assistance to another. All good."

"You are forgetting the Dre'kalak, Captain," Spock pointed out. "I believe they would disagree."

"Yeah, well, they took something away from this, too. The knowledge that the Federation is not to be messed with. They came and went angry at the Perenoreans for some reason, not at us."

"That is true." Spock likewise turned his attention to the ongoing discussion that was taking place between the Si-Boronaan and Perenorean leaders. As had everything else up to this point, it appeared to be going well. "Even so, the warning left by the departing Dre'kalak seemed to have been made in deadly earnest. It is illogical. I see little to fear from the Perenoreans. Unless it is more artfully concealed than we are able to detect, their ship is equipped with defensive weaponry only. They have not given any evidence of possessing even personal sidearms. To all outward intents and purposes, they are exactly what they claim to be: innocent colonists made refugees by misdirection and instrument failure who were forced to flee for their very lives."

Kirk was eminently satisfied with how things had turned out. "We'll escort them to DiBor and see to it that they get transferred safely to the surface. Any further help will have to come from the SiBoronaans, though once Starfleet has received my full report, I'm sure they'll want to send out a formal delegation to cement the new relationship."

The science officer stiffened. "Such consequences had not entered my mind, Captain. As a member of a refugee group, the opportunity to aid another party of similarly disadvantaged sentients is all the recompense I require."

Kirk grunted. "Well, it still won't hurt to have this on your record. A couple more like this and you'll probably be offered your own command."

"As you say, Captain." As usual, the science officer's perfectly neutral tone revealed nothing of what else he might be thinking.

7

The true extent of SiBoronaan generosity was confirmed when Kirk, Spock, and McCoy beamed down to the surface of DiBor. The planet-sized moon was lush with a huge variety of quasi-coniferous growths and native fauna. Unsurprisingly, much of it was related to the indigenous life-forms found on nearby SiBor. Multilegged ruminants grazed peacefully in great pinkish-brown herds on low rolling plains carpeted with thick-bodied grass-like plants. The Perenoreans were delighted to discover that these parted down the middle of their four-sided stems as neatly as if zippered to reveal a host of tasty and nourishing square-shaped seeds inside. Subsisting generally on a diet of supplements and elaborate synthesized dishes, veganism was yet another important characteristic the settlers shared with their SiBoronaan benefactors.

Turning his gaze back from the distant line of high hills

that lay beyond a lazily winding river, McCoy watched from a low rise as energetic Perenoreans began to unfold extensive shelters that had been unloaded from the *Eparthaa*'s shuttles. As ship's doctor, he was especially sensitive to matters of diet. The fact that the colonists shared a similar nutritional philosophy as their hosts had not escaped him. It was hardly unique in his experience. The three men started down the gentle slope toward the site that had been chosen for the new settlement.

"I sometimes wonder, Jim, if humans are among the last sentient species to raise and slaughter other animals for food." He glanced over at the science officer. "Didn't Vulcans used to eat meat, long ago?"

"We are omnivorous, as are humans. The decision to cease consuming animal flesh was both a cultural and a practical one. Cultural because our ancestors gradually came to realize that the killing of another creature for food went against all that our civilization was becoming, and practical because on a desert planet like Vulcan . . . was . . . the amount of energy and resources required to raise livestock was far greater than what was required to produce the same amount of nutrients in plant form." As if to emphasize what he was saying, he was careful to step over a red-stemmed plant atop whose pale mauve blossoms several small brightly colored arthropods could be seen feeding. "Were it possible to do so, we would prefer, philosophically, not even to have to destroy plant life and survive entirely on synthetics. However, we have not yet mastered the necessary nutritional science to permit this."

"But you could still eat meat if you had to," Kirk challenged him.

"Yes. Our digestive systems are still genetically coded to tolerate the intake. It is our ethics that would be damaged."

Kirk was shaking his head as he kept pace with his first officer. "Come on now, Spock. Didn't I read somewhere that Vulcans enjoy seafood?"

"It is true that the purely vegetarian and synthetics diet I have just described is not universal among my people. I confess that I often wonder about tasting such things myself, though I have restrained myself. I suppose that by way of an experiment I could request that the ship's food synthesizer prepare fish."

"If you're going to 'experiment,'" McCoy suggested, "try lobster." He smacked his lips. "Although as far as I'm concerned no synthesizer, no matter how advanced, can duplicate the real thing. And we won't even discuss barbecue. 'Barbecue' and 'synthesized' are two words that should never appear in the same sentence together. Or in the same galaxy."

"I am aware of the terrestrial crustacean to which you refer, Doctor, but I am afraid any such experiment on my part will have to proceed in a different direction."

McCoy made a face. "What's stopping you, Spock?" He grinned. "The mental picture making you queasy?"

"No, Doctor. It is the fact that the ocean-dwelling creature to which you refer reminds me entirely too much of a certain diplomat I've met. Who, needless to say, I cannot envision eating."

Kirk chimed in. "One of these days we're liable to run into

an intelligent species that through convergent evolution has developed to look like your basic farm animal." He looked over at McCoy. "Imagine the delicate diplomatic dance that would arise if that happened."

The doctor shrugged and nodded toward the horizon. "Damn shame. Lot of meat on the hoof here that's going to go to waste."

Spock's tone was reproving. "The 'meat on the hoof' would doubtless hold to a different opinion on that, Doctor."

For the site of their initial settlement, the Perenoreans had selected a bluff that protruded into and partly created a bend in the river. With grassy plains behind them and dense native forest on the opposite bank, it offered excellent prospects for development as well as a permanent water source. DiBor's gravity being slightly less than that of either SiBor or the Perenorean homeworld, everyone was able to move about and work with ease and efficiency, and for longer periods of time than would normally have been the case. The enhanced feeling of health and well-being extended to the visitors from the *Enterprise* as well.

Additional supplies and assistance had also begun to arrive in the form of promised local aid. Disgorging supplies and equipment from their cargo bays, several bulky SiBoronaan shuttles were visible off to the south of the settlement site. SiBoronaan spacecraft were only adequate for exploring their own solar system, but they were more than up to the task of bringing in prepared building materials and other goods from the home planet that could be used to boost the growth of the burgeoning Perenorean colony. Parked beside the settlers' far sleeker and more advanced shuttlecraft they looked like so many old-style football linemen squatting among gymnasts.

As they wandered through the construction site, the *Enterprise* officers could not help but notice the ease with which the bipedal Perenoreans and the monopole-multipodal SiBoronaans worked side by side.

"This is going better than anyone could have hoped." McCoy couldn't keep a smile from his face nor a touch of satisfaction from his voice as they walked between newly erected living quarters and other structures that were rising with admirable speed. "Look over there."

A trio of slender SiBoronaans was assisting a single Perenorean in setting water lines. The tubing emerged in a continuous flow from a single large, nearly silent mechanism. The process involved no welds, rivets, or fasteners of any kind. The comparative silence as well as the absence of any visible connectors linking lengths of tubing was what tipped the three officers to the fact that the device was one that the Perenoreans had brought with them on the *Eparthaa* and was not one that had been provided by their agreeable but less technologically sophisticated hosts.

"Truly as gratifying an example of interspecies cooperation as any we have seen, Doctor," Spock commented. "But . . ."

McCoy sighed. "What is it this time?"

The science officer wore a pensive look as he continued to observe the cooperative effort. "First, the machine that is doing the work is of Perenorean origin, though the raw materials may have been supplied by the SiBoronaans. Second, if you look carefully you will see that the SiBoronaans appear to be having some difficulty keeping up with the pace of the work. The Perenorean is repeatedly having to pause to explain some aspect of the process to them."

McCoy was unmoved. "The Perenoreans come from a more advanced civilization. It's only natural that there are certain aspects of their technology that will take some time to explain to the locals. You'll note that they don't appear to be holding anything back, or trying to keep any secrets from the SiBoronaans." With a sweep of one arm he took in their busy surroundings. "Everywhere we've been we see them giving freely of their knowledge to their new friends."

"Anything else, Spock?" Kirk asked curiously.

The science officer gestured in the direction of the ongoing hydraulic project. "The Perenorean supervising the work is not a diplomat or linguist, yet she seems to be conversing effortlessly with the SiBoronaans in their own language. I can detect no evidence that translation equipment is in use."

"So?" the always argumentative McCoy replied.

Spock continued to study the ongoing installation effort as he spoke. "It is surprising that someone as busy and burdened with other responsibilities as Leaderesque Taell would have the time to master even a small part of the local language prior to the ceremony. It is more understandable that a Perenorean linguistics specialist might manage it." He looked at the continuing work. "But to see that a Perenorean mechanical engineer has also been able to do so strikes me as quite remarkable."

Still McCoy refused to give ground. "Uhura said they might be natural linguists. What about it?"

"I am constructing a thesis, Doctor." For a second time Spock pointed at the work taking place in front of them. "This is but another piece of data."

"What is your theory, Spock?" Kirk asked him as they resumed their walk through the settlement site.

"Captain, I do not yet have enough data sets to lay out my theory."

"I hope we won't have to wait too long." McCoy smiled pleasantly.

Spock eyed him imperturbably. "If it turns out to be anything like I think it may, Doctor, you will be interested in the final result."

That prompted a shift in McCoy's attitude, but despite being pressed to elaborate, Spock would say no more.

Another piece of the data manifested itself later that afternoon. Having consumed the simple but nourishing lunch of concentrates they had brought with them, the three officers had descended from the bluff on which the settlement was being constructed in order to stroll along the pleasant river beach. The mix of sand and gravel hinted at the presence beneath the flowing water of something akin to a freshwater coral. Kneeling, Spock scooped up a sample of the fine-grained pink and yellow grit and placed it in an empty concentrate container for safekeeping.

"Something to study back on board ship," he explained unnecessarily.

McCoy offered his tricorder. "You could analyze it here."

The science officer straightened. "I have much on my mind, Doctor. Examining this will provide a welcome diversion."

Kirk was ignoring both of them. Instead, he was squinting at something on the other side of the river. "Speaking of diversions, gentlemen, one appears to be coming our way."

Turning, his subordinates joined him in examining the smooth-surfaced watercourse.

At least, the majority of it was smooth surfaced. The part that was not was presently a scene of considerable commotion. Having unfolded a small boat from the stores that had thus far been shuttled down from the *Eparthaa*, a trio of Perenoreans had crossed the river to explore the opposite bank. They had been joined by a couple of SiBoronaans. Now the five of them were expending a considerable amount of energy in their haste to get back, the craft's waterjet engine working at maximum thrust.

Speed was necessary because the creature that was currently in pursuit was larger than all five of them put together, plus their boat. Wide and flattened of body, it looked like a giant river stone, albeit one covered with protrusions, bumps, and warts. In comparison to its body, its eyes were small and set low on the sides of its skull. Additional bony protrusions covered its head and the short double tail. Six legs provided excellent locomotion in the water. The broad, horizontal mouth in which rows of interlocking triangular brown teeth were clearly visible, and from which the occasional reverberant bellow emerged, was just about wide enough to swallow the boat and its frantic occupants in one gulp.

"It would seem," Spock observed with his usual calm, "that this scouting party has disturbed an example of the local fauna."

McCoy had already begun to back up. "As usual, Spock, your powers of understatement are unmatched." He glanced at Kirk. "Jim, I don't suppose you brought a phaser with you?"

Kirk was likewise retreating. "Why? Carrying phasers among peaceful colonists and friendly locals would only make us look aggressive. Besides"—he was moving faster now—"it was assumed the SiBoronaans knew all about their moon and would warn us of any danger."

Spock had not started to join his companions in quickly retracing their steps. "It would appear, Captain, that in that regard they may be guilty of an oversight."

"Oversight?" McCoy was openly aghast. "How do you overlook a carnivore that's bigger than a shuttlecraft?"

"We'll ask our hosts," Kirk commented. "Later. Spock, we need to get *out* of here."

"I'm afraid I cannot do that, Captain."

"Spock, come on!" In the face of the very real oncoming danger McCoy had set aside his teasing sarcasm. "You can analyze *this* later—from the images."

Instead of joining them the science officer had begun to move in the opposite direction. "Go with the captain, Doctor. I have to stay and try to help my fellow refugees and their hosts."

The boat was nearly on shore and Spock was now running to meet it. Behind the scouting party the wailing DiBoronaan carnivore had closed the gap and was now kicking its way across the river gravel as much as it was swimming. As soon as its massive, pillar-like legs got a purchase on the rocky bottom it would be able to shrink the distance between itself and its prey even faster.

Kirk and his companions were not the only ones who had taken notice of the chase. On the bluff above the beach both SiBoronaans and Perenoreans had gathered to watch. Individuals of both species were pointing and gesturing. A couple of SiBoronaans had brought forth primitive projectile weapons and were firing at the rampaging predator. Most of their shots missed. The few that did strike home only served to increase the determination of the thrashing predator.

Kirk and McCoy caught up to the science officer. "Interesting," Spock observed serenely as they neared the rapidly approaching boat.

"'Interesting'?" McCoy gaped at his fellow officer. "What'll be damned 'interesting' is if we don't get our backsides out of here before that monster gets onshore!"

"What's interesting, Spock?" a less panicky Kirk inquired.

Turning, the Vulcan shaded his eyes as he looked up and back to scrutinize the edge of the bluff above them. The two SiBoronaans who had been firing at the oncoming carnivore had been joined by a third.

"Our SiBoronaan hosts have brought weapons with them. Either they harbor secret fears of us or their new neighbors, or it clearly implies that they were aware of the presence of dangerous fauna on this moon. Yet when discussion of permitting the Perenoreans to settle here was ongoing, such potentially hostile obstacles to development and exploitation were never mentioned." He glanced at McCoy. "In one of our many conversations I believe you once delineated a human term for this sort of thing, Doctor."

"What? I never . . ." The doctor's voice trailed away into thoughtfulness. "Oh. I see what you're getting at, Spock." He began to nod knowingly. "'Horse trading.'"

The science officer turned back to face the water's edge. "We now have another and perhaps overriding reason why the SiBoronaans have not settled their very habitable large moon. It is not because they are technologically incapable of doing so. Nor do they necessarily lack the will or the desire. It is because the local life-forms may be too much for them to handle." He pointed toward the incoming watercraft and its increasingly frantic passengers. "As a species, the SiBoronaans are physically very stable—but also quite slow moving. Even a casual predator would be able to run them down."

Kirk had no trouble following the argument. "I get it. So they invite the Perenoreans to settle here in the hope that the colonists will bear the brunt of dealing with dangerous local fauna. Following which the SiBoronaans can start putting up settlements of their own while the Perenoreans do the dirty work." His expression was taut. "Sounds like we may have been underestimating the ambition of our hosts."

Spock had started forward again. "If we do not do something soon, there will be two less of them, Captain, and three fewer colonists . . ."

McCoy hung back, spreading his hands. "We're unarmed,

Spock! What can we do? By the time Mister Scott could get a sufficient fix to beam all of us out of here that moving mountain will be on top of us!"

"I suspect that this particular large predator buries itself in the ground, perhaps in the softer sand and soil along the riverfront, and waits for prey to come its way. If you will notice, its dorsal side is a perfect analog of rocks and soil. A most excellent example of offensive camouflage."

"Yeah, well, right now all I can see *is its teeth*." Muttering to himself, McCoy remained with his colleagues.

Propelled by its waterjet, the folding Perenorean boat scooted up on shore before being brought to a halt as the weight of its passengers caused its convex hull to dig into the sand. Immediately the sides of the craft folded down to allow those inside an easy exit. The Perenoreans moved quickly, but their SiBoronaan guides could not.

Which was where Spock's determination to lend assistance proved itself. With he and Kirk hefting one of the SiBoronaans between them and a puffing, steadily complaining McCoy and two of the Perenoreans picking up the other, they raced to get away from the beach. Beneath the lightweight fabric that wrapped around its pole-like body Kirk found the SiBoronaan unexpectedly heavy.

They were just starting up the slope that led to the top of the bluff when the enormous, hulking carnivore erupted from the water and began lumbering up the beach after them.

As McCoy glanced back over his shoulder, his eyes widened. "We're not gonna make it, Jim! The damn thing's too fast!"

"Courage, Doctor." Across from his friends, Spock was all but pulling the two assisting Perenoreans along with him in addition to carrying the bulk of the SiBoronaan's weight.

This time, however, McCoy was right: if they maintained their current pace they were not going to make it. As the wide, stocky head of the predator loomed over them and started to descend, they were forced to abandon the two SiBoronaans and dart sideways to avoid the downward plunge of the massive skull. The broad mouth opened wide, and teeth like worn saw blades descended.

Propelled by their broad spray of pseudopods, the SiBoronaans could not move faster than a brisk walk at best. But their tall cylindrical bodies did permit them to roll rapidly. Tucking in their eye flaps and single multidigited limb, the two scouts did just that. The carnivore's massive jaws slammed into the beach where prey had stood only a moment earlier. Raising its mouth and spitting out sand and gravel, the monster made a deep grunting noise like an antique combustion engine unable to turn over. As it slung its head from side to side it continued to spit out the remnants of its unpalatable mouthful.

Brave intentions could only do so much, Kirk reflected as he scrambled for higher ground. McCoy was right behind him. Even Spock saw the futility of trying to stand and fight the thundering killer. Having expelled the last bit of inadvertently gulped ground, the predator looked to its left. One of the SiBoronaans had just struggled back to an upright stance. With the bluff on one side and the predator on the other, it had no room to roll free a second time and did not possess a tenth of the speed necessary to flee. Growling, the monster took a multilegged step toward it. At least, Kirk thought, they might be able to save the other guide.

Something liquid arced in a tight narrow stream from the bluff above. It looked like a gush of melted marshmallow. From the slightly off-white color Kirk recognized it as the same material that encased not only Perenorean equipment but much of the interior of their starship as well. It splattered against the monster's face, giving it pause as the terrified SiBoronaan scuttled away in a futile attempt to get clear. Kirk realized what was happening as a second stream from overhead joined the first. The Perenorean engineers had turned the nozzles of two of their unique foam devices onto the predator.

Hardening on contact with the air, the white stuff slowed the huge carnivore almost immediately. Bellowing and roaring, it struggled furiously beneath the twin spew of rapidly solidifying construction and insulation material. Whatever its composition, the white goo was not strong enough to permanently restrain the monster. As soon as a segment of the flow hardened, a mighty twist or angry kick shattered the material into snow-like shards. But the continuous jets of white did more than slow its movements. More importantly they also served to distract the predator while a cluster of fast-moving Perenoreans dashed down the slope, picked up the remaining SiBoronaan, and carried him to safety atop the bluff.

It seemed that their valiant and selfless effort was only a temporary reprieve. Bursting completely free of its hardening white bonds, the predator started upward in pursuit of its stolen prey, following a wider and gentler ascendable slope than the one taken by the retreating Starfleet officers. Once it got atop the bluff, there was nothing to stop it from wreaking havoc among the incipient colony. Shouts and whistles, clicks and hoots from the vicinity of the construction site had begun to fill the air.

Having reached the near side of the settlement Kirk debated whether or not to hail Scott to use the ship's phasers, but it would be hard to target just the predator. Or Scott could beam down phaser rifles, maybe with enough firepower that they could blast the lumbering carnivore into nodule-ridden cutlets. The only thing that caused him to hesitate was where the weapons could be beamed down, and in the meantime there was no telling how many of the colonists and their SiBoronaan hosts would die. Even so, that course of action seemed the best option out of a continuously shrinking number of bad ones.

Kirk had his communicator out and was preparing to make the request when a pair of Perenoreans appeared in front of the ascending carnivore. As it was about to crest the top of the bluff, from which other colonists and SiBoronaans had fled, the two refugees halted. One was carrying something long, slim, and tubular on a shoulder. As he knelt, his companion bent to make some sort of adjustments to the large oval shape at its terminus.

The monster put first one thudding foot pad over the rim of the bluff, then another. As it did so something tiny and bright flashed from the end of the cylindrical device resting on the Perenorean's shoulder. The second Perenorean had stepped to one side and out of the way. The blast of light that emerged from the oval opening of the tube shot in front of her.

The dart that had been fired by the kneeling Perenorean struck the predator, barely finding a purchase on the thick skin. As the tube wielder rose and started to retreat, a second bright flash came from the place where the dart had hit. A shudder ran through the monster from its jaws to the tips of both tails. Slowly, ponderously, like a gigantic boulder coming to rest at the bottom of a hill, its six legs folded beneath it. Without taking another step it came to rest where it had fallen. With the bulk of its mass still lying over the rim of the bluff, it began to slowly slide backward. Rushing to the edge, Kirk and his colleagues looked on as the carnivore slid down to the beach, creating a small landslide with it.

When it had been struck by the dart the creature had not made a sound. The weapon had only crackled twice: once when fired and once when the embedded dart had done—what?

"Quietest kill I ever saw." McCoy wore a look of awe. "Except for the little bang when the dart went off it's almost as if it just went to sleep."

As other anxious Perenoreans and SiBoronaans moved to help the exhausted scouts, the *Enterprise* officers confronted the pair of colonists who had intervened so decisively. The Perenoreans, one male and one female, made no effort to conceal the device they had employed, and answered questions freely.

"It is something we have among our supplies," the female explained without hesitation. "We could hardly be certain that the world upon which we settled would be wholly free of inimical life-forms." Multidigited hands and double-jointed arms gestured across the river. "It is just that we had none ready when the scouting group was attacked. They did not take the device with them on their expedition because we were not warned that dangerous life-forms would be present here."

"Yeah, our agreeable hosts, the SiBoronaans, neglected to mention that little fact to us too," a perspiring McCoy said.

"No matter," she declared cheerfully. "The incident, like the predator, has been put to rest."

Spock was examining the long, oval-tipped tube. "I am curious to know exactly how such a large and powerful carnivore, about which your people knew nothing, and have never before encountered, was so effectively 'put to rest.' I heard only a small detonation."

The male Perenorean who had fired the weapon was eager to explain. Yet again Kirk was struck by their willingness to share their own knowledge, no matter how potentially sensitive. Was nothing held back? Did the Perenoreans even have a word in their language for "secrecy"?

"The *lagarouth* fires a projectile that contains a powerful electric charge. A lethally flexible battery, your kind might say. The projectile is connected to the *lagarouth*, at the rounded end of the device"—the Perenorean did not say *weapon*, Spock noted—"which holds a more powerful charge. As soon as it penetrates a target, the projectile performs an instant analysis of the subject's neurology and delivers enough of a jolt to paralyze the nervous system and stop its heart. If the charge carried by the projectile is insufficient to accomplish this, it can draw upon the greater charge stored in the end of the *lagarouth*. Linear broadcasting of energy permits transfer of sufficient power to carry out the termination." He bobbed his head slightly; a sign of deference mixed with politeness. "It is not the use we prefer to put our technology to. But our species' experience has shown that colonists must expect to occasionally encounter native life-forms that cannot always be persuaded by reason."

Spock nodded knowingly. "A situation in which I find my own self more often than I would like."

"Right," commented McCoy, "except that when you're about to lose an argument you don't respond by electrocuting your debate partner."

An eyebrow lifted. "That is true, Doctor. I confess that on occasion the desire to do so has manifested itself."

Kirk was studying the motionless bulk of the monster. "A clean, quick, and comparatively painless death." He turned back to the pair of Perenoreans. "I continue to be impressed by your people's efficiency. Maybe one of these days you can even give us some pointers."

"Pointers?" The female Perenorean was stumped.

"Instruction. Suggestions." Kirk smiled as he explained. For some odd reason he felt gratified that the supple alien could not perfectly comprehend the meaning of what he had said.

"Ah." She looked away. "I do not think that either I or any of my fellow colonists would presume to offer correction or instruction to those who saved us from the Dre'kalak and succeeded in helping us to secure our new home."

"But you are happy to answer questions if they are asked." Spock indicated the *lagarouth*. "Such as when we inquired about the operation of your weapon."

"It is not a weapon." The male Perenorean was quick to correct the science officer. "It is a tool whose use is sometimes regrettably necessary to ensure that a settlement is safe." Holding the long metal—or was it metal, Kirk wondered as he saw it close up—tube with both seven-fingered hands, the shooter offered it to Spock. "Would you like to inspect the interior? I would welcome your observations on its engineering and construction."

Spock demurred. "Perhaps another time." His attention shifted to the other side of the river. "Given the recent dramatic encounter and the apparent reticence of the SiBoronaans to go into detail about the local life-forms, I suspect you may have need of it again soon. It will be decidedly useless to you if it is lying in pieces on a table somewhere."

Moving up alongside the science officer, McCoy joined him in gazing out across the sea of green and blue boles that dominated the far bank.

"You think another one of these things is likely to follow in the wake of the first, Spock?"

"I do not know, Doctor. But I do know that where one large predator is encountered, there are likely to be others."

Kirk turned his attention back to the bustling, incipient settlement. "I think we should have a talk with the SiBoronaans."

8

Maybe their timing was just bad, Kirk told himself. Or maybe they had used up their quotient of luck. Vulcans were willing to entertain theories of convergence, and were content to discuss coincidence, but to ascribe them to luck was an "invention of emotionally effervescent humans." In fact, Kirk found himself thinking as he ran for cover, he was not even sure there was a word for luck in the Vulcan language, or if they simply employed the human term as a courtesy.

Could use a little of what the Vulcans insist doesn't exist right now, he thought anxiously as he ducked beneath a track-wheeled bulk carrier. At least this time he was armed. Ever since the encounter with the giant riverine predator, no one beamed down to the Perenorean colony without a phaser.

In a panic situation that could be an issue, as he discovered when a blast of energy disrupted the air in the immediate vicinity of his left ear. He whirled furiously.

"Hell, Bones, watch where you're shooting!"

Behind him and huddled deeper beneath the massive yet streamlined Perenorean construction vehicle, McCoy lowered his weapon and looked abashed.

"Sorry, Jim. I'm a little out of practice." He glanced down at the phaser clutched tightly in his right fist. "In fact, I never had much practice. Starfleet expects its physicians to heal wounds, not inflict them."

Kirk peered out from beneath the carrier's overhanging front end. Chaos had descended among the settlement's partly erected buildings. And that was not all that had descended.

Even in the midst of the hysteria caused by their arrival, Kirk had already learned that the SiBoronaans did not have a name for the aerial carnivores. While they had failed to warn the Perenorean settlers of the presence of the giant forest dweller, at least they had been aware of its existence. The swarm of membranous-winged killers that was presently assailing the settlement site was of a species and number unknown to the SiBoronaans. Their limited technology had allowed them to visit DiBor but not to explore it fully. Each expedition, the captain had been told by a SiBoronaan fleeing the swarm, returned home with new information. Unfortunately, none of these earlier visits had included mention of the two-meter-long flying predators.

The carmine-green segmented cylindrical bodies of the attackers were quadsymmetrical. Each body section featured a single eye that gazed hungrily at the world around it from the leading edge of a leathery wing. The location of the eyes on the four opposing wings was unusual but understandable, since there was no room for oculars or any other identifiable sense organ on a tiny head that was almost entirely mouth. About as large as a human eye, the circular maw was lined with sharp, inward-pointing teeth. When a wide-eyed McCoy described the first one he saw, appropriately enough, as a flying mouth, for want of a better or a local term Kirk promptly dubbed the indigenous carnivores *flyjaws*.

As he and McCoy gazed out from beneath the loader where they had taken refuge, a Perenorean technician came running toward them. He was flailing futilely at his back. His double-jointed arms allowed him to grasp at the creatures clinging there but he was not strong enough to pull them off. That was because the pair of flyjaws that had attacked him had locked their mouths onto his flesh, their circular jaws ripping through his clothing to fasten themselves to his back. One continued to flap two of its wings while its companion had all four folded flat against its body. In a couple of seconds the uppermost of the pair also folded all of its wings against its sides. Uttering an intermittent high-pitched meeping, the terrified and tormented Perenorean began to slow, his stride surrendering to a stagger as the blood was methodically drained from his body.

"Here's a better use for your hands, Bones." Gripping his phaser tightly, Kirk started out from beneath the protection of the loader. Glancing upward, a hesitant McCoy followed.

"Hundreds of other worlds out here," he muttered. "Why can't one of them look like Kentucky?"

"Bones!"

McCoy whirled, ducked, and fired as a flyjaw struck at his back. His shot went wild, but Kirk's did not. The energy burst ripped into the chittering predator and tore it from mouth to wing. It face-dove into the ground, the head snapping and sucking at the long open wound.

Having already reached the rapidly weakening Perenorean technician, Kirk was firing at the flyjaws attached to his back. "Bones, cover me!"

"Cover . . . ?" While the doctor didn't have a great deal of experience with Starfleet weapons or particularly good aim, it didn't mean McCoy could not be effective. Standing close to Kirk and the injured Perenorean, the doctor fired off burst after burst. Though several struck home and caused a brace of flyjaws to tumble from the sky, McCoy felt no sense of achievement. In firing repeatedly and blindly upward, he was bound to hit something.

Because the sky overhead was dimmed by the presence of no fewer than a thousand circling, cackling, saliva-dripping flyjaws. And more of them arriving every minute.

Though he had shot both of the DiBoronaan predators clean through, Kirk still had to holster his phaser and use both hands to rip them away from the Perenorean's body. Each flyjaw left a bloody circle on the technician's back. With one of his arms draped over his shoulders, Kirk hauled the weakened Perenorean toward the shelter of the loader as McCoy did his best to supply covering fire.

Once beneath the impenetrable overhang the doctor commenced an examination of the moaning Perenorean's wounds. Swapping phaser for medical tricorder, he passed the sophisticated instrument slowly over the alien's body. Having been downloaded with every bit of medical information on their species that Masteresque Founoh and his colleagues had been able to supply to their human counterpart, the tricorder quickly analyzed the damage and prescribed a course of treatment. This demanded a transfusion of synthesized Perenorean body fluids and far more work than McCoy was presently equipped to perform; the best he and Kirk could do was try to stop the bleeding and keep the injured technician calm until his own people arrived.

Mixed with the kind of desperate meepings the female had been uttering were the hysterical chirps of fleeing, panicky SiBoronaans. The flyjaws were a thoroughly opportunistic class of predators, more than happy to suck nurturing body fluids from any prey that might present itself. Having already demonstrated a fondness for Perenorean blood, Kirk felt certain they would be just as glad to attach themselves to any unfortunate human.

As McCoy tended to the injured technician as best he could with the limited equipment that was available, Kirk hazarded a glimpse outside. He had been so occupied with defending McCoy and himself from the initial assault that he'd not had a chance to get anything more than a quick look at their fast-moving attackers. A single glance upward showed that, despite the steady toll being taken on the attacking flock by the defenders of the settlement, there were now far more of the ravenous bloodsuckers circling overhead than there had been earlier.

They must send out some kind of signal when they've found a tempting food source, Kirk decided as he continued to watch from cover. *Like bees or ants.* A high-pitched squeal, or something olfactory in nature. If that was the case, then it was likely the colonists were going to have to kill every last one of them before the creatures could contact others of their kind. Unless the swarm first sucked the life out of every Perenorean and Si-Boronaan on the bluff. Squatting there while McCoy worked desperately to keep the Perenorean technician alive, the captain of the *Enterprise* considered his options.

Sulu and Chekov had proven adept at the use of the *Enterprise's* weapons. But while a starship phaser burst or two directed at the flyjaw swarm from orbit would doubtless exterminate most if not all of them, the unavoidable collateral damage would be unacceptable. A cleansing blast of such force would probably result in the deaths of the majority of colonists and their SiBoronaan saviors.

Kirk was not concerned for himself. Should the situation become hopeless he, McCoy, and Spock could beam back aboard the *Enterprise*. Utilizing the transporter, Scott would try to save as many of the others as he could. Maybe Spock would have a better idea. He looked around, frowning.

Where the hell *was* Spock, anyway?

With his free hand, Kirk pulled his communicator. Behind him McCoy, quietly cursing his lack of equipment, continued to work feverishly on the injured Perenorean technician. The colonist's moaning had ceased, though whether from the salubrious efforts of the doctor's ministrations or because he had died, Kirk did not have the heart to turn and find out.

"Spock! Where are you? What's your location?"

"Coming your way and closing, Captain."

Kirk was relieved to hear the familiar voice. As usual, Spock sounded as calm and controlled as if they were back on the ship.

"I am not alone."

The science officer came into view moments later, racing around the corner of a half-finished structure. Kirk had a bad moment when he noticed something alien and cylindrical clinging to his second-in-command's back. He was in the process of raising his phaser and taking aim, hoping he would be able to free the science officer without hitting him, when he saw that Spock was burdened not by a bloodsucking flyjaw but a SiBoronaan. Flapping like loose flags, pieces of the alien's garb trailed behind.

They safely reached the cover of the loader, thanks to Kirk methodically blasting first one hungry dive-bombing flyjaw and then a second out of the sky. Breathing hard but evenly, Spock unloaded his passenger. It was impossible to tell if the SiBoronaan was scared stiff because their normal posture was one of innate rigidity. Both eye flaps, however, were in constant motion, beating fretfully back and forth like the wings of a small stingray and making it impossible for Kirk to meet either or both of them with his own gaze.

Spock looked past his friend. "Doctor McCoy is tending to the injured, I see."

Still frustrated by his lack of appropriate medical material and medication, McCoy spat a reply. "I'm doing everything I can short of mouth-to-mouth—and I haven't ruled that out yet."

Anger and anxiety churned within Kirk as he turned to— or rather on—the fortunate SiBoronaan Spock had rescued. At the moment, the *Enterprise* captain was in no mood to be diplomatic. He made sure his translator was functioning.

"First that hulking great mountain of a meat eater whose existence here you people 'forgot' to mention comes lumbering out of the riverside, and now *these*." After gesturing skyward, he stepped past Spock and, utterly heedless of protocol, reached up with both hands and grabbed the two fluttering eye flaps, stilling them. "Look at me when I'm talking to you!" Kirk hoped that his translator was fully conveying the anger and frustration underlying his words. "What's next? Tell me! Giant worms that swallow buildings? Lethal parasites? Poisonous night predators? No wonder your people were so willing to let the Perenoreans settle here. The place is a hellhole seething with dangerous carnivores!"

"No, nay, negative, Captain Kirk." The SiBoronaan was plainly more worried about the airborne predators circling overhead than he was of the human holding him by the eye flaps. "We are innocent of such accusations! Yes, true, we knew of the existence of the giant river-forest dweller. It was something to be mentioned later, as the Perenoreans grew more comfortable in their surroundings."

"Helping folks avoid being eaten while they're building their home is one way of making them feel 'more comfortable in their surroundings.'" McCoy made his point while he continued to minister to the injured Perenorean tech.

Either the SiBoronaan did not properly comprehend the doctor's sarcasm or else chose to ignore it. "But as has been confessed, these aerial killers are new to us also. Until this day, we knew no more of their existence than did you."

"Great. Wonderful," Kirk commented tiredly as he released the SiBoronaan's eye flaps and stepped back. "Just what's needed here. A mutual learning experience." Turning, he looked back out at the blood and chaos that threatened to overwhelm the colony before it could even get started. "Spock, any ideas? We could beam armed personnel down to join the fight."

Spock shook his head. "Impractical, Captain. A gratifying notion on the face of it, but tactically ineffective. Not a solution. While another few dozen phasers would of course have an impact on the attacking creatures, they would not bring an end to their assault. Not as long as they somehow continue to call upon others of their kind to join in the attack. While it is true that the ones here now must be killed or driven off, it is even more important that more of their species be convinced not to come this way—as additional hundreds, perhaps thousands, are doubtless doing so even as we speak."

"Then what do we do, Spock?" McCoy indicated his breathing but unconscious patient. "We're responsible for these people settling here. We can't just beam back aboard the *Enterprise* and abandon them."

"I concur fully, Doctor." Spock joined Kirk in peering out from beneath the loader's overhang and, occasionally, letting loose a killing burst from his own phaser. Though dead flyjaws were piling up everywhere, each time Kirk snuck a look skyward, there seemed to be more of them, reinforcements arriving every moment.

And each new cluster was as hungry and determined and ferocious as those who had preceded them.

The concentrated fire from the Starfleet officers as well as those SiBoronaans and Perenoreans who were armed exacted a steady terrible toll among the circling, swooping, diving predators. Being unfamiliar with advanced weaponry, they dove fearlessly at armed as well as unarmed colonists and SiBoronaans. By now the majority of Perenoreans as well as their SiBoronaan "benefactors" had taken shelter inside the first nearly complete settlement structures. Slamming up against windows and portals, the flyjaws were not heavy or strong enough to break in. These strange and previously unfamiliar obstacles to the food huddled within only drove them to greater heights of feeding frenzy.

Trapped beneath the loader, Kirk pondered his next move. Even if Scott could somehow manage to transfer every one of the embattled colonists as well as all the SiBoronaans onto the *Enterprise*, it would provide only a temporary solution. It would do nothing to solve the problem posed by the existence of the swarming flyjaws. In order to ensure the continuing safety of the settlement, the predators attacking the site not only had to be destroyed or driven off, but a way had to be found to discourage them from broadcasting their still unidentified attack signal to their fellow flyers. And those who were already on their way had to be convinced to change their one-track minds.

While trying to come up with an answer, Kirk continued to pick off any flyjaw that came too near their hiding place. His efforts and those of his companions were too late to save many Perenoreans and SiBoronaans who had been unlucky enough to have been caught out in the open. Even from where he and his fellow officers had taken shelter, Kirk could see the numerous bodies lying motionless on the ground while chittering, writhing flyjaws twisted and coiled above them, fighting each other for the last drops of Perenorean or SiBoronaan blood.

Next to him Spock took aim, fired, and dropped a patrolling flyjaw as it glided along the street in front of them. As the phaser beam tore into it, the predator let out a high-pitched whine, snapped at itself, and crashed into a pile of containers filled with liquid construction material. Flailing furiously at its wounds, it crumpled to the ground. Its movements slowed quickly, and then it was still.

"We cannot continue this indefinitely, Captain." The Vulcan checked his sidearm. "Our weapons need to be recharged. If they empty while we are still here, we will have no choice but to ask Mister Scott to beam us back aboard. Our lives are in comparatively little danger." Leaning forward, he checked the sky. It was growing increasingly dark as more flyjaws arrived to join the vast circle of winged bodies wheeling overhead. "The same cannot be said for the Perenoreans or the SiBoronaans. Mass evacuation would be difficult and dangerous."

"I've already come to the same conclusion, Spock. There has to be another way." Kirk took aim at a passing flyjaw, noted that the power indicator on his phaser was running dangerously low, and slid his finger off the trigger. The airborne killer soared past untouched.

McCoy looked back and up from where he continued to monitor the injured Perenorean's condition. "Here's a thought. How about we just evacuate the Perenoreans and leave the SiBoronaans to deal with this second little 'oversight' of theirs?"

"I believe the SiBoronaans are being truthful when they claim to be guilty of nothing more than an honest omission, Doctor." Spock's tone was disapproving of the physician's half-serious suggestion. "Their exploration of this satellite world has been limited at best. It is entirely possible they were unaware of the existence of and the danger posed by the species Captain Kirk has designated as flyjaws."

McCoy grunted. "Still should've cautioned us and the Perenoreans that there were aggressive predator types living on this moon. Didn't have to be specific. A general warning would've been useful."

"With that I certainly agree, Doctor. But however justified, anger and frustration will do nothing to resolve the present difficulty in which we find ourselves."

"You're right about one thing, Spock. We can't stay here forever." Kirk started to rise from his crouching position. "If nothing else, we ought to be consulting with the colonists and their SiBoronaan advisors." He gestured with his free hand. "The central administration building for the colony is almost

complete. If I'm remembering right, it's only about a half kilo-
meter sprint from here. Once inside, we can caucus with the
settlers and try to figure out the best way to deal with this."

"Only a half klick?" McCoy sounded doubtful. "Fine for
you maybe, Jim, but running was never my favorite exercise."
He indicated the wounded Perenorean. "Especially when
carrying a patient."

Kirk's expression was grim. "We have to move from this
place, Bones. If only because our phasers are running low."
Holstering his phaser, he started toward the Perenorean. "I'll
carry him. He's lighter than a human. You and Spock flank me."

"No." His breathing still labored, the Perenorean raised a
hand and spread all seven fingers wide.

"'No'?" McCoy gaped at the supine alien. "What do you
mean, 'no'? If we leave you here, the moment we step outside
and make a run for it, there'll be half a dozen of those bloodsuckers in here draining the life out of you."

"There is no need for panic." The Perenorean's response
emerged half-natural and half via his translator. "I know that
my people are capable of dealing with this problem. Before
leaving our homeworld, we were trained to cope with every
conceivable threat."

"Well, either your training overlooked the possibility of
an attack by thousands of airborne carnivores," McCoy countered, "or else it's taking an awful long time to kick in."

"Patience, please." The pain in his back caused the Perenorean to flinch. Seeing someone who was multiply double-
jointed "flinch" was an education in alien physiology all by

itself, McCoy reflected. "I know that my fellow colonists are preparing a response. Do not risk your lives to carry me from this place." Vertical golden pupils focused on the doctor. "I could not live with myself if harm came to you, Masteresque McCoy, after what you have already done for me."

The doctor turned contemplative. "'Masteresque McCoy.' That has a nice ring to it."

"Enjoy it while you can, Bones." Kirk looked back to Spock. "It's good of our patient not to want to see us come to harm, but we really need to consult with the other colonists and the SiBoronaans. After we've done that and made sure that everyone is on the same page, we can proceed." He tried to sound encouraging. "Assuming of course that we can come up with a next step."

Turning, he moved past McCoy. The doctor stepped back out of the way as Kirk slipped one arm beneath the Perenorean's right arm and the other under the alien's leg. Hoisting the protesting colonist onto his shoulders, Kirk repositioned the weight slightly before turning back toward the street. Outside, multiple incarnations of winged death awaited.

"Spock will cover me on one side," he told the doctor. "Even if you're only half as good with a phaser as you are with your medical tricorder, we should make it to the administration center." Taking a deep breath, Kirk started forward. "Let's go. And if I fall, pick up this guy first." He juggled the Perenorean lying across his shoulders.

They had gone maybe fifty meters when they were set upon by the first flyjaws.

Spock methodically began shooting the attackers out of the sky, beginning with the nearest predator and then moving on to the next. McCoy was less systematic but no less enthusiastic. Torn and shredded, a ragged line of dead and dying aerial predators took shape behind the sprinting officers. But for each flyjaw that went down, two or three more were called to the attack.

It was growing more difficult to hold them off. One actually clamped itself to the back of a cursing, frantic McCoy until Spock shot it off. When the science officer's phaser finally died, he had to quickly switch weapons with Kirk. And they were still barely halfway to the administration center.

Then the sky landed on them and they were shoved to the ground.

One minute they had been sprinting between unfinished buildings and piles of construction material; the next, they found themselves forced into prone positions. It was as if the irresistible hand of an unseen giant had descended to push them into the ground. The hand took the form of near-hurricane-force wind.

A wind that was blowing straight down. And in contrast to the usual temperate daytime temperatures, it was freezing cold.

Struggling to rise against the howling gale, McCoy found that he could barely lift his head off the ground. Lifting his arm and the hand holding his phaser proved next to impossible. The steady tornadic force that was being applied against his back was not painful, but it was unrelenting. He could hardly move. Twisting his head to his left he saw that Spock was similarly pinned, as was Kirk. The injured Perenorean had rolled away from the captain and off to one side. As a horrified and helpless McCoy looked on, a flyjaw came hurtling out of the sky to slam directly into the science officer's back.

But it did not bite, did not attempt to drill through the Vulcan's uniform to sink its saw-toothed circular mouth into the soft areas on either side of the science officer's spine. Instead it flapped its four wings madly in a desperate attempt to regain control and climb back into the air. Despite its most strenuous efforts, it could not get more than a couple of centimeters off the ground before the howling wind shoved it back down again.

Around them McCoy could see one flyjaw after another plunging sharply downward. It was then that he realized they were not attacking. They were desperately fighting to stay airborne. Forced into the ground by the same relentless gale that had pressed the three Starfleet officers into the dirt, one after another of the aerial predators were smashed into the unyielding surface. Massing far less than any of the four sprawled bipeds and entirely dependent on their wings for maneuverability, those still capable of movement flopped about helplessly on broken limbs, torn ligaments, and snapped tendons. Putting forth a considerable effort, the doctor managed to tilt his head back enough to look skyward.

It was raining flyjaws.

Forced groundward by the strange storm, they crashed into the settlement by the hundreds. Bouncing off buildings, clawing at one another, they struggled impotently to return to the air. Where they formed a pile of bodies, those still relatively intact resorted without hesitation to cannibalizing their less fortunate fellows.

Kirk placed both hands flat against the ground and pushed with all his might. He had not been weakened or injured: he could feel the strength coursing through his arms. But he could do no more than briefly raise his upper torso off the surface. When he tried to get his legs under his hips, the downward-thrusting tempest that had knocked him off his feet all but collapsed his arms beneath him. Giving up any further attempt to stand he lay there, pinned and helpless, aware that his ultimate effort had been doomed to failure. If the much stronger Spock couldn't raise himself up, Kirk knew there was no way he could manage it. But he'd felt compelled to try.

It was the injured Perenorean who provided an explanation both for their inability to move and the sudden mass collapse of the attacking flyjaw swarm.

"I told you that my people would respond. I see that they have the weatheranse operating."

"The what?!" Teeth chattering from the sudden onslaught of cold, McCoy had to shout to make himself heard above the roaring in his ears.

Though pinned to the ground as decisively as his human rescuers, the Perenorean was sounding increasingly confident. "It is a simple device that is included with all colonial supplies. As the weather at this site has thus far ranged from tolerable to invigorating, there was no need to set it up. Our engineers have obviously recognized that it can be a useful means of dealing with these unforeseen predators and have reacted accordingly." His tone turned apologetic. "It is to be regretted that it has taken this long to do so."

"Excuse my ignorance," a shivering Kirk shouted, "but I don't understand how a single machine located somewhere in the settlement can generate anything like this kind of wind—much less keep all of it blowing in one direction—down!"

The Perenorean's clarification came without hesitation. "Among my kind, a weatheranse is a useful and proven means for controlling the climate in the immediate vicinity of a settlement. Its most important function is to provide precipitation on demand. But it can also variegate the climate in other ways. Clouds can be called forth to shade new growths that are sensitive to sun." He looked upward. "In this instance, I would say that the device has been utilized to alter temperature and atmospheric density in such a manner as to generate the meteorological forces we are presently feeling."

Kirk gaped at the alien, then struggled to turn toward his science officer. "Mister Spock, is that possible?"

"We are living proof of it, Captain. The Perenorean device is apparently capable of rapidly and severely lowering the temperature of the DiBoronaan atmosphere in our immediate vicinity. Generating a dense cold-air pressure system within a sharply confined area would generate the kind of powerful—and cold—winds we are presently experiencing." He looked upward. "They have somehow generated a miniature arctic climate directly above us."

"I follow you, Spock," Kirk shouted back, "but why are the winds blowing straight *down* instead of sideways?!"

"It would seem that the Perenoreans can also control wind shear, Captain. How, I do not know. But while we only suffer from the resultant gale by being forced to lie flat on the ground, the same wind is powerful enough to render flyjaw flight impossible. The situation is not dissimilar to one that might be encountered on Earth where in a category four or five hurricane, humans cannot walk but can survive by lying prone while small flying creatures are blown about helplessly." He looked over to where piles of dead and dying flyjaws were rapidly accumulating. "It is an elegant and eminently efficient solution to the problem. Instead of dealing with these airborne predators on an individual basis as we have been doing with our phasers, the Perenoreans have initiated a means for dealing with the entire swarm at once."

Spock's gaze shifted skyward and he squinted against the airstream. "If, as we have surmised, the flyjaws do communicate across long distances with one another, then the same method they have been using to continuously call forth others of their kind should now be employed to warn newcomers away from the sudden and fatal onset of weather in this vicinity. Until this clever and skillful counterattack concludes, I suggest that we remain where and as we are." So saying, he looked downward and sought to use his hands to cover as much of his face as possible.

Kirk's inability to rise mitigated any further attempts to try and make it to the colony administration center—much less continuing to take aim with and fire his phaser. He no longer had a functional one anyway, and there was no point in trying to get it back from Spock. So he swallowed his yearning to strike out at the plummeting carnivores and did his best to imitate the science officer's example by burying his own face in the ground.

Only McCoy did not retreat into immobility. Crawling on his belly at the rate of one violent adjective per meter, he worked his way across a small patch of open ground while the unrelenting tempest did its best to push his nose into the dirt. Like Kirk and Spock, the doctor could have stayed where he had first been forced to the ground. Physically it would have been much easier for him to do so. Mentally and ethically, for him to remain in place and do nothing was something else entirely.

He had a patient to look after. He had no choice but to try and continue to give comfort to the injured, even if the surrounding conditions made treatment more difficult than usual, even if the tips of his fingers were turning numb from the cold.

9

The unremitting howl that was the wind from above and kept them pressed to the ground died with a suddenness that left the three Starfleet officers gasping. It was as if someone had thrown a switch. Which, in effect, was exactly what had happened. As soon as the Perenorean device was shut down, normal atmospheric equilibrium returned and the wind stopped.

Rising slowly to their feet, the battered visitors and the injured Perenorean saw that Spock's supposition had been correct. Not only was the sky overhead devoid of predatory flyjaws, so was the air above the winding river, the forest, and the mountains that demarcated the far boundaries of the settlement site. The few remaining flyjaws that had managed to survive the horrific and consistent down rush of air were fighting to gain altitude as they dispersed in all directions, desperate to escape to anyplace where the weather was stable and the winds less likely to suddenly turn mad.

The stench of death that was beginning to rise from hundreds of crumpled flyjaw bodies reminded everyone in the colony that construction would have to pause until a settlement-wide cleanup could be completed. While the relieved and more than slightly dazed SiBoronaans stumbled about on their pseudopods, struggling to recover mentally as well as physically from the swarm's attack, the Perenoreans set to work. Before the last dispirited flyjaw had disappeared into the distance, the settlement site filled with a quiet frenzy of activity.

Perenorean medics tended to the wounded, and the respectful removal of the deceased. As other settlers set to the disagreeable task of removing piles of dead flyjaw bodies, McCoy marveled at the calm being displayed by the colonists.

"You'd think they did this sort of thing all the time."

He gestured toward a peculiar vehicle that was vacuuming up broken corpses several at a time and depositing them in its capacious, bulbous interior. Designed and built to remove construction debris, it had been quickly modified to deal with the unexpected avalanche of organic detritus instead. A pair of Perenoreans followed patiently behind, picking up and tossing into the ventral vacuum chute the smaller body bits that the vehicle missed. Though these "smaller bits" consisted of heads, entrails, pieces of wing and other body parts, the two Perenoreans never blanched. The fact that their seven-fingered hands and lower legs were slick with flyjaw gore did not appear to trouble them in the slightest. It was a scene that was being repeated throughout the colony.

"At this rate," an admiring McCoy commented, "they'll have the whole site cleared by tomorrow."

"They are indeed proceeding with remarkable efficiency." Hands folded behind his back, Spock was following the cleanup with as much interest as the doctor. "In fact, from what we have been able to observe, it would appear that the Perenoreans are a people who go about every task they take on with equal eagerness and expertise. If they do not know how to do something, they are quick to ask, and even quicker to learn. I have never heard of a species that learns so fast and so thoroughly."

"Come on now, Spock." Kirk smiled pleasantly as they continued their stroll through the bustling colony site. "Humans are quick to learn, and no one is faster at picking up new things than Vulcans."

The science officer paused to watch a group of Perenorean youngsters at play. They were building something out of fly-jaw bones that had not yet been collected for disposal. As the Starfleet officers looked on, the outlines of the juveniles' architectural effort rapidly became visible. They were building a perfect replica of the automated navigation tower that had been erected at the far end of the shuttle landing site. Supply shuttles traveled in a steady stream between the *Eparthaa* and the colony.

Exiting the field hospital, McCoy strode over to the steadily rising osseous edifice, the young Perenoreans deferentially moving aside, leaving him alone to appreciate what they had built. Putting his left arm around the gently tapering tower and ignoring the blood from the bones that threatened to add more stains to his uniform, he turned to face his colleagues.

"How are the wounded?" the captain asked.

"Recovering rapidly. Get an image, would you, Jim? I feel like playing tourist."

"What could you possibly want with a picture of . . . ?" Kirk caught himself. "Oh, right—bones." Pulling out his tricorder, he made a recording of the scene. As McCoy stepped away from the graceful yet grisly plaything, he nodded his thanks to the youngsters.

"You are most welcome, Masteresque McCoy," the eldest told him without the aid of a translator.

Startled, the doctor blinked at the youth, who gazed back innocently. "Yeah, okay. Uh, have fun."

Spock immediately stepped forward. "You have learned our language already? When have you had time to receive formal instruction?"

"No formal instruction." A second slightly smaller and younger Perenorean sculptor spoke up cheerfully. "The details of the language you are using were disseminated widely among us as soon as they became known. We have all been studying it since our ship first made contact with yours."

Spock's tone did not change as he bent slightly toward the speaker. "You are required to do this?"

The three Perenorean youths looked at one another. It was left to the eldest to reply. "Required? You mean, was it demanded of us?" Spock nodded, and it was evident that his youthful audience was as familiar with the gesture as they were with the visitors' words. "Among our people, learning is never a requirement. It is a joy, a delight. A new piece of knowledge acquired is . . . is . . . ." He struggled for the right term.

"Exhilarating," trilled the youngest member of the trio.

"Is there something new you can teach us?" The second youth, a bright-eyed female, regarded the science officer eagerly.

"Not at the moment." Spock straightened. "My friends and I must return to our ship. Now that you are properly established here and safe from the Dre'kalak, we have our own work to do and we must prepare for our departure."

"Oh-weh." All three youngsters looked disappointed. "Perhaps we could come with you?" The eldest's earnestness was unmistakable.

Kirk eyed the slight figures arrayed before him. All three appeared to be deadly serious. "You mean you'd leave your friends, your parents, to go off on a strange ship crewed by a species that until just recently had never been in contact with your own kind?"

"In a twinkling!" A flurry of liquid gestures indicated that all of the oldest youngster's companions were in agreement. "What Perenorean could pass on the opportunity to learn so many new things all at once?"

McCoy clearly approved. "These kids are a teacher's dream!"

Spock's reaction was considerably more reserved. "Perhaps, Doctor . . . perhaps. In some ways they remind me of my young self. I was always striving to acquire new knowledge, to master as many disciplines as possible. And yet I sense a difference here that I cannot yet properly define."

"I'm sure it'll come to you." McCoy guffawed softly. "It always does, whether those around you want it or not."

"Maybe you can visit us another time." Kirk smiled paternally at the visibly disappointed youngsters. "Maybe when we have a chance to clear that kind of extensive visit with your parents."

"That is not necessary." Like her companions, the young female displayed a maturity beyond her age. "The acquiring of new knowledge supersedes everything, including birthing authority."

Kirk's smile changed to a slight frown. The desire to gain new knowledge was all well and good and to be admired. But the intensity of interest being shown by these youngsters carried with it a whiff of the fanatical. "Nevertheless, that's the way it would have to be."

"Oh, I see." The eldest of the trio gestured comprehendingly. "While the granting of such permission is not a requirement of our society, it is of yours." He stepped back. "We must of course live with our disappointment and defer to your superior cultural stance."

The three officers took their leave of the youngsters. As Kirk was walking away he looked back to see that they had returned to their macabre building. Squinting at the replica of the navigation tower, he marveled at how they had been able to erect such a haphazard yet sturdy structure out of such improbable building materials—and without any glue or bonding agent of any kind. Not to mention any apparent squeamishness. Plainly, Perenorean youth were as adept at improvisation as their parents.

Improvisation. Ever since they had been forced off course only to subsequently find themselves attacked and pursued by the Dre'kalak, these people had been compelled to improvise. True, without the intervention of the *Enterprise* and its crew they might very well have been destroyed by the Dre'kalak. But ever since that providential rescue they had managed everything, from contact with the SiBoronaans to establishing this first settlement. The *Enterprise*'s crew had helped, but it was plausible the Perenoreans could have done it without them.

That was a good thing, Kirk told himself. The possibility that, after all they had been through, the colonists might fail was one he preferred not to contemplate. It was too depressing. Much more pleasant to envision a burgeoning and successful Perenorean civilization taking root on DiBor, ready to put themselves forward as friends to the Federation and helpmates to the SiBoronaans.

"You should be pleased, Spock. As a refugee yourself you've been instrumental in the survival of refugees of another species."

"I am pleased, Captain." Striding along beside him the science officer appeared even more contemplative than usual. "Yet something continues to trouble me. No, that is not entirely accurate. It persists with me though its specifics are not yet defined."

"Well, that's clear as crystal," McCoy noted sardonically.

They were due to beam up soon. Kirk was looking forward to a full meal and some solid sleep. The latter would come easily now that this latest threat to the colony had been dealt with, even though they weren't exactly sure of all the technical details of how it had been done.

"What's on your mind, Spock?"

The science officer made a sweeping gesture to take in their immediate surroundings: the rapidly disappearing mounds of dead flyjaws, the prefabricated buildings that were going up all around them with astonishing speed, the vehicles and machines that had been transported down from the *Eparthaa* and put to work almost immediately.

"Everything we have seen and experienced of Perenorean culture leads me to believe that they come from a society where conflict is avoided and belligerence is scorned. They are non-aggressive, dislike fighting, and above all else seek to expand and enhance their existing store of knowledge. Whose extent, I should point out, remains unknown to us. And yet . . ." His voice drifted off.

"And yet?" Kirk prompted him.

"There remain contradictions that puzzle me. Consider the effectiveness the Perenoreans demonstrated in holding off an assault by three warships of a hostile species. Three *warships*, Captain. Given a similar set of circumstances, how many Federation colony vessels would be capable of doing the same?"

"They were on the verge of being blown to bits when we showed up," McCoy pointed out.

"Quite so, Doctor. Had the *Enterprise* not arrived when it did, I am quite convinced not a single Perenorean would now be preparing to make their home on this SiBoronaan moon. Yet the Perenoreans' accomplishment prior to our intervention cannot be overlooked and must be taken into account."

"Into account for what, Spock?" Kirk stepped to one side to give a peculiar single-tracked Perenorean vehicle room to pass silently by.

"The contradiction that exists between their declared pacifism and their ability to partake effectively in combat. Consider: first their colony ship, utilizing only defensive weaponry, survives for a long time battling to a standstill a trio of enemy warships. Later, on this moon, and only when forced to do so, they produce a device called a *lagarouth* that turns out to also function quite well as a weapon." He gestured at the rapidly gentrifying surroundings. "Now, when confronted with a massive assault by flocks of native aerial predators, they bring forth still another new device. Designed to manipulate the local weather for the benefit of agriculture and other nonhostile purposes, it too has more forceful capabilities—to which hundreds of dead flyjaws can attest." He turned to face Kirk. "I hardly need point out how useful such a new and as yet incomprehensible technology would prove in a battlefield situation."

McCoy shrugged. "Just because they have equipment in their colonizing stores that can be jury-rigged for defensive purposes doesn't mean any of it was designed and built with such a dual purpose in mind."

"In mind, indeed, Doctor. None of this is what deeply troubles me."

Kirk frowned. "Then what *is* bothering you, Spock?"

The science officer's tone darkened slightly—though not emotionally. "Embraced by their exceptional and admirable actions, Captain, I find myself wondering what other 'dual purpose' technology they possess that has yet to be revealed to us."

McCoy made a disgusted sound. "I didn't know Vulcans were subject to paranoia."

Spock raised one eyebrow. "Not paranoia, Doctor. Merely prudent curiosity based on what we have observed thus far."

Kirk deliberately picked up the pace. "As soon as we've conveyed our formal final farewells to both the SiBoronaans and the Perenoreans, we'll be on our way out of here. We have an interrupted mission to resume."

Spock halted so abruptly that his two companions nearly stumbled in response. "Captain. I am intrigued. I ask permission to remain here on DiBor, both to offer continuing advice to the colonists and to delve more deeply into a slowly coalescing thesis of mine."

"Denied and denied, Mister Spock." Kirk's tone was unyielding. "As to the first, the Perenoreans have their new friends the SiBoronaans to help them. As to the second, I need my science officer on the *Enterprise*. Your presence and your advice are not replaceable."

"I am not swayed by flattery, Captain."

Kirk stared past him. "It wasn't flattery, Spock. It was a statement of fact. Your request to remain behind is denied.

You will beam back aboard and we'll hear no more about it." Seeing the science officer stiffen, Kirk added, "You can write up your observations in a formal report and we'll see that they get to the appropriate Starfleet division for in-depth analysis as soon as possible. If the Federation decides to delve deeper into your theory, I'll see about recommending a temporary leave of absence so you can join any approved investigations."

Spock relented. "Thank you, Captain. While I would rather stay here to pursue such studies, I understand." He glanced at McCoy. "I suppose that my presence on board the *Enterprise* is indeed irreplaceable."

Refusing to take the bait, McCoy said nothing.

Final farewells took place in the colony's administration building—the first structure in the new colony to be finished, it had been completed with astonishing speed. In the absence of the Perenorean equivalent of a traditional meeting hall, Kirk, Spock, and Uhura found themselves standing on a paved area in front of the gleaming new white and blue structure. As with Perenorean attire, the building was swathed with swirls of alternating color.

Perenorean dignitaries crowded close to one another, each hoping for a chance to bid their Federation saviors a personal goodbye. Taell was there, as was Masteresque Founoh and many of the other senior Perenorean operatives the *Enterprise* officers had come to know over the preceding days.

They could have simply bid the colonists and their Si-

Boronaan benefactors farewell from orbit. But Uhura felt the formalities were important. Not only because they might represent the last contact for some time between the Federation and a newly contacted sentient species, but because they would also serve to further cement relations between the Federation and the SiBoronaans.

The three Starfleet officers stood in the mild warmth of SiBor's sun and took turns accepting gifts from both species. Traditional arts from the SiBoronaans, exquisite and sometimes baffling abstract constructions from the Perenoreans. Then Thirty-four Narlekt, the appointed permanent SiBoronaan government representative on DiBor, trundled forward and launched into a long, rambling speech lauding the efforts of the Federation to assist a people in need. Following this, Taell eloquently praised the gift of territory from their hosts.

He spoke, Uhura noted admiringly, in perfect SiBoronaan. How the Perenorean commander had found the time to master the difficult language while still overseeing the landing of settlers and supplies and supervising the establishment of the colony she could not imagine. SiBoronaan was not an easy tongue. She felt she would have needed at least a year to match his fluency.

When he had finished, the leaderesque of the *Eparthaa* turned to the trio of watching Starfleet officers and switched effortlessly from SiBoronaan to Federation Standard.

"We have already told what we owe you. At present, simple words are all we have to offer in way of thanks." Spreading his arms and bending them in ways no human or Vulcan could duplicate, he took in the nearly completed colony administration building and the rest of their surroundings. "We hope one day soon to be able to offer the Federation a more solid example of our gratitude. Until then, we give freely all that we have and all that we will have: the knowledge accumulated by our species, our poor skills, and our friendship." His left arm stabbed skyward and his voice rose to a shout. It was, Kirk reflected, one of the few times since encountering the species that he had heard a Perenorean raise its voice.

"Arekalvo!"

"Arekalvo, arekalvo!" The cry and the sky-reaching arm thrust were repeated by every Perenorean present. Since neither Taell's declamation nor the crowd's shouts were directed toward him, Kirk's translator could not quite execute the translation. Kirk leaned toward his communications officer.

"I'm assuming they're not yelling 'Federation go home.'"

Uhura smiled while mentally running through her laboriously acquired store of Perenorean words. "It means something like, 'We admire,' or 'We praise.' As in 'All praise to you!' An exclamation indicative of general glorification. I remember chatting with Chekov once about Russian. They have a word, *slava*, that connotes approximately the same feeling. There's a whole chorus during the 'Procession of the Nobles' in a Rimsky-Korsakov opera, *Mlada*, that repeats the word over and—"

"Over." Kirk cut her off. "I get it." He surveyed their surroundings. "Rescuing the Perenorean colonists, striking a bargain with the SiBoronaans to let them settle on this moon, everything that's happened here since, would make a pretty good opera of its own, I think."

She eyed him. "Why don't you write it, Captain? The ship's entertainment software would help a great deal and . . ."

"Several reasons, Lieutenant. First, as captain of the *Enterprise* I don't have the time. Second, I can't sing worth a damn. And third—I don't like opera."

"Oh, well, then." Her smile broadened. "Other than that . . ."

He nodded. "Look at the Perenoreans. They're planning something." He tensed slightly.

The colonists were indeed planning something. As one, they turned toward the trio of Starfleet officers and in unison executed the same full-body genuflection that Taell had performed in front of the SiBoronaan leadership when they had first arrived. Every Perenorean present dropped to their knees and bent forward, their spines forming dozens of body arcs all around the administration complex. They remained like that until an increasingly embarrassed Kirk admonished them to rise.

"Okay, you're welcome, that's fine, that's enough." Approaching the prone Taell he reached down and took the leaderesque by one arm to urge him upward. "You've already thanked us more than is reasonable."

Indicating that he understood, Taell stuck out his right hand. The Perenoreans had been almost as quick to pick up human gestures as human speech. Taking the proffered hand of friendship, Kirk shook it gently. The leaderesque's grip was firm without being overbearing, the extra two fingers involved notwithstanding.

"Will we ever see you again, Captain Kirk?" Looking past him, Taell added, "Or you, Commander Spock, or you, Lieutenant Uhura?"

"It's not up to us." Kirk was quick, and grateful, to pass the buck. "We go where Starfleet tells us to go. If by chance our orders should bring us back to this part of the quadrant, we will of course make every effort to arrange an official visit." He gestured past the leaderesque. "I for one will be very curious to see how you progress."

"Intensely curious," Spock added without elaboration.

The last image Kirk had of Taell was of the leader of the colonists waving in a very human-like manner as the transporter beam took hold of them.

After the greenery, bustle, and fresh air of the colony, stepping off the transporter platform back on the *Enterprise* was a shock to the system as well as the mind. It always was, Kirk reflected as Spock and Uhura headed straight for the bridge.

The familiar and welcome face behind the transporter stepped out from the console to greet him. "How did it go, Captain?"

"Fine, Mister Scott. No, better than fine. I believe this little diversion from our mission has resulted in the cementing of relations between the Federation and not one but two sentient alien species. While neither is likely to strike fear into the hearts of potential Federation enemies, an ally is an ally. One of them is deliberate and resolved, the other energetic and"—he hesitated briefly—"still something of an enigma. But steadfast to a fault, I think." He clapped the chief engineer on the shoulder. "We should be back on our planned course and schedule in a few days. After what we've accomplished here, I don't think Starfleet will begrudge us the detour."

Spock was waiting for Kirk on the bridge. As soon as Kirk appeared and before he could make his way to the command chair, Spock drew him aside.

"Captain, may I have a word with you?"

"Of course, Mister Spock." Still basking in the lingering glow from the gratifying farewell ceremony, Kirk was determined not to let the science officer's characteristic dourness spoil the mood. He allowed himself to be drawn over to the science station.

Instead of a tridimensional projection, Spock had restricted the current large readout to a screen. Kirk immediately recognized an enhanced long-range image of the new Perenorean colony. The administration building in its center was unmistakable, as was the bluff on which the settlement sat, the nearby forest and plains, and the slow-moving river that wound through them.

"Nice view," he commented. "What about it, Mister Spock?"

"Keep looking, Captain."

The science officer adjusted his instrumentation, widening the view. The settlement shrank rapidly, as did the rocky promontory on which it was being constructed. More of the river became visible, along with several of its tributaries. Then it too shrank from a broad watercourse into a narrow winding stream, and finally a mere rivulet. As Spock manipulated the controls the downward view shifted to the east and began to zoom in on another part of the DiBoronaan landscape. A clearing appeared in a deep forest atop a wide plateau. The view was magnified even more. Thickets of more massive vegetation stood out among shorter growths. So did individual shapes within the clearing. Kirk did not need his science officer to interpret them for him. He eyed his science officer querulously.

"Buildings?"

"Probable, Captain, as they are still under construction."

Kirk regarded the stolid Vulcan. "The SiBoronaans have outposts of their own on parts of their moon."

Spock shook his head. "Indeed they do, Captain. However, this is not one of them. I could increase the magnification still further but at this distance resolution would suffer. Anyway it is not necessary. In style and design, these are clearly Perenorean in origin."

Kirk considered. "Okay—so the Perenoreans are setting up a second settlement. According to the terms of their treaty with the SiBoronaans they have every right to do so. No one expects them to confine themselves to one community, much less one part of the moon."

The science officer studied his friend evenly. "It does not trouble you that no word of this second settlement was mentioned to us?"

"No." Kirk's gaze narrowed. "Why should it? Not mention-

ing it doesn't prove any effort at deception on the part of the
Perenoreans. You know how straightforward they are. They don't
waste time. If one of us had asked if they were planning or starting construction on any additional settlements, I'm sure they
would have replied openly and honestly. They have every other
time." He shrugged. "None of us thought to ask, that's all."

"I concur completely, Captain."

Kirk surveyed the rest of the bridge. His crew were at their
stations, waiting for him to issue the departure orders. His
tone turned irritable. "Then what is the purpose of this revelation, Mister Spock?"

"Look again, Captain." Once more the science officer adjusted the instrumentation, and once again the view pulled
back only to zoom in a second time.

This time the rising settlement was set in a deep cove on
the portion of continental coast nearest to the main river system and the initial touchdown site. Kirk did not need Spock
to tell him that the structures that were rising in the excellent
natural harbor were of Perenorean and not SiBoronaan origin.
His impatience showed in his expression as well as his words.

"Okay, I see. There's a third settlement going up. Any more
you want to show me?"

Straightening, Spock dragged a fingertip across a control
strip and the view on the monitor died. "I have only been able
to find these two."

Kirk gestured curtly. "Then the show's over. We've done
what we came to do and it's time to leave."

"Once again I agree, Captain." As Kirk turned to go, the

science officer restrained him with a few last words. "I did not show you these two additional settlement sites to suggest that the Perenoreans were engaged in anything deceitful, Jim."

Having started toward the command chair, Kirk now paused and looked back. "Then why did you show them to me, Mister Spock?"

"To reinforce an observation already made. That these people are not just remarkably resourceful, but that they are capable of achievements even the best-prepared and best-equipped humans could not duplicate. Nor could my own people. The fact that in such a short time they have embarked on the establishment of not one but three settlements, I find nothing short of astonishing."

Kirk didn't waste time in profound contemplation of the science officer's assertion. He had a starship to command.

"Desperate sentients are capable of extraordinary feats, Mister Spock. Take the example of Vregon VI, where the human population had to move its entire civilization—living quarters, farms, industries, everything—from one location to another because of rapid continental subsidence. That required a far more extensive hasty mobilization of resources than setting up three settlements instead of one."

"I am familiar with the example you employ, Captain. It is not human fortitude and determination that I am comparing to the Perenoreans, but sheer speed. They make decisions and act on them with a swiftness I believe to be unprecedented."

"Well, I say good for them. The faster they establish themselves, the sooner their colony will be ready to apply for full membership in the Federation. And maybe they can drag their slower-moving hosts the SiBoronaans along with them." He smiled. "Speaking of moving fast, we've delayed here too long. I suggest you ready your station for departure."

"Aye, Captain." His expression betraying nothing, Spock turned back to his console and took his seat. Kirk turned to the rest of the bridge.

"Mister Sulu, Mister Chekov—prepare for departure. Mister Chekov, I presume you have a recalculated course so that we will resume our mission?"

"Plotted and entered, Captain," the navigator replied.

Kirk nodded once. "Lieutenant Uhura?"

"Communications are open and scanning, Captain," came the response from her station.

Settling himself in the command seat, Kirk leaned forward slightly and addressed the chair's pickup. "Mister Scott, ready for departure?"

"The sooner the better, Captain. Sitting in one place gives me an itch in the—"

"Thank you, Mister Scott," said Kirk quickly, cutting off the chief engineer. He straightened. "Mister Sulu, warp five. We're in no rush now."

"Aye, Captain."

Sulu caught up to Kirk in a corridor late the following day.

"Captain? I was just wondering about something."

Kirk grinned. "Wondering, Mister Sulu? On a starship on patrol in deep space? If you're trying to shock me, you're failing miserably."

The helmsman smiled back. Although he was Sulu's superior, the captain had a way of putting everyone at ease.

"I wasn't trying to do that, Captain." The smile faded and his tone turned more serious. "It's actually something that's been bothering me since our time at DiBor." When Kirk said nothing, simply stood and waited, the helmsman continued. "One of the Perenoreans who was allowed to visit the *Enterprise* joined me when I was exercising. You know that I'm quite fond of the martial arts."

Kirk gestured for him to continue. "So were some dead Romulans. Go on."

"I was practicing fencing. Épée, specifically. This Perenorean watched for a while and then asked if I could show him how it was done. I didn't think anything of it, and no orders had been issued forbidding that kind of interaction, so I went ahead."

"Very accommodating of you, Mister Sulu. Is that what's been worrying you?"

Sulu's concern showed in his expression. "No, Captain. What bothers me is that after only a few lessons, the Perenorean was beating me. He wanted to learn how to use other edged weapons too. Everything and anything else that I could teach him."

"I'm not surprised. The Perenoreans are a very curious species. Interested in everything. Not unlike our own."

"I understand that, Captain. But as proud as I am of my

own accomplishments in the field of martial arts, I can't see myself ever defeating an accomplished alien in its own fighting specialties after only a brief instruction. It's just amazing. Especially for a member of a non-warlike species. Aren't the Perenoreans supposed to be peaceful?"

Kirk realized what was unsettling his helmsman. "Fencing is a balletic art, Mister Sulu. As physically flexible and fluid as they are, it wouldn't surprise me if the Perenoreans have an elaborate and long-established tradition of dance, or something very much like it. Wouldn't a dancer, and an inhumanly agile one at that, be able to pick up fencing's technical moves more easily than an ordinary untrained human?"

The helmsman's sudden introspection showed that he had not considered this line of reasoning. "So what you're saying, Captain, is that some pacifistic art—dance, to use your example—might predispose an otherwise nonaggressive species toward a skill set very similar to a martial one." Sulu found himself nodding in agreement. "That makes sense. He never said anything about being good at dance."

The captain had had many interactions with the Perenoreans and consequently knew a little more about their culture and civilization. He did not use this to chastise Sulu for jumping to conclusions. Only insecure and morally inferior individuals used superior knowledge to dominate or embarrass the less informed. Having spent part of his life feeling inferior to just about everyone around him (except when it came to fighting and seducing), James Kirk was now the last person to lord over anyone.

"Did you ask him?"

Sulu looked surprised. "No, Captain. It never occurred to me. When the alien made his request, I assumed he was starting from zero knowledge and experience."

Kirk chuckled. "Maybe you should have made inquiries. Who knows? The Perenoreans might have an analog to traditional human sword fighting and your eager 'student' might have been an expert among his kind."

The helmsman looked abashed. "I hadn't considered that, Captain. I might be completely wrong—but the possibility that you might be correct makes me feel better about losing."

Kirk clapped him on the shoulder. "Nothing more soothing to the injured ego than a comforting fiction. Don't worry about it, Sulu. Even if your first supposition is the correct one, you have to remember that the Perenoreans are amazingly fast learners." Turning, he resumed walking up the corridor. "Keep practicing. Maybe we'll run into these people again and you can ask for a rematch."

"I'll do that, Captain. And—thank you."

"*Now* what?"

Lying on the divan beside Uhura, Spock continued to gaze upward and reflect. This despite the wonderful display the ceiling was currently putting on, showing the night sky as it appeared above the brandy-colored lake of Teleris on Cuoulphon IV. The lambent stars and flaring aurora being imaged overhead could not draw his mind back to the present. Nor could the woman who was reposing supplely beside him. This was not for lack of trying. Uhura was doing her best. Eventually she gave up, sat up, and glared down at him.

"When you put your mind to something, Spock, there's no one who can accomplish more. But when you let it wander, there's no one further away." Her tone softened as she rested a hand on his chest. "I can't be with you if you're not here. And don't go all spatial physics on me and tell me you're actually here or I swear I'll slap those pointy ears right off your head."

He blinked, looked away from the ceiling display and back to her. One hand reached up to stroke her right arm.

"I'm sorry, Nyota. Something is vexing me that I cannot shake."

"I'm asking you again: What is going on? Maybe I can help."

"It is kind of you to offer, but as I am still formulating my theory, I must continue to deal with it. Alone."

She lay back down beside him. "Can you at least give me a hint?"

That, at least, he could provide without hesitation. "It involves this newly contacted species whose colonists we rescued."

"The Perenoreans? I found them pleasant enough to be around. Charming, even, if at times a bit obsequious. *They're* what's been bothering you for days? I can't imagine a first contact that could have gone better."

"I know." He let out a measured sigh. "I wish the captain had allowed me to remain. There are many questions I still would have liked to ask. However, orders are orders. I am sure the captain is correct that Starfleet would brook no further deviance from our original mission."

She snuggled closer. "So what is it, exactly, about the Perenoreans that bothers you?"

"They are not merely fast learners; they are *remarkable* learners. They pick up new knowledge with unparalleled speed and ease."

She shrugged diffidently. "How is that a bad thing? Haven't they promised to freely share all their accumulated knowledge with us? The more knowledge they acquire, the more knowledge they have to share with us. Isn't that why we are out here?"

"Yes. I suppose I worry unnecessarily."

"I can confirm that, Spock. Why would you worry about them learning quickly? They'll learn all about their new planet, and they'll learn how to manage it fast. So what?"

He turned toward her. "It is not what they learn about their new home that concerns me, Nyota. It is what they learned during their brief visit to the *Enterprise* that concerns me. That, and the speed with which they learned it."

"What? Fencing? Chess? Food preparation? I think it's time you think about something else," she murmured. "Maybe I can divert your thoughts to other concerns."

Meeting her gaze directly, he pursed his lips. "A most logical supposition with which I am unprepared to argue."

10

The urgent communication from Starfleet reached the *Enterprise* just short of four months into its journey. Uhura announced its arrival to a quiet, smooth-running bridge whose occupants had settled comfortably into the daily routine of running the great ship.

"Incoming call from Starfleet, Captain." She wore a look of surprise as she turned toward the command chair. "Priority one."

Kirk had been chatting with McCoy. The captain flashed his friend a look that said "I had a feeling this was coming," and swiveled to face the communications station.

He had been expecting something of the kind ever since they had filed the official report on rescuing and making contact with the Perenoreans, negotiating successfully with SiBor to secure a new planet for them, and waiting to depart until the *Enterprise* was sure that the refugees had established themselves.

From beginning to end it had been a laudable—*enterprise*, he thought proudly. He was feeling very pleased with himself, and looked expectantly at his communications officer.

This is it, he told himself. Maybe an official commendation for the *Enterprise* and a formal acknowledgment of the crew's achievements. The medal that had been presented to him for dealing with the Romulan threat was getting lonely. It needed company.

Perhaps the delay in recognition, Kirk told himself as he waited for Uhura to bring up the transmission, was due to the need for the appropriate authorities to decide exactly how large and ornate his new commendation should be. It wouldn't do to be too ostentatious.

But it should be a *little* ostentatious.

"Put it up on the main viewscreen, Lieutenant," he instructed her grandly. The captain settled back to view the incoming communiqué. He would be unpretentious in response. Humble and self-effacing. All those things that he knew would be right and proper. He would accept the congratulations of his comrades with soft voice and modestly lowered eyes. After all, someone who had achieved so much so quickly could afford to be generous with his gratitude.

Everyone on the bridge recognized Admiral Yamashiro. Odd, Kirk mused as he studied the image. The admiral was not smiling. Furthermore, no medals or commendations of any kind lay on the desk before him. In point of fact, a rapidly deflating Kirk thought, the diminutive but wire-tough admiral appeared to be quivering with rage. At least, his mustache was.

It soon became clear that the admiral's fury extended well beyond the short hairs that quivered above his upper lip.

"For the record: Am I speaking to James Tiberius Kirk, captain of the U.S.S. Enterprise?*"*

Uhura hurried to lower the incoming volume even as the automatics tried to respond. Sulu slid a little lower in his chair while Chekov edged to the right as much as possible without abandoning his station in the hope that he might succeed in moving just out of range of the bridge's visual pickup. Spock did not move at all. But eyebrows were raised.

"Yes, Admiral." A greatly diminished Kirk replied as authoritatively as he could. "From the tenor of your voice would I be correct in assuming that something is not right?"

"From the tenor of my voice, Captain, you may assume that Starfleet Command would like to have you keelhauled!" The admiral was visibly struggling to contain his emotions. *"However, this is—regrettably for us, and fortunately for you—the wrong century for that sort of thing. As much as some of us would like to have you keelhauled. In deep space."*

Kirk blinked and leaned forward slightly. "Sir?"

"Starfleet has received an official communiqué from the government of SiBor. Although overtones in alien communications can be difficult to interpret, this one might best be described as—frantic."

Sitting in the command chair to which he was rapidly becoming accustomed, a bewildered Kirk tried to make some sense of the admiral's words. His sole consolation at the moment was that judging by the looks on their faces, his crew was equally baffled. He threw a quick glance toward the science station. The brief shrug a silent Spock offered by way of response was neither encouraging nor revelatory.

"'Frantic,' sir?" he managed. Sooner or later he knew he would be required to say something beyond repeating the admiral's words.

"I would say more than frantic. Panicky would be more like it." The grim-faced admiral folded his hands on the desk in front of him. *"Starfleet has been trying to bring SiBor and its good-natured, hard-working people into the Federation for some time now. But as you no doubt found out, they are a cautious species. Negotiations have been protracted and delicate, but the diplomatic corps felt it was making progress."* He leaned forward to glare into his pickup. *"Now all that hard work has been blown out the airlock. I'm told we'll have to start all over again—if the SiBoronaans will let us, and if we can somehow fix this mess you and your people have created."*

Kirk sat up straighter. Accustomed to being bawled out, his natural reaction was to fight back—admiral or no admiral.

"Are we"—he hastened to correct himself—"am *I* being charged with something, sir?"

"Individual and collective stupidity, perhaps. I'm sure the experts in JAG are hunting for the proper charges as we speak. We're still not sure of the extent of the problem you created. In addition to being tenuous, the SiBoronaans apparently can be frustratingly nonspecific. Also, I'm told that the more panicky they get, the more garbled their communications become. What we have *been able to pick out is that they are claiming that the Federation has foisted a stealth takeover on them. A furtive coup."*

"I don't . . ." Kirk's voice steadied. What could have gone so utterly wrong in a matter of a few months? "I can't imagine where this is coming from, sir. All we did was aid a single Perenorean colony ship. The solution we found was, I'd like to point out, advantageous to the Federation. The Perenoreans were settling down on the SiBoronaan moon. When we left the system they were cooperating fully. I can state with confidence that both species were on the best of terms."

The admiral let him continue.

"Surely this message from SiBor can't have anything to do with our efforts to help the Perenoreans? They showed themselves to be nonaggressive and peaceful, their gratitude to the SiBoronaans as well as to the Federation was sufficiently effusive as to border on the embarrassing."

"*I wouldn't know,*" the admiral snapped. "*I've never met a Perenorean. But I* have *read both your official report and the subsequent analysis of it by Starfleet xenologists, and I admit that there is something going on here that just doesn't make sense.*" He threw up his hands. "*Maybe this is a SiBoronaan idea of a joke, though from the tone of their communiqué I doubt it. Maybe it's a simple matter of misperceptions, or cultural conflicts. All I know is that Diplomatic Corp is all over Command, and that this situation needs to be resolved* immediately." He smiled wolfishly. "*That is assuming you would like to continue your career in Starfleet as a captain and not as a waste extraction engineer.*"

Kirk stiffened. "I'll assume that's a rhetorical question—sir."

Yamashiro looked to his right. "*The* Enterprise *is to proceed immediately to the SiBor system and to the SiBoronaan capital of*

EmouValk. They are expecting a response from us. The fact that you are already familiar with their civilization and procedures should speed understanding of the problem and point to a resolution that is satisfactory to all parties. Or . . ."

"Or—sir?" Kirk kept his voice perfectly neutral.

"Or when they learn that it's the Enterprise *that's been sent to sort out the problem, they may decide to kill you on sight. When you beam down you'll need to be prepared for anything. Just because the SiBoronaans have a reputation for pacifism doesn't mean you can rely on it."*

"We'll take all necessary precautions, sir."

"Your pardon, Admiral. Commander Spock speaking."

Yamashiro's gaze shifted slightly to one side. *"What is it, Commander Spock?"*

"Is Starfleet certain that the distress communication from SiBor was not more specific? Merely informing us that they are being 'taken over' and that the *Enterprise* is somehow responsible gives us very little to go on, and nothing with which to prepare a response."

"I realize that." The admiral finally seemed to soften a little. *"You'll just have to improvise. That's part of your mission anyway."*

"Sir, if I may," Spock continued, "if the SiBoronaans are agreeable, we could suggest that they send a delegation directly to the *Enterprise*. That would greatly improve our ability to safely manage both our security and theirs while also allowing us to get a preliminary handle on the problem. Having already met and dealt with individuals of their species, I suspect they would be flattered by the offer and eager to take advantage of it."

"An excellent suggestion, Commander. Captain Kirk, upon your arrival at SiBor, you may act on Commander Spock's suggestion. Proceed as you see fit—although permitting you that sort of leeway doesn't seem to have worked well in this particular situation." He sighed heavily. *"At the risk of making things worse, and given the level of anxiety expressed by the SiBoronaans in regards to finding a solution to this situation quickly, I'm afraid I'm going to have to allow you to"*—he winced visibly—*"use your own judgment."*

"Thank you, sir. We'll be careful, and whatever the problem is that has arisen, we'll put it right."

"I hope so, Captain. Diplomatic Corps hopes so. We all hope so. Yamashiro out."

The admiral had hit Kirk with a challenge and an accusation. The first had piqued his curiosity. The second had made him mad as hell. As McCoy would have been the first to point out, the combination often saw the captain perform at his best. Kirk hoped it would be good enough.

Prepared to send down a landing party, Kirk was greatly relieved when the clearly distressed SiBoronaan delegation agreed to beam aboard the *Enterprise* to explain the state of affairs that now afflicted their society. Meanwhile, Kirk put the ship on alert status—just in case.

Kirk, Spock, Scott, and Uhura did not carry phasers to the meeting. In addition to making a bad impression, it was unnecessary. Unless all the delegates were bent on premeditated suicide, they could not get home unless the *Enterprise* beamed them back. No matter how upset they might be, they were unlikely to cause trouble. At least, not of the physical kind.

While there was no equivalent on the *Enterprise* of the Si-Boronaans' formal, decorated meeting hall, the ship's shuttle-bay offered a suitably spacious venue. An honor guard stood at attention off to one side while the *Enterprise* officers awaited the arrival of the native delegation from the transporter room. When the slow-moving SiBoronaans arrived, Kirk was pleased to see that it was headed by Four Amek and Six Jol.

"The Federation once again extends its manipulative digits and reminds the great SiBoronaans of its eternal friendship." He waggled the fingers of his right hand in imitation of the corresponding SiBoronaan gesture for formal/polite greeting. "It's good to see you again, Four Amek, even though I and my colleagues are informed there is some difficulty on SiBor that we might be able to help you with."

"There is difficulty, and it is not small." The slender Si-Boronaan did not mince words, and his eye flaps worked themselves back and forth rapidly enough to risk a sprain. As near as Kirk could tell based on what little he knew of Si-Boronaan biology, the delegate standing before him was both angry and exhausted. In fact, he thought to himself, the entire delegation looked beat. The single SiBoronaan limb with its multiple branchings and grasping digits rose to flail wildly in the captain's direction. "And it is your fault! All your fault. You deceived us!"

Taken aback by the straightforward accusation, Kirk struggled to come up with a reply that would be formal and friendly. "We did nothing secretly, Amek. Everything we did from the moment we contacted you, everything that followed, was done openly and in full consultation with your people. There was no attempt to deceive." Peering past the fuming speaker Kirk tried and failed to interpret the agitated gestures that were being executed by the rest of the delegation. Given their evident rage, perhaps his continuing incomprehension was just as well.

Spock took a step forward. "What, precisely, is the nature of your difficulty?"

"Precisely? Specifically?" Turning, Four Amek consulted with his colleagues. Their conversation was as animated as any Kirk could remember seeing among the SiBoronaans. While they conversed, he leaned over and whispered to Uhura.

"My translator's not getting any of this, Lieutenant. Can you understand anything they're saying?"

Straining to pick up as much of the alien conversation as she could, the communications officer looked hesitant.

"There are a lot of untranslatable exclamations, Captain. Some of them are accompanied by fore and aft adjectives that—let's just say it's better if they don't go into the official log. As to the rest"—she frowned—"they seem to be arguing over which offense is the most heinous."

" 'Which'?" Kirk gaped at her. "You mean there's more than one?"

She nodded gravely. "Many more, Captain. I believe they are preparing a list."

How long a list? he found himself wondering. *And what could possibly be on it?* Maybe an interruption would be in order.

"Please, could you give us, uh, an example of what's troubling you," Kirk prompted Four Amek. "So that we can get an idea of what's going on here, and what has you so upset."

Pivoting on his central axis, the SiBoronaan delegate turned around to face Kirk instead of merely shifting his eye flaps.

"For one thing, Captain Kirk, SiBor's largest and most settled continent of MaFir now has a swiftly expanding new rapid transit system for delivering goods and travelers. This highly efficient scheme is already being extended to Second and Fourth MaFir."

Kirk succeeded in looking thoroughly confused. The SiBoronaan's words seemed totally at odds with his irate tone. "I don't understand, Amek. This new system doesn't work properly? It pollutes the atmosphere or the ground? It's too costly for your people to use?"

"No!" Even though Kirk's translator automatically lowered the volume of the exclamation, the SiBoronaan's vehemence still came through. "It works perfectly! Not only does it not pollute the sky or the earth, its mechanism actually takes pollutants from the air and renders them harmless." His gurgling voice rose to a shout. *"It is cheap to operate and everyone can afford to make use of it!"* His digits retracted. "We are *outraged.*"

If possible, Scott was even more bemused than his befuddled captain. "Sounds like an engineer's dream. I confess I cannot see the problem."

"The problem?" Four Amek turned on his support-ive pseudopods to face the *Enterprise*'s chief engineer. "The problem is that the entire system was envisioned, devised, and designed by Perenoreans! They also had to supervise the construction—because we were incapable of doing so with suf-ficient efficiency. The SiBoronaans supplied the labor and the raw materials and the manufacturing facilities, but that was all. Everything else was done for us by the new colonists."

Scott was shaking his head in disbelief. "I still don't see the difficulty."

Six Jol scuttled forward. The smaller delegate's voice was notably higher than that of Four Amek. "The difficulty is that only the Perenoreans understand the system. Therefore only they can run it. Some of our own engineers have tried, but the complexity and subtleties of the computational mechanics and the devices that keep them operating at peak efficiency defeated them. Without Perenorean supervision, the entire system would quickly collapse."

"What you're saying," Kirk replied slowly, "is that the Pere-noreans have helped you to build a better ground transporta-tion system, but that they control it."

"Exactly." Four Amek sounded relieved that the message had made it across the language barrier.

"If the situation bothers you, why not," Scott wondered, "go back to the old one?"

"Because," Six Jol explained, "the new transportation sys-tem *is* better. For all the reasons Four Amek has given you, it is as if they knew! If the government were to try and go back, even

if we declared that it was for the ultimate good of the Num-
bered, there would be great anger. And commerce would surely
suffer. Having wholeheartedly adopted the system offered to us
by the Perenoreans, we now find ourselves prisoners of it."

Spock was nodding understandingly. "It would appear
that the Perenoreans are, quite openly and obligingly, making
themselves, their knowledge, and their abilities invaluable to
their hosts."

Uhura had come to the same conclusion. "I get it. It's like
a big company that has only one person who really understands the corporate finances. She's the one person the company can't fire."

Scott grinned. "Or like the chief engineer on a starship
bein' the only officer who truly understands all the workings
of the ship."

"You said there's more." Kirk waited expectantly for either
of the two delegates to continue. Both responded.

"We have a much more sophisticated orbital staging system for our spacecraft," Six Jol aggrievedly told him.

"Five new varieties of genetically engineered food plants
have been developed and planted. Each shows more promise
than the last." The tips of Four Amek's digits were quivering
with agitation.

"A new device for extracting valuable minerals from sea-
water is now in operation at five sites in the western ocean,"
delegate Jol bitterly informed the Starfleet officers.

Four Amek was running out of steam, perhaps from
waving his digits so often and so vigorously. "Our capital

EmouValk has been gifted with new forms of art, music, and literature."

"And these are insulting to your SiBoronaan culture?" Kirk ventured hesitantly.

"No!" Four Amek shouted. "They are all each and every number of them honorable and worthwhile. The art dazzles the eye, the music thrills the heartpipes, and the literature is of the most compulsive kind." A deep earnestness had crept into the delegate's voice. Earnestness, and desperation.

"I think I understand." Spock was taking notes on a data slate.

"Well then, maybe you'll be so kind as to share your revelation with the rest of us, Mister Spock." A plainly baffled Scott stared hard at the science officer. "From where I stand, it sounds to me as if the Perenoreans have done nothing wrong except bequeath one gift after another to their hosts."

"That is quite correct, Mister Scott," Spock agreed. "Just as they promised to do for us prior to our departure. They have given freely and expansively of their knowledge and abilities to their new hosts." He turned his attention back to the delegation. "This realization is critical to understanding why the SiBoronaans are so upset, why they sent a distress call to Starfleet, and why they feel they have been deceived."

Scott's expression twisted. "Mister Spock, can you unravel it any better than that?"

The science officer drew himself up. "I shall endeavor to do precisely that, Mister Scott. Using you as an example." For a change it was Scott's eyebrows that rose.

"Suppose," Spock began, "that a newly arrived ensign knew how to maintain full warp engine power while cutting dilithium drain in half?"

The chief engineer glanced around at his companions before turning back to the science officer. "Why, I'd offer him me heartiest congratulations, adopt his methodology, and recommend him for a commendation!"

Spock continued: "Suppose that despite your best efforts you proved incapable of understanding the new process? Suppose that other ensigns, his friends, were assigned to the ship to oversee the necessary conversions? What if this ensign and his friends kept suggesting improvements—improvements that worked, and none of which you could comprehend despite your extensive experience? Might you not soon find yourself eased out of your position in favor of one of the newcomers who did understand all the changes?"

The chief engineer digested this, looked slightly stunned at the conclusion he arrived at, and stammered a response. "Why, I dinna think that would . . . it couldn't happen because . . . it isn't likely that . . ." He broke off, stared at the science officer, looked dazedly at Kirk, and finally turned back to once again face the muttering delegation from SiBor.

"*Help ma boab!* Now I get it." He looked back at Spock. "Na wonder the SiBoronaans think they've been deceived. The bloody Perenoreans are helpin' them so much that they're takin' over! 'Tis conquest by gift giving!"

Spock gestured affirmatively. "Albeit without such intent in mind. Plainly the difference in knowledge not only of technology but of aesthetics as well as other fields is so great that the SiBoronaans cannot compete. Yet everything the Perenoreans have done and continue to do for their hosts arises out of a feeling of gratitude and a desire to be of help."

"Och, aye," commented the chief engineer, "they're helpin' themselves to control of the SiBor system, they are."

"By making themselves and their gifts irreplaceable." Kirk understood the science officer's point. "The SiBoronaans now find themselves trapped in a deepening spiral of free help and good neighborliness. If they refuse gifts that improve life on SiBor, whatever segment of the SiBoronaan population that stands to benefit is bound to raise a stink. And if they accept them and only the Perenoreans can make the gifts work, then that leaves the colonists in control of one more aspect of Si-Boronaan society. Brilliant!"

"A caution, Captain." Spock eyed his friend intently. "I am not at all certain that this represents some carefully thought-out devious plan on the part of the Perenoreans. It may be nothing more than what it appears to be: a general and generous outreach on their part to be of assistance to their benefactors." He turned his attention back to the delegation. "That does not, of course, obviate the attendant consequences that have so upset the SiBoronaans."

"And as you point out, Spock," Uhura added, "they're trapped. Turn down future presents and some segment of their society will protest. Continue to accept them and take the damning consequences along with them."

"There is one possible solution."

Kirk sighed as he waited on his science officer. "All right, Spock: let's have it."

"It is very simple, Captain. If they wish to continue to dwell on DiBor, the Perenoreans must be persuaded to stop assisting the SiBoronaans. Furthermore, the SiBoronaans must be educated to master the Perenorean gifts."

"And the alternative?" Kirk asked him.

The science officer eyed the waiting delegation as its members continued to argue among themselves.

"Unless this is done, I fear that, quite unintentionally, the SiBoronaans will become second-class citizens if not outright slaves in their own planetary system."

11

While the members of the SiBoronaan delegation continued to debate furiously among themselves, the Starfleet officers turned introspective as they pondered the ramifications of Spock's solution. Captain Kirk finally broke the silence.

"So then. We've just been told that the SiBoronaans have become reliant on the Perenorean contributions. How are we going to slow that down?"

"I've got it!" Scott's expression brightened. "If you'll permit me an engineerin' analogy, it strikes me that these Perenoreans are like a runaway nuclear reaction. They're so full of ideas and concepts and obligin' hints that they need an outlet for their energy or they'll just explode. What they need are the social equivalent of carbon rods to soak up all their excess neutrons—excuse me, excess energies." Having caught the attention of his colleagues, he swiftly continued. "In this case 'tis the Si-

Boronaans who are both the beneficiaries and victims of all that energy. Now, if we can substitute a more effective system of control for all this Perenorean 'helpfulness' and find them a locale better suited to soakin' up all their surplus energy . . ."

Kirk eyed his chief engineer with admiration. "That sounds like a fine idea, Mister Scott. A fine idea." He looked to his right. "Mister Spock?"

The science officer's reaction was considerably more restrained. "I am not sure, Captain. It sounds plausible. Time should be taken to study all the possible ramifications." He looked at Scott. "I presume you have some suitable source in mind for the 'soakin' up' of the Perenoreans' excess energy?"

"Why, of course!" The chief engineer spread his arms wide. "Where better to release a wealth of new ideas than in the Federation!"

Kirk frowned. "The Perenoreans are already well established on DiBor, Mister Scott. Moving them into the Federation would mean uprooting everything they've managed to accomplish thus far."

"Nay, Captain," Scott argued. "The ones who have put down roots should stay. But if we offer some of the best and most active minds among them the chance to move back and forth between their new home and a suitable location in the Federation, I think that they would jump at the chance. Mister Spock?"

The science officer considered this. "Perhaps that is indeed what the irrepressible creativity of the Perenorean demands." He turned to Kirk. "With regard to Mister Scott's suggestion, I

urge caution, Captain. But I suppose escorting a small delegation of the Perenoreans' brightest and most fecund minds to
Earth could be a solution. Removing them from the current
equation might well serve to dampen the speed with which
their people are apparently taking control of activities on
SiBor. It would also provide an excellent opportunity for us
to study them in greater depth. The time that some of them
spent aboard the *Enterprise* was insufficient to develop a complete picture of any one individual, much less how they act in
groups when exposed to alien surroundings. I would welcome
the opportunity to study with them on a more extensive basis."

Uhura chimed in. "And I could produce a better lexicon of
the Perenorean language than what I've been able to compile.
There's no better way to learn what someone means than to
spend extended time in their company listening to them speak
their native tongue."

Spock coughed slightly. "I must concur with Lieutenant
Uhura's assessment."

The active chatter and deep glottal stops of SiBoronaan
conversation filled the shuttlebay. Though their hosts seemed
to have forgotten them, the circumstances that had brought
them aboard continued to generate so much excitement among
the delegation that they did not notice any oversight.

"That's it, then." Kirk turned back to the SiBoronaan
delegation. Seeing their host beckon for their attention, they
ceased their conversation. "Based on what you've told us, we
see no way short of outright hostilities that can prevent the
Perenoreans from continuing to make contributions to your

society. We can't turn back the clock." His mouth twisted into a wry smile. "What we propose is to shift the attention of the Perenoreans, especially that of their most helpful and intelligent individuals, away from SiBor and to the Federation itself. SiBor is only one world. The Federation is comprised of hundreds. There will be ample opportunities within it for the energetic Perenoreans to contribute all the ideas they wish.

"To convince them that it's better to share these with all the peoples of the Federation rather than just the SiBoronaan, we plan to ask them to put together a delegation to visit Earth. Once their attention is drawn elsewhere, we believe they will be inclined to direct less of their immediate attention to SiBor. We will insist that they stop, step back, and teach you everything you need to know to use, run, and create at their level. Your people will regain control of your society."

While harsh to the human ear, the collective squalling this proposal ignited among the SiBoronaan delegation was the clamor of approval. Only Six Jol was reluctant.

"But will the Perenoreans agree to this? To remove their most oppressing—your pardon, their most 'helpful'—people from our world in order to become part of this delegation you describe?"

"As someone who lives to seek new knowledge," Spock told the reluctant SiBoronaan, "I do not see how beings of the Perenorean temperament will be able to refuse."

"And," Kirk added, "when they come back and report on the opportunities that exist within the Federation, more of their most innovative individuals will want to transfer to where they can exploit their suggestions to the fullest. Those who remain should be too busy teaching and maintaining their new home."

"One hopes," the science officer cryptically whispered.

This time the caucus among the delegates was brief. Four Amek turned back to Kirk.

"We find in favor of your initiative, Captain Kirk. If there is anything you require of us, anything we can do to aid in its implementation, you have only to ask."

Kirk smiled. "I think we will handle it."

"We wish to learn to improve ourselves, and our planet. Not to be treated like second-class citizens," Amek replied disconsolately.

"Easy there, now. We're goin' to fix it for you." Reaching out as if to give the delegate a friendly pat on the shoulder, Scott had to awkwardly withdraw his hand as he realized that the SiBoronaans were wholly lacking in this particular physiological feature. He settled for a brief, cheering smile.

Kirk watched the SiBoronaan delegation shuffle back to the transporter room. There was no reason to suppose that Starfleet would not be equally gratified. The SiBoronaans had arrived agitated and angry. They were departing mollified, if not entirely appeased, convinced that the Federation intended to immediately address their unexpectedly difficult state of affairs. This had been accomplished without threats of violence. And if Mister Scott's suggestion could be carried out, there would be no violence. The SiBoronaans would be content, the Perenoreans would be happy, and Starfleet would be satisfied. There was only one potential problem.

"Spock, are you *sure* the Perenoreans will agree to gather together their best people and send them away from the colony and off to Earth? Or to wherever Starfleet thinks appropriate?"

"I don't see why they would turn down such an offer. Their new home here is established. Too established, according to the SiBoronaans. The Perenoreans may want a diversion as badly as the SiBoronaans need it."

Kirk nodded contentedly. "It should be interesting having more than a couple of them on board ship for an extended period of time. Although we're more advanced than the Si-Boronaans, we still might learn a thing or two."

"Indeed we might, Captain. We should be open-minded about such things."

"Why, Spock, haven't you learned by now that I have an open mind on everything?"

The science officer's brows drew together. "Do I detect a reference in your comment to something other than the matter at hand, Jim?"

Kirk, Spock, and McCoy beamed down to DiBor. They soon found themselves sitting on gracefully curving Perenorean benches in a lightly silvered but otherwise transparent sphere that ballooned from the top floor of the completed administration center. Looking around, the doctor could not stop babbling about the bubble.

"This is an amazing piece of engineering." Peering down,

he could see the busy street directly below. "It hardly seems strong enough to support a cat, let alone the four of us." He returned his gaze to Taell, their host. "You've had a haircut. Or a fur cut."

Taell's golden eyes glanced down at his right shoulder, which was exposed between two folds of the mauve-and-black fabric that was wrapped tightly around his body. The patterns presently etched there were indeed different from those he had sported when contact had first been made with the *Enterprise*. His mouth flexed.

"You have a remarkable eye for physical detail, Masteresque."

McCoy shrugged. "I'm a doctor. Taking note of physical variation is my job."

Spock was equally intrigued by the ethereal alien engineering. "If I may ask, Taell, what is this material that forms our present enclosure?"

The leaderesque of the Perenoreans set aside the tall cylinder he had been holding with four pad-tips of his right hand. "The nearest human term I can find in my poor, limited vocabulary is 'gossamer.' I do not think our name, which is specific to the Perenorean science of materials engineering, can translate better. We call it *ku!ralpt*."

McCoy pursed his lips. "I'll stick with gossamer, thanks."

"It is fashioned by a special machine," Taell continued. "Within the apparatus, the raw materials are blended in a flux and then quickly extruded into the desired shape." Reaching out, he drew several finger pads down the inside of the nearly perfect transparent fabric. In their wake, spreading ripples of silver appeared briefly before fading from view. "It will flex slightly with the weather and bond instantly to any construction material. I am told this involves amalgamation at the molecular level. But I am not a materials physicist."

Kirk began smoothly, "We have a proposition for you. One with which the SiBoronaans already concur."

"Ah, our great benefactors!" As the leaderesque sat back on his bench McCoy feared that Taell was going to fall over backward. But the Perenorean's multiple joints allowed him to "relax" in ways that would have put a human at risk of bodily injury. "I fear they are distressed with and confused by certain aspects of our feeble attempts to repay them for what they have done for us."

And what you've done to them, Kirk thought. "A number of their representatives were quite upset. We think we may have come up with a solution that will satisfy their concerns while opening a whole realm of new prospects for the Perenoreans."

Taell straightened on his bench. "We are always eager to hear of new opportunities. Especially those that might allow us to help those who have helped us."

"Then you should be pleased with this one." Kirk set his libation aside. It looked like a simple metal utensil; however, the gleaming Perenorean drinking cylinder had managed to change the taste of its contents three times since it had been handed to him. Maybe the drink possessed the ability to change flavors all by itself. He made a mental note to inquire once the meeting had concluded.

"We would like to extend an invitation to two dozen of your best and most energetic people, each experts in their own field, to come and visit Starfleet Headquarters on Earth." He fought to keep any hint of condescension out of his voice. "At the same time, the SiBoronaans want to learn everything about the . . . gifts you've given them. They insist, and we agree, that a pause in your generosity is necessary, until they can understand them and work beside you."

Taell appeared overwhelmed by the offer. "This is a wonderful opportunity! I cannot convey enough thanks for this expression of trust and generosity. I am sure my colleagues will approve." He indicated the street and new buildings that had taken shape outside the bubble. "As you have seen, the colony here is well established, with two others already striving to match the First Settlement in energy and expansion. I am certain we could spare some of our best people to visit Earth to observe and to learn." His voice fell slightly. "I only worry about how our great friends the SiBoronaans will manage in our absence. They seem to have some difficulty managing some of the assistance we have given to them."

McCoy controlled his expression as well as his voice. "I think they'll muddle through somehow. Don't underestimate them."

Taell looked shocked. "Oh no, never, never! The SiBoronaans are a brilliant, compassionate, persevering people. They just need a little bit of support here, a line of information there, which we are thrilled to be able to supply."

"I know it will be hard on them to have their Perenorean

supervisors take a leave of absence," Kirk declared dryly, "but as Doctor McCoy points out, they should be able to get by." He looked to his left. "Spock? You're being mighty quiet. Thoughts?"

"Hmm?" The Vulcan drew himself back from whatever his contemplations had been. "Oh, to be sure, Captain."

Kirk frowned. Whatever had been bothering Spock for some time now continued to maintain its grip on the science officer's thoughts.

"I do have one fear, though," Taell confessed. There was no hint of artifice in the Perenorean leader's response.

Kirk smiled reassuringly. "Your people have nothing to fear from the Federation or from Starfleet."

"No . . ." the leaderesque agreed. "It is a fear of the unknown and how it may impact on us. How will they react when they find themselves confronted by your superior technology and its unfathomable advancements?"

"I don't think you have to worry on that score." McCoy was forthright in his assurance. "Your medical representatives should be able to keep up with anything, I can vouch for that from my own experience working with them. In fact, whoever you choose to represent that field might even be able to offer a useful idea or two of their own." He grinned broadly. "We doctors can be stubborn, but we're always willing to listen to new techniques."

"I know, I know." Taell stared at the dark contents of his own drinking cylinder. "But still I fear for the mental stability of the specialists who will be chosen to go." He brightened.

"Yet this is an offer that cannot be disregarded. I myself will see to the selection of the fortunate twenty-four. Despite the uncertainties to which I have just referred, there will be considerable competition within each field to see who will be among the elect. Except for one area, where no competition will be necessary."

"Which one would that be?" Kirk was only mildly curious.

"Why, interstellar travel, of course." Taell's ears snapped straight back and stiffened while golden pupils widened as much as possible. "I am availing myself of your invitation to be one of the representatives of my people."

"That's . . ." Kirk glanced at McCoy, whose nod was not only approving but enthusiastic. "That's fine, Taell. I feel like we've become more than just allies. In the time we've spent together and gotten to know one another, I feel that you and I have become friends."

The fur on the Perenorean's exposed sloping shoulder rippled, gleaming in the light. "Captain Kirk, you embarrass me. Not in my deepest dreams would I dare to contemplate such an eminence as yourself as a personal friend."

"Well, I . . ." Kirk tried not to blush. "That's very kind of you, Taell."

"And you, great Doctor McCoy—might I presume to count you as a 'friend' as well?"

"Why, sure!" McCoy flashed a ready smile. "I'm happy to be friends with anyone who shows the kind of concern for others that your people do. You're compassionate and protective. Who wouldn't want to be friends with you?"

"Certain of the SiBoronaans, I fear." Spock voiced the re-joinder so softly that his translator did not pick it up. But Kirk and McCoy overheard clearly enough. Both of the Vulcan's fellow officers shot surprised looks in his direction. Noting them, the science officer added by way of explanation, "Lest we forget why we returned here."

"Oh, right." Kirk relaxed. Spock was, as always, making sure none of them got carried away by circumstances, no matter how benign they appeared to be.

Though the captain was sure the science officer's translation unit had not rendered his cautionary words into Perenorean, Taell nonetheless focused his eager gaze on the Vulcan.

"And what of you, Mister Spock? May I count you as a personal friend along with your colleagues?"

The *Enterprise*'s first officer did not hesitate. "Certain aspects of Vulcan culture are different from those of humans, Leaderesque Taell. Without wishing in any way to appear aloof, I have to say that when it comes to establishing close personal relationships, Vulcans are somewhat reticent. I am willing to declare that the personal relationship between you and I falls somewhere between pleasing familiarity and cordial acquaintance."

Although his translator seemed to have some difficulty parsing the fine line the Vulcan had drawn, Taell appeared sufficiently pleased with this response.

"Thank you, Commander Spock. I am most thankful for your thoughtfulness."

"You are welcome," the science officer replied.

Kirk felt it necessary to preempt any continuing uneasiness. "Don't feel that Mister Spock's response is slighting you in any way, Taell. It's a fact that his people really are less extroverted than humans."

"There's an understatement if I ever heard one," McCoy put in dryly.

Kirk threw the doctor a look, then turned back to the leader of the colonists. "My people make friends quickly and without reservation. Vulcans tend to be circumspect." He smiled encouragingly. "We're more emotional, they're more logical."

"I very much understand, Captain." To Kirk's relief, the leaderesque did not seem the least insulted, nor even put off by Spock's restraint. Taell turned his wide yellow eyes on the science officer. "I regard Mister Spock's reserve as a challenge. Before our voyage to Earth is completed, I will make him my good and close friend! Such a thing is easier than navigating a route between the stars or fighting off the brutal Dre'kalak."

McCoy mustered a wry grin. "I wish you luck, my friend."

12

ontgomery Scott beamed the chosen twenty-four representatives aboard. Since the majority of the Perenorean delegation
were new to the experience, each small group was accompanied
by a member of the *Enterprise*'s crew. For a sentient who had
never before undergone transport, teleportation could be unsettling. Just the awareness that one's body and very self were being
destroyed only to be precisely assembled elsewhere was sometimes
sufficient to induce severe anxiety in the prospective transportee.

To their credit, not one of the Perenoreans suffered the
slightest psychological issue as a consequence of the transport.
On the contrary, they arrived aboard the *Enterprise* marveling
at the experience and wanting to know every detail about how
it had been accomplished. Instead of allowing themselves to be
escorted to their assigned quarters, they frustrated their guides
by besieging a busy Scott with questions relating to the process

and the science behind it. With several more groups still to be beamed aboard, Scott was afraid he might have to beat them back with something stronger than sharp words. Their enthusiasm was unbridled—and a bit overwhelming.

"Nay, I cannot explain right now exactly how the transporter works. It'd take me a whole bleedin' work break just to show you the math." As he spoke, another inquisitive, energetic Perenorean arrived behind the transporter controls and began to cast queries at the chief engineer so fast that Scott's translator could barely keep up with her questions. The loose ends of the alien's swirling pearlescent ochre-and-bronze garb threatened to entangle Scott's legs.

"See here now, lassie, do not touch that!" Reaching over, he gently but forcibly pulled seven pad-tipped fingers away from the top of the console. "You want to scramble up your friends while they're in transport? The result would not be a pretty sight, I promise you." With a sigh of exasperation, he yelled at an ensign posted to another part of the chamber. "Servantes! What are those two doing over there?"

The harried ensign looked up from where she was standing helplessly above two of the recent arrivals. Both Perenoreans were lying on their backs across the transporter pads with their heads hanging over the rear lip of the platform as they chattered incessantly between themselves.

"I don't know, Mister Scott, sir! The translator I was issued can't keep up." The ensign paused a moment to listen. "I think they're talking about energy requirements. Or maybe loop geometry. I'm not sure."

Though he admired their intense curiosity, Scott was more than a little annoyed. Several groups of the Perenoreans and their handlers were still waiting to beam aboard, and he knew the captain was anxious to get underway. All of the aliens' personal belongings had already arrived on board. All that remained was to beam the remaining visitors up to the ship. Meanwhile the transporter room was turning into a circus.

"I don't care if they're debatin' the ingredients for a sauce for Perenorean haggis—get them out from under there and take them to their quarters! Carry them if you have to." He indicated the console in front of him. "I've still got a full pack of their nosy cousins to bring aboard and a ship to prepare for the jump to warp. Tell them they can ask all the bloody questions they want once we're on our way."

"Yes, sir, Mister Scott!" Kneeling, Ensign Servantes spoke urgently to the probing visitors. The three of them had hardly moved clear of the critical zone before a dyspeptic Scott had the transporter energized once again.

It seemed to take forever for the increasingly exasperated ensign to get the pair she had been assigned to their quarters. Part of her frustration stemmed from the fact that in order to make room for the two dozen Perenorean guests, a number of the crew had been compelled to temporarily double up with colleagues. Federation starships were not passenger transports. They did not travel with empty holds or guest cabins. Every centimeter of space was valuable and accounted for. Wide corridors were intended to provide psychological comfort by eliminating feelings of claustrophobia, while the spacious engineering deck supplied ample room in which to work, add new equipment, and allow for flexible space in the event of emergencies.

While it was not her cabin that had been requisitioned to provide living quarters for the two Perenoreans, Ensign Servantes still felt a certain communal proprietorship toward the space. Its usual occupant had put into temporary storage all items of a personal nature; however, the cabin still retained a lived-in feel and the lingering essence of its permanent habitant. As to the Perenoreans' own modest personal effects, these had already been delivered to the room.

"My name is Ensign Ermina Servantes. I have been designated your personal contact while you are on board the *Enterprise*.

"I'm sorry there's only one bed," she told them. Both of her charges were male. Knowing nothing of Perenorean culture, she introduced them to the cabin's facilities without any preconceptions.

"Wonderful!" was the comment that greeted everything she said or showed them. They had no difficulty comprehending the functions intrinsic to the small living area. Their only disappointment surfaced when they inquired about access to the ship's computer and she had to explain that it was, at least for now, unavailable to them.

"Each crewmember has a personal code. Additionally, auditory and ocular recognition is required to enable access." Servantes smiled at the two yellow-eyed visitors whose ears seemed to semaphore all over the place as they listened intently.

"Not all of your crew are humanoid. I have seen others

whose eyes are very different." Reaching up, one slender multi-jointed finger indicated a large yellow orb. "Wouldn't it be a simple matter to program ours, and our voices as well, into your security system so that we could have access?"

Servantes was immediately on guard. "Why are you so anxious to have access to the ship's computer? You and your people are our guests on board. As guests of Starfleet, everything possible will be done for you. All you have to do is voice your request."

The slightly taller of the pair looked at his companion, then back to their escort. "But we want to learn how to do things for *ourselves*. You are already doing so much for us, simply by having us on board and taking us to Earth. Hospitality is a hallmark of our species. We don't want to do anything to take you away from your normal work routine."

"Or your schedule for relaxation," added the other alien. "It seems so unfair, so unnecessarily troubling, when we could do so much more for ourselves."

"Besides," finished the larger Perenorean, "we do not want to waste an instant of this miraculous, valuable experience that has been granted to us. Our purpose in accepting your wondrous invitation and undertaking this journey is so that we can learn more about you and the Federation. How can we learn if we do not have access to your store of information?"

"Ask a lot of questions, I suppose." *Though not of me*, Servantes thought tiredly. Just the number of queries the pair had posed en route had exhausted her. "I'm sure that once the necessary procedures have been run through and suitable safeguards put in place, you and your companions will be allowed access to appropriate portions of the ship's computer." She tried to make her response sound as reassuring as possible.

For a second time, the Perenoreans exchanged a glance. This time it was the shorter of the pair who spoke first. His bewilderment was sufficiently profound to come through in translation.

"Security procedures? Are we— Is it possible that our presence on board your breathtaking vessel is considered to be a threat?" Rising to his face, both seven-fingered hands covered his eyes in a gesture indicative of deep shame.

Servantes didn't know what to say. Even more embarrassed than his comrade, the other Perenorean had turned completely away from her. Reaching out instinctively, she put a hand on the narrow shoulder and was surprised at the degree of lean musculature she could feel through the lightweight wrapping. A gentle tug was enough to turn the humble creature back toward her.

She smiled comfortingly. "It's normal procedure. Unless they arrive pre-cleared, no one brought on board a Starfleet vessel is allowed immediate access to its computer. Surely you can understand that? These regulations apply to everyone. Your people are not being singled out. I'm sure access is just a matter of time." Finding the following silence distinctly awkward, she edged toward the door.

"I showed you how to call for help if you have any problems or difficulties operating the cabin's amenities. Given what I and the rest of my shipmates have been told about you, I doubt you'll need much in the way of assistance." Servantes was at the doorway now. "The reports say that you're highly adaptable and fast learners."

Some of the distress slipped away from the two visitors. "We are just anxious to learn new things, that's all."

His companion gestured affirmatively and Servantes found herself fascinated by the intricate and supple movements of the double-jointed arm and its seven manipulative digits.

"Your Masteresque—Doctor—McCoy compared us to a simple ocean-dwelling creature of your world called . . ." The Perenorean paused a moment to remember. "A—a sponge. Yes, a sponge. He said that we are constantly soaking up new information and new things." As he stood a little straighter the coils of material that made up his attire glistened in the cabin's subdued light.

Doctor McCoy's observation might be flattering as analogy, she thought. Her personal take was that while their constant flow of questions could be decidedly annoying, these two were nice. Yes, that was it. Just plain nice. Although a little too fawning for her taste. No doubt the captain lapped it up.

"You know how to operate the communication instrument." By now the ensign was halfway out the door. "If you need anything of a *personal* nature, that is, anything immediate that doesn't involve the supplying of answers to general questions, please don't hesitate to call on me. My regular duties have been adjusted so that I can be available to assist you when and if necessary."

The two Perenoreans promptly dropped to the floor and

arched their backs. Now it was the ensign's turn to experience a bout of embarrassment.

"We thank you from the center of our beings for your kindness and understanding," the smaller of the pair murmured liquidly.

"Yes, well, you're welcome." Decidedly ill at ease with the visitors' profound humbling, which bordered on groveling, she backed out into the corridor.

Really nice, she decided as she headed for the next deck up and resumption of her regular assignment. *Easy to get along with, easy to understand, and anxious to make friends.* If she could get them to limit their incessant questioning, she could see herself enjoying their company for the duration of the journey to Earth.

Over the next few days, Ensign Servantes did see them, and they did chat pleasantly, and she did enjoy their company. It never struck her that not once did they have to call for help with the cabin's human-friendly and non-Perenorean facilities.

Specialist Wissell was supervising the last of first meal, also known as breakfast, when the alien appeared. As Wissell was very particular about his domain and about general hygiene in the food preparation area, he viewed the unannounced intrusion warily. Orders were that as guests, the Perenoreans were to have access to all nonsensitive sections of the ship; other sections would be opened to them when they were cleared and accompanied by an authorized escort. While the specialist was privately miffed that food preparation was not included among the departments classified as sensitive, there was nothing he could do about the designation.

He could, however, try to minimize both the intrusion and the interruption as courteously as possible.

"Greetings."

To Wissell's surprise the alien extended long fingers as if he had been shaking hands all his life. The specialist took it automatically. The grip was firm except for a distinct softness detectable at the padded tips.

"I am Couthad." Yellow eyes roamed the web of intricate machinery that took raw materials and from them synthesized food for the crew. "Having been made aware of this counterpart to a similar installation on our colony ship that was my responsibility, I have come to admire it for myself. Your work is amazing and your end product delicious beyond imagining."

"Yes, well." Taken aback by the unexpected flattery, Wissell was not so easily sidetracked. "We're still serving first-meal requests. I don't have time to show you around just now."

He peered harder at his deferential guest. Everyone on board had been briefed with all that was known about the Perenoreans together with suggestions on how to deal with them. Based on what the specialist knew, something appeared to be absent from this Couthad's attire. The spiraling garb was eye-catching, just as in the images he had seen. Was he missing something important? Then he relaxed. There was no translation gear.

"I entreat you, Nurturesque Wissell. For days now, I have delayed asking questions of you out of fear that my lack of understanding would only magnify my ignorance. Please do not amplify my shame by turning me away!"

"Well, I . . ." The specialist hardly knew what to say. His visitor's command of Standard was flawless. No one had ever "entreated" him before.

"All right. I suppose my team can manage without me for one morning. Escoffier knows they've done so before. You say that your responsibilities on the *Eparthaa* were similar to mine on the *Enterprise*?"

Couthad accompanied his nod with a hand gesture that was the Perenorean equivalent. "I am responsible on DiBor for the providing of all synthesized nutrients." Gazing past the specialist, the alien visitor eagerly scrutinized the complex of food-making apparatus. "While at first glance it would appear that our machinery is somewhat different in design, save for specific supplements such as trace minerals and vitamins the nutritional requirements of our respective species are not so very different."

Wissell was agreeable. "No reason why we shouldn't be able to eat each other's foods. We're both carbon-based omnivorous life-forms." He chuckled. "I'll let you in on a little something, Couthad."

The alien's command of the specialist's language did have its limits. " 'Let me in on' . . . ?"

Wissell lowered his voice. "A little joke among the fraternity of nutrient-synthesizer specialists. You do have jokes among your people, don't you?"

The round mouth could not flatten to form a smile, but the alien managed to give an impression of the expression nonetheless. "The Perenoreans have as well-developed a sense of humor as any species we have ever encountered. Most intelligent species seem to appreciate humor of one sort or another." His gaze narrowed. "Except, perhaps, for the Dre'kalak."

"Yeah, from what I was able to see and learn of them, they didn't strike me as an excessively jovial type, either." He moved a little closer. "See, every time the Federation makes first contact, the first thing everyone on the vessel wonders about is whether the new race will be friendly and what they'll look like. But for food specialists like myself, we have this secret desire—never fulfilled, of course—to wonder what they might . . . taste like." He stood back. "Can't help it. It's part of our intellectual and professional makeup, I guess. How about you? Do specialists like yourself among the Perenoreans have similar feelings?"

Couthad ruminated a moment. "No. We do not wonder what other intelligent species might taste like. We do not think about eating every animal we see."

"Oh." Wissell was disappointed. "Ah well, no matter. It was just a joke." *One that has fallen decidedly flat,* he told himself. Turning, he gestured grandly at the equipment complex behind them. Outside, the last first-meal eaters were finishing their breakfast. In a little while it would be time to gear up for second meal. The specialist was confident his subordinates could handle the routine process. "What would you like to see first?"

Couthad did not hesitate. "I would very much like to view

your system for synthesizing and reconstructing the genomes that form the basis of the food products you provide."

Wissell blinked. "Excuse me? We, uh, we don't do that here. We're given prefabricated supplies of multiple nutritional building blocks. These are broken down by category, then parceled out and reconstructed or rehydrated into specific menu items as requested by the crew." He peered harder at his guest. "You use a different procedure?"

"Yes. Although I am sure it is not nearly as efficient or satisfying. We synthesize the genomes necessary to brew ten to twenty basic organic soups. Using these broths by themselves and in combination with a large variety of additives, we can duplicate almost any foodstuff required or requested. The availability now of natural ingredients on DiBor and additional imports from SiBor have greatly expanded the nutritional options available to the colony."

Wissell studied his visitor. "What you're describing is beyond anything I trained for. I just supervise the combining of prefabricated nutritional components. We don't build them from scratch here. Certainly we don't work at the molecular level." He frowned. "You sure you're just a food specialist?"

"Certainly that is what I am," Couthad readily admitted. "Of course, I am also a qualified molecular biologist and trained DNA recombinant engineer."

"Of . . . course," Wissell murmured. "I've got to say I'm impressed. I wish I could—"

The alien quickly interrupted him. Out of sheer enthusiasm, the specialist was certain, and not out of disrespect.

"I could teach you how to create food through this process. We would need to make adjustments to your equipment. I think it could be done."

"Hmm. Start with the genomes of the food base, you say? I could probably get a paper out of that, could distribute it throughout Starfleet. Might even be a promotion in it." Wissell looked behind him, back into the depths of the food processing complex. "I'd have to work closely with you every step of the way, Couthad. Security."

"Oh, certainly, certainly! I would not think of trying to do such a thing by myself. I would merely make the necessary suggestions to you. You could then run them through your computer to check on their viability and safety before actually implementing them."

"Sounds promising." The initially wary specialist began to reflect a little of his visitor's contagious excitement. "This is very thoughtful of you, Couthad. Really. Very thoughtful."

The Perenorean food specialist lowered his gaze. "I am only seeking to return the graciousness your kind has extended to mine, and that you have shown me personally."

Wissell chuckled to himself. "But I haven't shown you anything yet. We've only talked. You've just had the most superficial glance, and from a distance." He gestured at the processing complex behind them. "Don't you want to have at least a quick look around before we start?"

"There will be ample time, and I am sure I will see everything I wish to see in the course of our cooperation. Shall we begin?"

"Absolutely." It took Wissell a moment to find his tricorder.

"You don't mind if I make a record of our collaboration? I don't want to overlook any details."

"Not at all." Couthad sounded proud. "Anything that will aid you in remembering my small suggestions and serve to underline the usefulness of our work together is welcome."

Wissell responded enthusiastically. "I have a feeling that some of the molecular bio stuff might be a bit out of my league."

Couthad's ears fell limp in a gesture of infinite patience. "I will go slowly and repeat where necessary so that you do not miss anything, friend Wissell."

"Sir, two of the Perenoreans are here."

Montgomery Scott noted that Ensign Pearson was dirty and apologetic: both good. A dirty engineer was a busy, working engineer, and the man's apologetic tone indicated he was anxious to get back to what he had been doing. Scott was busy as well, and he understood why the visitors were being fobbed off on him. It had been his idea to bring them aboard in the first place. So now, in addition to seeing to the smooth operation of the *Enterprise*, it was also his responsibility to attend to any of the Perenoreans who were cleared for engineering. Each of the ship's section heads had been prepped on how to handle the interminably inquisitive guests—"inquisitive" being the polite, formal adjective that had been employed in the reports. Had he been asked his opinion, Scott would have said the Perenoreans more properly ought to be described as "pests."

Which was another way of saying that he had work to attend to, and that he did not especially look forward to having to play tour guide to a couple of the visitors. But orders were orders, and diplomacy was diplomacy.

Now if the three of them could just sit down around a bottle . . .

They were waiting for Scott outside. By now everyone on the ship had learned the subtle differences that allowed an observer to determine the sex of Perenoreans. A good thing, too, Scott decided as he regarded his guests, since their attire was essentially identical. The male introduced himself as Jiwarth, the female as Ouroum.

"We would be most interested in comparing your antimatter system with ours, as typified by the drive system installed on the *Eparthaa*." Jiwarth's golden pupils focused hopefully on the *Enterprise*'s chief engineer.

I'll bet you would, laddie. Aloud, Scott said, "And I'd love to show it to you and discuss it in detail, but there are sections of the ship that due to security reasons are off-limits to visitors."

The pair of Perenoreans exchanged a look, then turned back to their host. Mechanical translator notwithstanding, Ouroum succeeded in sounding downright hurt.

"Is it then decided that we are not trustworthy? After all that our species and those of the Federation have accomplished by working together?"

" 'Tis not that." Though no diplomat, Scott could be tactful when the situation demanded. "You should not feel singled out." He gestured behind him. "For security reasons, certain sections of Starfleet vessels are off-limits even to members of their own crew. It's a natural precaution."

Jiwarth sounded confused. "A precaution against what?"

Could it be that these folk had no security procedures on their own vessels, or that the very concept of internal security was unknown to them?

"When you're visiting Starfleet Headquarters, you can ask the regulation writers. I do not make the directives; I just follow 'em." He gestured to his right. "While I cannot show you the facility you're askin' about, I don't see why we can't have a look at a dimensional model. There're no regulations against that."

Ouroum was visibly disappointed. "We are of course happy to partake of any new knowledge however it is offered to us." Her ears went straight back. "It may be that the viewing of schematics combined with your own unequaled insightfulness into the actual physics and mechanisms may be sufficient to answer our questions."

Scott nodded encouragingly. "I'll show you everything I'm allowed to show you. We don't have to worry about what's been designated as off-limits because the ship's computer will automatically block those from appearing."

Jiwarth mimicked the nodding, careful to bob his head in the best human fashion. "We will just have to substitute informed suppositions as best we can, then. And if you are constrained from answering certain queries, we will of course understand."

The problem, as Scott soon discovered, was not that they asked questions he was forbidden to answer. It was that they were soon asking questions he did not understand. While the mathematics and mechanics of warp-drive systems were well known, it quickly became clear that both of the Perenorean engineers had a grasp of the theories behind them that was far in advance of anything Scott had studied. As tactile holo-images hovered in the air between them, the Perenoreans did not hesitate to repeatedly thrust their spatulate-tipped fingers into the intricate mix of colored lights and lines.

"If your dilithium system was realigned *so*," Ouroum declared with conviction as she moved one bit of engineering around in midair, "wouldn't that improve control, especially at maximum warp?"

Scott squinted at the consequences of her deft manipulation. "Well now, I dunno, lassie. It's one thing to reposition components within a schematic and quite another to reengineer and rebuild them in reality." He stuck a finger into the depths of the complex projection. "For example, what's to keep this from suffering from critical overload due to the increased power it's now bein' asked to manage?"

Standing beside him, she scrutinized the small but critical subjunction he had singled out. Her eyes seemed to glow as if their very reflection was analyzing the problem he had posed.

"A just concern, Mister Scott." Once again long fingers slid into the projection, their double joints allowing them to move and manipulate it in ways no human could manage. "It would take a complete redesign of the redirect to handle the new load."

"Exactly. That's why it's not possible. Because there's no

way to redesign the module in question without having to re-work the entire dilithium lensing system."

"But Mister Scott." Her fingers never stopped moving, even as she protested softly. "I am reworking it even as we speak."

He chuckled condescendingly. "Now, lassie, I'm sure on your own ship where you're intimately familiar with the work-ings it might be possible. But this is the *Enterprise*. She's the latest and most-advanced vessel of her kind. Her inner work-ings are alien to you and to ask anyone to do something like what you propose is . . ."

His words trailed away and his lower jaw dropped slightly as a pair of tiny green lights appeared in the depths of the float-ing projection. Leaning closer, he stared at the glowing seg-ment from which she was carefully withdrawing her left hand.

"C'mon now—it's not possible." He stared over at the Pere-norean engineer. "Starfleet engineers and physicists have been working on refining the lensing system for years. Nay, for de-cades." He turned his gaze back to the interior of the hovering schematic. Both green lights glowed bright and strong where her manipulative digits had been a presence. "You cannot fix such a problem in a matter of minutes!" Even as he voiced the objection, he had sufficient presence of mind to reach for the nearest wall and hit a control so that the design impossibility he was looking at would be recorded.

"Of course, I cannot be certain of the ultimate efficacy of my poor efforts, Mister Scott." Ouroum's tone was modest. "But I think if you can make the necessary adjustments to the

Enterprise, you will find that the next time you engage your warp drive, your energy efficiency will have improved by ten to twenty percent, with no loss to the dilithium structure."

Standing nearby, Jiwarth said, "Or more. It's really just a matter of seeing a new way of controlling an old design."

Scott frowned at the holo. "'Old design.' Now wait a minute here, my over-fingered friend. Didn't I just tell you that the *Enterprise* is—"

"Look at this hydration system." Ouroum had moved around to the far side of the projection and was singling out a section filled with conduits and pipes. "It must supply the whole ship. Allowing for access for necessary maintenance and repair, there is substantial wasted space and duplication."

"You don't have to tell me about the ship's hydration setup." Scott walked around to join her in scrutinizing the indicated sector. "I know it intimately. Too intimately, if you must know." He squinted at the hovering imagery. Unlike the ship's warp system, nothing about hydration and filtration was off-limits. "I don't know about you two, but I'm tired of squintin' at a projection. I'm sorry I can't show you the drive nacelles and related sections, but we *can* have a look at anythin' that involves water." He smiled at the wide-eyed Ouroum.

"So you're sayin', based just on what you can see in this projection, that you've already been able to identify areas of wasted space?" She nodded. "Do I presume correctly that you have an idea or two in that slender little skull of yours on how to improve it?"

"We are always happy when we can make suggestions for improvements!" The Perenorean engineer was clearly delighted that her host was willing to listen.

"Then why are we standin' here? Let's go."

Jiwarth chattered away as he paced the chief engineer on his right. "It is very good of you, Mister Scott, to give us this opportunity to be of some assistance. We wish nothing but to try and find ways and means of repaying you and your colleagues for this magnificent opportunity that has been granted to us."

"Well, if you can help me improve hydration and filtering so that the ship has access to better water more efficiently, then I'll be the first to toast your suggestions!" After a moment's pause, Scott added less exuberantly, "With the first freshly filtered water that passes through an improved system, of course."

13

asteresque Founoh watched carefully as McCoy passed the episealer across the open wound. Now that the edges of the gash in the crewman's calf had been drawn together, the doctor carefully sprayed a few puffs of synthskin over the wound. Drying almost instantly, the artificial skin would not only keep the wound closed, but except for a slight sheen, would match the surrounding undamaged surface perfectly.

"We're done, Harper." As the crewman sat up, McCoy smiled and slapped him on the back. "That should be fine in a few days. A week and you'll never know you cut yourself."

"Thanks, Doc."

As the repaired crewman donned his pants and prepared to check out of sickbay, McCoy led Founoh to the main medical console. Taking a seat, he gestured for the Perenorean to sit down opposite. His guest had no trouble accommodating his slighter frame to the human furniture. Truth be told, given the flexibility of the Perenorean form, Founoh could probably have made himself comfortable on the console.

"Drink?" Reaching under the console, McCoy fumbled around in a small cabinet. "Coffee, fruit derivative, green tea?"

"Just water, thank you, Doctor. Something in the first makes our eyes hurt and in the second there are compounds we should still analyze for safety. I do not know the third."

"Green tea's not bad." McCoy opened a container and waited for it to chill. "Fellow crewmember introduced me to it. We differ on a lot of things, but not on the merits of the stuff." He handed his guest the container of water. "Here. The coolant will chill it to what it thinks is the proper drinking temperature based on the body temperature of whoever's holding it. You can disable the function by sliding your finger along that embedded strip on the side."

Founoh proceeded to do so. "Room temperature will be fine." After enjoying a swallow, he indicated the surgery. "You are fortunate that the simple structure and design of your bodies allows you to make such rapid diagnoses and to apply the applicable treatment almost as fast."

McCoy said, "I suppose we are. When I was on the *Eparthaa* I did notice that it took longer to treat what we would consider to be minor wounds. I didn't have a chance to watch you perform surgery. Despite the outward similarities conveyed by the principles of convergent evolution, your internal makeup is more complicated than ours?"

"I believe so." One hand gestured fluidly in the direction of

McCoy's computer. "We could confirm such discrepancies if I could access the biological records contained in your ship's computer." He lowered his head. "But as you know, that access has been denied to us."

McCoy pondered for a long moment. Then he set his drink aside and swung around in his chair. "The medical section has access to the ship's main library computer, of course, but it's also accessible as a separate entity. It has to be able to operate independently in the event of damage to the main." His fingers moved over instruments and a holo-screen appeared above the console. "What would you like to know? Beyond what you can see with your own eyes and what you've already learned, of course."

Founoh edged his chair closer to that of his host. "This is very kind and thoughtful of you, Doctor."

McCoy smiled. "You already know what we look like on the outside. I can't see the harm in letting you see what we look like on the inside. I just wish I had access to equivalent information."

"But you *can* have that, Doctor McCoy." From a pocket in one of the swirls of his garb, Founoh withdrew a small device. It was compact, sleek, and like every other instrument of Perenorean design, almost devoid of external controls. "This would be our equivalent of your medical tricorder."

McCoy examined the instrument. "I saw them in use on the *Eparthaa* and also on DiBor. It's smaller than the ones we use, and with what looks like a much cleaner interface." He smiled again. "I just supposed that's because it's not designed to do as much."

Without commenting on the implication, Founoh slid two fingers along one featureless side of the device. A second tridimensional projection appeared alongside the one that had been called forth by McCoy. The senior Perenorean physician gestured.

"We can compare information side by side and you may record anything that appears. By the time we reach Earth, you will be the leading expert on Perenorean physiology."

"I thought I was already." McCoy worked the interface. "Can I record everything, you say?"

"Everything and anything. The sharing of this knowledge is but a small gift from my kind to yours." The round mouth flexed. "Besides, who knows but that one day you or your fellow medical experts may again be needed to aid injured Perenoreans."

"Hopefully not ones fleeing from the Dre'kalak." McCoy shook his head at the memory. "They really did go all out to convince us that you were dangerous. Maybe your eagerness to help can be overwhelming. I'm looking forward to learning all I can from you about your people."

"And about your own." Founoh gestured agreeably.

"Excuse me?" McCoy's joviality and smile gave way to obvious puzzlement. "I already know about humans."

"Of course you do," Founoh said pleasantly. "It is just that in the time I and the other submasteresques have spent in the company of your species, we have noticed one or two things that you seem unaware of and where a small suggestion or two on our part might prove useful."

"Is that so?" McCoy bridled. "What 'one or two things'?"

"Well, this matter of some of you not being able to sleep as well as others, for example." As he spoke, Founoh manipulated not only his own projection, but also the one McCoy had called up from the medical console. "In our bodies, neurotransmitters communicating with our equivalent of the human cerebral cortex fire at a more constant rate. This results in Perenoreans spending almost eighty percent of our sleep time in what you call deep sleep, where humans usually spend about twenty. As deep sleep is the most restful and useful kind, we awake feeling more invigorated than you do—and with having spent considerably less time asleep."

McCoy was duly impressed. "Maybe that's the reason, or at least a contributing factor, to why you people are so intense all the time; always on the move, always asking questions." When his counterpart did not comment, the doctor continued. "Are you telling me that you have some kind of secret formula or something that could improve the quality of sleep for humans, and maybe also let us get by with less sleep?"

"It is not a secret. With us, this extended deep sleep comes naturally. There are physiological underpinnings. It is not a cultural achievement, but a matter of biochemistry. Biochemistry, as you know, can be manipulated to produce desired results. Even for something as seemingly simple as extending sleep periods."

Gesturing at the holo-image being projected by his instrument, he enhanced the interior of the skull. Longer and narrower than a human brain, in the angular Perenorean skull the critical organ was set on a vertical rather than horizontal axis. But it did not look smaller than a human brain, McCoy decided. It would be interesting to compare volumes and see if it was the same size.

"Let us work together, Doctor," Founoh proposed. "We will compare neurological pathways, chemical composition, brainwave activity and centers, and perhaps when we are through with this we will have found a way for humans to enjoy a deeper, sounder, more rejuvenating rest."

"Hell yes. After all, it's just sleep we're talking about. What could be the harm?"

The cabin door was open, yet Uhura still hesitated. Faced with a similar situation involving members of the crew, she would never have walked in. Was it permissible to enter when a door was open? Was it perhaps even an invitation? In that case she would be derelict in her duty if she did *not* enter.

She came to a quick decision. Communications were her specialty, and she fully intended to communicate. But she would do so as unobtrusively as possible so as not to startle the guests.

Part of her current assignment was to make regular checks to ensure that the Perenoreans were adequately communicating their needs. Having already made contact and exchanged pleasantries with half their number, she anticipated no difficulty with the couple occupying this cabin.

As she eased into the cabin, she could see that the two Perenoreans who had been assigned to Ensign Servantes were not sick or injured. Instead, they were so engrossed in studying the pulsating readout from the cabin's information terminal that they failed to notice her approach. Not wishing to startle them, Uhura stood quietly and waited for the pair to finish their immediate research. As she waited, casual curiosity impelled her to strain forward to see what they were doing. They couldn't read standard text, of course, and as no audio translation was audible she assumed they were just enjoying whatever images they had managed to call up. Whatever it was had to be localized and for security reasons they had been denied unfettered access to the ship's main computer. Except . . .

She took another step forward and frowned. While she was no engineer and didn't recognize the schematics the pair were scrutinizing, even a casual glance on her part suggested these were more detailed and elaborate than what one would expect to find in general access.

"Excuse me . . . ," she began.

On DiBor she had seen that Perenoreans could move fast, but the speed with which one confronted her while the other got behind and between her and the doorway was shocking. It happened so quickly she did not even have time to cry out. They had merely changed position with unexpected speed without any threatening gestures.

The female who now stood before her spoke in the familiar exceptionally polite tones that were a characteristic of her kind.

"Forgive us. We did not mean to alarm you. Our reflex reaction was because you startled *us*."

"I'm sorry. I didn't want to disturb you and I was just on my usual rounds to make sure everything is okay." Leaning to her right, she managed to peer around the intervening body of the alien. The cabin's screen had gone dark. "I was wondering what you were studying so intently. It didn't look local."

The male had come around to rejoin his companion, leaving access to the door unencumbered. "We were playing." He made a gesture indicative of humor. "Humans are not the only ones who enjoy amusing themselves. Despite what some of you appear to think, we do not spend all our waking moments asking questions."

Uhura had to laugh. "I suppose we do tend to look at you all as unrepentant workaholics. What were you playing at— if you don't mind my asking?"

"Not at all. As Yoronar and I are both engineering specialists, we were entertaining ourselves by redesigning this cabin to better suit the needs of our kind. It was simply a matter of importing templates from the *Eparthaa* onto your ship. A harmless diversion." She turned and gestured at the now quiescent unit. "Would you like to see?"

"No, that's all right. I still have other checks to conclude." Uhura indicated the portal through which she had entered. "Your doorway was open."

The male gestured understandingly. "Such openness is in our nature. But we also wish to conform to the mores of our hosts. In the future we will keep it closed."

"It's not necessary," Uhura told them.

"That is good to know," Yoronar replied without committing either to continued openness or newly respected privacy. "You can proceed on your way without concerning yourself about us, Lieutenant Uhura. We are doing fine and there is nothing that we need."

The communications officer smiled. "That's what I expected to hear. It's what I've heard from every one of your colleagues. It's what I hear from all of you every day."

The male tried to smile back, but his mouth simply could not manage the necessary muscular contortions. "We would never do anything that would cause you undue stress. The less trouble we can be, the better we will feel about this wonderful gift you are giving us."

She nodded and bade them goodbye until the next day's check.

Uhura headed straight for Spock's cabin.

"Lieutenant." A quick glance up and down the corridor showed Spock that it was empty. "Nyota, I do not expect to see you while you are on shift."

"Are you going to put me on report?"

"Perhaps not on report." He stepped back into the cabin and she strode past him. The expected kiss that followed as the door to the corridor closed behind them was far briefer and considerably less intense than usual. As he usually had to be the one to break it off, its transitory nature was surprising.

"Something is troubling you." He sat down on the bed

while she took the chair opposite. "I can only hope it has nothing to do with me."

"No," she assured him quickly. "It has to do with our guests."

"I see. My first assumption would be communications difficulties."

She shook her head. "Not unless you count prevarication as a communications difficulty."

Immediately interested, he sat up a little straighter. "Intentional? Or possibly a misunderstanding?"

Her tone turned impatient. "If there's one thing that I, as chief communications officer, have learned about the Perenoreans, it's that they don't misunderstand anything. Their speedy mastery of our language continues to amaze me. Even though I've requested reports, I haven't a single case of linguistic confusion. Spock, I just caught two of them in a lie. They tried to cover it up, and they were pretty clever about it, but I didn't buy it. Although I let them think I did."

"What kind of lie, Nyota?"

"I walked in on them. The door to their cabin was open. An accident, I have to believe. I caught them studying restricted engineering schematics. I only got a quick look—but they were of the ship's weapons systems."

As usual, Spock's expression did not change. But his tone did. "Access to that area has been forbidden to them."

Uncertainty colored her response. "I might have been mistaken, Spock. But I'm fairly confident."

He considered. "Whose cabin have these two been assigned to?"

"Karin Luo-wong." Her gaze met Spock's. "She's a medical orderly."

"An unlikely subject to have detailed engineering specs." He rose from the bed. "The Perenoreans have been denied right of entry to the *Enterprise's* main computer. They should not have access to *any* of the ship's engineering diagrams."

"What do I do?"

He started toward the door and she followed. "I will discuss the matter with the captain. Meanwhile, I suggest you resume your duties as though you have encountered nothing out of the ordinary."

She nodded thoughtfully, then smiled and put her arms around his neck. "Aye, aye, sir."

Ensign Draper was the fourth member of the crew to report in as sick that morning. If McCoy's gut was right as to the nature of Draper's problem . . .

"Hi, Doc. Sorry to bother you, but . . ."

The ensign displayed the same hangdog attitude as those who had come before him, McCoy noted. His face showed the same listless, wan expression. The doctor raised a hand.

"Wait. Let me guess. First, what's your section?"

Though briefly taken aback by the query, Draper responded quickly. "Nourishment and physiological maintenance. I work with Mister Wissell. I'm the primary organizer of the relevant portion of ship's inventory."

"Got it—you're in food prep. I'm going to base a preliminary diagnosis on that."

Draper stared at him. "But Doc, I haven't even told you
what's wrong."

McCoy grunted softly. "Allow me to tell you. I'm going
to assume that one of our Perenorean guests has taken a look
at your work and figured out a better way to do it, thereby
leaving you with nothing to do except ruminate on how your
Starfleet specialty has just been made obsolete and you have
been practically if not officially downgraded from traditional
to outmoded."

The ensign gaped at McCoy. "How . . . how did you know
that?"

The older man eyed him sourly. "Because you're the fourth
member of the crew to come to me this morning with a nearly
identical issue. As a result of some 'helpful' Perenorean intervention, you've suddenly and unexpectedly found yourself
superseded." He cocked his head sideways as he regarded the
ensign. "Or have I got it wrong?"

"That's not the worst of it, Doc." Even as he nodded
his assent, Draper was clearly struggling with a baffling set
of circumstances that had overtaken him with bewildering
speed. "It's that this alien's process for doing my job *is* better.
I don't quite understand how he figured it out, but there's no
denying the results. If they're adopted throughout Starfleet,
his suggestions will save time, resources, and effort." His gaze
dropped. "And as a consequence, everyone with my specialty
will have to be retrained, if they expect to keep their present

rankings. I know it sounds like a *good* thing," he added earnestly. "But . . ."

"I understand." Walking over, McCoy put a comforting arm around the distraught ensign's shoulders. "I'm going to speak to the captain. Maybe these seeming 'improvements' really aren't all that much of an advance on current procedures."

"But they *are*, Doctor McCoy. They are. Or at least, they are in my case. I don't know about what else you've been told." He shrugged, despondent. "I've studied the proposed changes and there's no doubt about it. I'm going to have to retrain or I'll risk dismissal from Starfleet. I just don't know how it happened so fast."

McCoy continued to speak soothingly. "Don't assume anything. That's what I told your colleagues. Go back to your duties. Forget about problematical Perenorean suggestions."

The ensign departed, still downcast but a bit less so than prior to his visit. McCoy watched him leave.

Four cases of acute depression in a single morning. One right after the other, each with a similar cause. He shouted to the nurse on duty, "Ayanda, I'm going to talk with the captain! I want you to notify me immediately if anyone else comes in seeking counseling or treatment for depression."

"Certainly, Doctor. Anything else?"

Having started out, McCoy now paused. "Yeah. If one of the Perenoreans comes in and offers to show you a better way to do your job, tell 'em . . . thanks, but no thanks." With that warning he disappeared out into the main corridor, moving fast and leaving the nurse staring bemusedly in his wake.

"Are you sure about this, Bones?"

Having turned away from his desk, Kirk faced McCoy in the confines of the captain's cabin. While not large, it was more than spacious enough to allow the restless doctor ample room to pace back and forth as he declaimed his thesis.

"I'm positive, Jim. Too many instances in too short a time for it to be a coincidence." Coming to a sharp stop, he eyed his friend and commanding officer. "The Perenoreans are giving the crew, one by one, a severe inferiority complex. This is leading to depression, loginess, and a feeling of uselessness that is not just bad for morale, but it's downright dangerous. I hardly need tell you that a crewmember who feels that they've been rendered obsolete is not one you want to rely on when going into a dangerous situation, much less in battle conditions." He paused for breath. "And that's not the worst of it."

Kirk's expression never wavered. "What is the worst of it, Bones?"

"I believe this is the same syndrome that's afflicted the Si-Boronaans. We've been thinking that because Federation civilization and technology is superior to that of SiBor that we were above that, but I'm starting to get a nagging feeling that we're not. And keep in mind that I've been a booster of the Perenorean cause." His expression contorted to reveal the internal conflict he was experiencing. "If only they weren't so damn insistent on being *helpful*. But I guess they can't stop themselves. It seems to be ingrained in their being, a critical component of who they are. It's either a species-wide attribute—or a species-wide defect."

McCoy's voice took on an unaccustomed intensity. "Jim, based on what I'm hearing from our despondent crew, the Perenoreans are smarter than we are. *Way* smarter. Not hostile, oh no. That's not their way. They may not have a belligerent bone in their multijointed bodies. All they want to do is be useful and show their gratitude. To *help* us." He snorted. "If the Perenoreans can do anything and everything better than we can, the human race will just fade away. We'll give up. Or we'll become the technological equivalent of manual laborers, serving our Perenorean masters. Nice, friendly, polite, kindly, helpful masters . . . but masters nonetheless."

Kirk dubiously eyed his friend. "Isn't that scenario a bit extreme, Bones?"

"No. There are plenty of precedents. Just look at human history. Whenever a more advanced culture comes along, the lesser one inevitably gets swallowed up or just fades away. Even when that advanced culture is acting out of the most altruistic motives. To 'civilize' the natives, or 'improve their standard of living,' or 'bring them the benefits of technology.'"

He leaned toward the captain. "That's what'll happen to us if the Perenoreans get themselves established on Earth the way they have on SiBor. And the scariest part of the process is that the less-advanced culture usually doesn't realize what's happening to it until it's too late. Because they're mesmerized by all the wonderful toys and tech the dominant culture bestows on them. Out of a desire to be helpful, of course, and to improve the lives of their poor, benighted 'friends.'

"I'm not predicting with a certainty that's what will happen. But based on what I'm hearing from the crew, the possibility is significant enough to make me want to say let's think this thing through before we start letting ultraclever Perenoreans and their helpful 'suggestions' loose on Earth."

Kirk was clearly torn. McCoy's turnabout was noteworthy and his passion undeniable—was that reason enough to cause a potentially serious rift with what up until now had been nothing less than a profoundly grateful species? A profoundly helpful species?

The door chime sounded. "Come." Granted admission, Spock strode into the cabin, halted as soon as he caught sight of McCoy, and curiously eyed the quietly seething doctor.

"Not to trespass on your area of expertise, Doctor, but your rate of respiration appears to be as elevated as your blood pressure."

McCoy restrained his irritation at the interruption. "What is it, Spock?"

"I have just come from meeting with Lieutenant Uhura." At this, McCoy made a sound that the science officer chose to ignore. "She reported that she had entered one of the cabins being used by our guests. Though they strenuously denied doing so, it appeared that they had managed to gain access to the ship's main computer."

Hearing this, Kirk immediately set McCoy's concerns aside. "That's impossible. They don't have the necessary biometrics to allow it."

"The lieutenant was positive, Captain. She said that they appeared to be viewing the *Enterprise*'s engineering schematics. Possibly those relating to ship's weapons."

Kirk looked back at McCoy. The doctor's mouth twisted. "Maybe they're just preparing to be helpful, Jim."

Spock's gaze flicked between the two men. "Is this something I should know about?"

"What is going on here?" Muttering, Kirk swiveled in his chair to face his desk once again. "First, Bones says that the Perenoreans are making a raft of 'useful' suggestions that are causing members of the crew to slide into depression. Then he says he believes that they're smarter than us. Now this." Raising his voice slightly, he directed his words to the pickup in the desk. "Computer, have the Perenoreans accessed the restricted areas?"

"*Negative,*" the pleasant synthesized female voice responded without hesitation.

Kirk continued, "Have any of them requested information that has been put off-limits to them; specifically, engineering diagrams?"

"*Negative, Captain.*"

Swinging around in his chair, Kirk asked, "Well, Spock?"

The science officer looked over at McCoy before turning back to the desk. "If Doctor McCoy is correct, then a clever intelligence aware that it has been banned from accessing the *Enterprise*'s main library computer would naturally take steps to conceal having done so." McCoy found himself nodding in agreement as Spock continued. "Either the Perenoreans are ingenious enough to have accomplished such a subterfuge, or Lieutenant Uhura is completely mistaken in her observations."

McCoy took a step forward. "Can we take that chance, Jim? If they're accessing our secure files and we don't even know that they're doing it, and they've managed to hide it from the main computer . . ." He did not need to finish the thought.

Kirk was thinking hard. "We have only Uhura's observations to go on. But that's not enough. I'm not willing to risk a burgeoning relationship with the Perenoreans. Spock, see if you can fully confirm what Uhura witnessed. The visiting elephant may be gone, but it will have left tracks." He shifted his attention to the doctor. "Bones, you really think that if the Perenoreans are allowed to move about freely on Earth, they'll start to take over?"

McCoy chose his words carefully. "I can't predict anything that apocalyptic for sure, Jim. But one thing I think I can say with some assurance: while on Earth or anywhere else in the Federation, they won't stop being 'helpful' wherever and whenever they can."

Kirk was visibly unhappy. "Dammit! You can't fight psychological threats with force."

Spock gazed stolidly past him, his eyes focused on a blank spot on the far wall. "One might even say, Captain, that in its unique and subtle fashion, this state of affairs is more complex than the *Kobayashi Maru* simulation."

Kirk took a moment to study his first officer. "We don't want to offend the Perenoreans. At least not until we can find a way to confirm or deny Uhura's observations. Until then, I'm going to order that computer access of *any* kind to the cabins they're occupying be locked down. And that from now on, the Perenoreans are to have no contact with the crew and that they be allowed out of their quarters only under close supervision." He eyed McCoy. "We can make up a story about there being some sort of potentially species-jumping virus active on board."

The doctor considered a moment, then shook his head. "Masteresque Founoh is too smart to fall for that."

Kirk shrugged. "If he has questions, put off answering them directly. For a while at least. It'll buy us some time until we can think of a better excuse for keeping them penned up. Once we get to Earth, we can arrange for them to be quarantined until Starfleet decides how to deal with them." He looked at his science officer. "Spock?"

"A not unreasonable scenario, Captain. I admit to being far more concerned about Lieutenant Uhura's report and the possibility that they may have accessed the ship's main computer. This matter of them inflicting feelings of uselessness and inferiority on individual crewmembers concerns me considerably less."

McCoy glared at him. "Is that your roundabout way of saying that while the Perenoreans might be smarter than humans, that there's no way they can be smarter than Vulcans?"

Kirk raised a restraining hand before the science officer

could reply. "Please, Bones. Not now." He looked back to Spock. "Vulcan emotional control would render you much less vulnerable to the kind of benign psychological manipulation the Perenoreans are apparently inflicting. I don't know about smarts, but it's a fact that humans are far more prone than Vulcans to suffer from psychological complexes such as inferiority, whether internally generated or imposed from outside.

"So that is another reason for restricting their movements until we reach Earth. Unauthorized computer access aside, the mental as well as physical health of my crew comes before any diplomatic niceties." He smiled thinly. "If the Perenoreans truly want to be 'helpful,' they won't raise any strenuous objections to the new state of affairs."

McCoy nodded slowly. "Even if they don't accept my reasoning, I suppose I can still find ways to stall them until Starfleet can take over." His expression was somber. "And if they don't, we might get our answer."

"Agreed." Kirk rose. "Bones, keep me apprised of any more crew seeking treatment for depression. Spock, get me some answers."

"Immediately, Captain."

Both men departed. Kirk blew out a long, frustrated breath, his mind racing. A number of days remained before they reached Sol. That ought to give them enough time to acquire some knowledge as to what was going on aboard the *Enterprise*. Kirk also couldn't help thinking that in alluding to the *Kobayashi Maru* simulation, Spock had been teasing him in his own way, but there was no mistaking the science officer's point.

Evrenth terminated the surreptitious connection and the view of Captain Kirk's cabin vanished. Turning his slim form around in the human chair, he faced his Perenorean superior.

"What shall we do now? If the humans do not allow us to circulate freely among them while on their homeworld, we cannot be of assistance to its people."

Leaderesque Taell did not have to deliberate. Perenoreans rarely wasted time in superfluous contemplation. He looked unhappy.

"Our good friends and benefactors are about to do themselves harm by refusing us such access. They have already hurt themselves by attempting, albeit unsuccessfully, to restrict our access to their knowledge." He emitted the Perenorean equivalent of a reluctant sigh. "We have no choice. It is our duty as good friends and grateful allies. We must protect them from their own poor decisions." He did his best to put as positive a spin on the situation as he could. "Most of them are, at heart, not illogical. Once they realize that we mean them only good, they will calm down and drop these foolish and unreasonable concerns."

With both seven-fingered hands, Evrenth gestured full understanding. "This is the same irrational fear we have faced among our other new friends, the SiBoronaans."

"Yes." Taell rose. "Continue to quietly monitor as much of Captain Kirk's movements and conversation as possible without letting him or anyone else become aware that it is taking place. Before our movements are restricted, I will inform the others and initiate an appropriate response. It is well that we prepared ourselves for such a contingency."

Again, Evrenth gestured knowingly. "I will never understand why such a response is necessary. One would think that, after multiple such interventions launched from the homeworld have demonstrated the value of our freely given assistance, other newly contacted species would simply and sensibly accept them."

"Yes. However, as we are from a displaced colony ship, these SiBoronaans and Federation peoples have no knowledge of the help we have rendered to other worlds and their eventually grateful inhabitants."

"In the end it will not matter," replied Evrenth. "It will be here as it has been elsewhere. One day, the descendants of their unreasonably suspicious progenitors will stand before us and proclaim their eternal gratitude for the advances and aid we shall freely dispense."

Taell was almost to the doorway. "Without question. And if we persist, one day we will surely also be able to include the inhabitants of the stubborn worlds of the Dre'kalak among those we have selflessly helped."

14

"Captain, cabin twenty-six is empty."

Kirk listened to the report from the security team and frowned. "Try the mess. The Perenoreans like to eat. Once again, when you pick them up, treat them kindly but be firm as you escort them back to their quarters." Movement behind him drew Kirk's attention and he turned. When he resumed speaking, it was more slowly and softly.

"Never mind, Anson. They're here."

The security officer's voice was anxious. *"Shall we come up to the bridge, sir?"*

Kirk briefly hesitated. "No. Move on to the next pair and deal with them. We'll handle the situation here. There are only two of them."

"Yes, sir." The officer sounded dubious but dutiful. *"Anson out."*

Kirk looked on as the two Perenoreans came toward him. Chekov glanced up from the navigator's station while Sulu attended to his work. At communications, Uhura paused in what she was doing to observe the quiet confrontation. At present, the science station was occupied by Ensign Marinsky.

Halting a couple of arm's lengths from the captain's chair, Taell peered down at Kirk while Masteresque Founoh lingered slightly behind. While the Perenorean voice was as subdued as ever, there was a new crispness to his words as he addressed the captain.

"We have learned that you plan to confine us to our cabins on the *Enterprise* until certain decisions can be made regarding our forthcoming visit to Earth. And that this decision was made because of certain misconceptions that have unaccountably taken hold. We also know that our visit to Earth might now be fully denied and that we may be returned to DiBor without being allowed to show our gratitude for what you have done for us."

"What makes you think that?" Kirk replied noncommittally even as he wondered how the Perenoreans had learned of this.

There was no false pride in Taell's response. "We are adept at knowing facts that relate to our survival."

"Your survival is hardly at stake if you're asked to stay in your cabins, or if you have to go back to DiBor."

The leaderesque was not appeased. "We cannot accept irrational restrictions on our movements or on our ability to aid those who would benefit from our suggestions and help."

By now, Sulu as well as Chekov had picked up on the tenor of the conversation. Separately and on their own initiative, both men touched fingers to drawers at their consoles. Reading and recognizing the relevant biometrics, both drawers silently unlocked. Stored within were phasers within easy reach.

Kirk smiled apologetically at the two visitors. There was no reason to worry. If they had been carrying any kind of weapons, numerous alarms would have gone off and the lift in which they had been traveling would have locked up and stalled long before its armed occupants could reach the bridge.

"Respectfully, you'll just have to accept them. Not only are your 'helpful suggestions' unleashing a wave of depression and feelings of uselessness among my crew, but the evidence is clear that you've also been accessing the ship's computer to view materials that were designated off-limits to you."

Taell replied: "Our natural curiosity compels us to acquire new information whenever and wherever it is available."

"That's just it." Kirk's tone hardened. "It *wasn't* available to you. Somehow you hacked into the ship's computer. I hope you haven't done any damage while you were poking around in there."

Taell looked shocked. "We would never do such a thing! We always take the utmost care with property that belongs to others."

"I wish I could believe that," Kirk told him stolidly. "You've lied about being in the restricted files—why should I believe you when you say you'd never do any damage?"

"Because it is integral to who we are," Founoh protested, speaking up for the first time.

Kirk smiled humorlessly. "Then you admit that you've been accessing material that was made off-limits to you?"

Off to the captain's side, Sulu quietly took out his phaser.

"I sense that you are filled with an unreasoning fear." Founoh advanced until he was standing beside the leaderesque. "What harm can our perusal of your stored and somewhat clumsily filed data do you?"

Kirk sat up straight in his command chair. "You and your companions are to be confined to your assigned quarters and allowed out only under armed escort. The computer access links to your cabins have been shut down. Hopefully, this minor misunderstanding can be resolved when we reach Earth. If Starfleet determines that nothing untoward has occurred, I'm sure your visit will be allowed to proceed as originally planned."

The two Perenoreans exchanged a look. "We understand, Captain," Taell finally told him.

Kirk looked surprised but pleased. "You do?"

"Yes." As the leaderesque stepped past the captain's chair, Founoh turned to leave. As he did so, he pulled something small and unseen from within the folds of his attire.

Both Perenoreans took aim and fired at the same time. Eyes widening at the sudden and incredibly rapid movement, Sulu tried to fire his phaser. Alongside him, Chekov was frantically fighting to do the same. Neither man's fingers made it to their respective triggers.

Passing unnoticed by the weapon detectors installed in the ship's turbolifts and on the bridge was a small personal moisturizer that had undergone radical modification. As compact as ever, the simple push-button sprays had been replaced with higher-power emitters as efficient as their design was complex. An engineer taking one of the devices apart would have been amazed at what had been cobbled together out of harmless components scavenged from isolated corners of the *Enterprise*.

The small spurt of fluid turned into a cloud of minuscule droplets before striking Sulu and Chekov. Another struck Uhura. Marinsky was engulfed as he tried to sound a warning. Kirk's right hand was sliding toward the alarm on his chair when he inhaled just enough of the mist Taell had sprayed in his face to be reminded of freshly mowed wheat.

Keeping clear of those they had sprayed, Taell and Founoh stood back to back, holding their small containers out in front of them. No one charged them. No alarm sounded. Design and assembly of the modified sprayers and their rapidly atomizing contents had not been difficult. Their fellow Perenoreans had been able to glean the engineering knowledge from Montgomery Scott, acquired the active ingredients from working with the food-preparation supervisor Wissell, and the necessary information on human physiology from Doctor Leonard McCoy.

Kirk blinked into the silence and said nothing. Then a slow, wide smile spread across his face and he swung his chair around to once more face forward. Eschewing the sidearm that was so near at hand, Sulu returned to supervising the helm, Chekov to keeping track of navigation, Marinsky to keeping watch over science, and Uhura to monitoring communications.

As soon as Taell was certain that the spray he and Master-esque Founoh had unleashed had produced the desired effect, he approached the back of the command chair. When Kirk did not react to his proximity, Taell walked around to the side.

"Greetings, Captain Kirk."

The broad smile having swiftly settled into a permanent facial feature, Kirk blinked up at the Perenorean. "Hi, Taell. Everything going well for your people?"

"Everything is quite satisfactory, Captain."

"Nothing else that you need?" Kirk's expression bordered on dreamy.

"No, Captain. Thank you. We have everything that we need."

"Well, that's just fine and dandy." Slumping slightly in the chair, Kirk half shut his eyes and entwined his fingers over his lap. "We should be arriving in Earth orbit shortly."

"I know, Captain."

For an instant, something like recognition transformed Kirk's expression. Recognition, and the slimmest suggestion of fear. It passed quickly and the all-embracing smile returned.

"You guys sure do know a lot."

"Sadly, we swim in a sea of boundless ignorance, Captain Kirk. But thank you for the compliment. We look forward to greatly expanding our knowledge when we arrive at Earth."

"Yeah," Kirk mumbled. "Great place for expanding your knowledge, Earth." He slid even lower in the chair, as if his mind had lost interest in his muscles. "You gotta 'scuse me. I'm feeling kinda tired alluva sudden."

"Certainly, Captain. One in your position of great authority needs his rest."

In moments, Kirk was asleep. Taell knew that if Founoh's formulation had done its work according to predictions, then the effects of the spray would last for some time. The bridge crew would return to active consciousness groggy and uncertain as to exactly what had transpired. They would be just aware enough to take care of themselves—and to allow them to respond to Perenorean instructions. Then another dose of spray would be administered. It was a pattern that could be repeated without difficulty until they arrived at Earth. At which time, the leader of the Perenorean delegation knew, more rigorous supervision of the crew would have to be instigated.

Given the success achieved through the use of the spray thus far, Taell anticipated no problems.

Yoronar and his three companions encountered no opposition as they made their way swiftly down the corridor. No one challenged their right to be there. The lack of confrontation suggested that Leaderesque Taell and Masteresque Founoh had achieved their goal of rendering the starship's bridge crew compliant.

Scott met them at the entrance to engineering. His gaze darted from one alien to the next. "Well then, my lanky lads, 'tis unusual to see so many of you in one place at one time. My understandin' is that you're usually dispersed about the ship. What can I do for you?"

One of the Perenoreans looked at her companion. "That strange human salutation again, wherein they offer assistance in the most general terms but never seem to follow through on it."

"What's that, lassie?"

Yoronar stepped forward. "Think of the most wonderful aroma you can imagine, Mister Scott. The most attractive fragrance. The most all-consuming scent."

The chief engineer guffawed softly. "I've no idea what you're on about, but that's an easy question. Fresh heather bloomin' in the Highlands, o' course. Why?"

From the twists of his colorful attire, the Perenorean engineer brought forth a small spray container. Though it looked pretty much like the one Scott kept in his locker, he noted absently that it was crowned by a small improvised mechanism that was far more complex than the usual top.

"That is such a coincidence," Yoronar continued, "because it is exactly what we have herein distilled." A delicate finger pad nudged a control on the back of the cylinder.

Alarmed, Scott tried to turn his face away from the emerging mist. A moist coolness settled on his cheeks, nose, forehead, and mouth, tickling his pores and cooling his skin. The perfume that accompanied the dampness possessed all the promise the alien had foretold; the fragrance was honeyed and refreshing. He suddenly felt unaccountably buoyant, as if all the cares and concerns of his job had been pulled from him like a bad tooth from an infected mouth. For the first time in recent memory, he was completely relaxed.

And why not? No need to worry about the engines and such trifles. Not on a modern starship as automated and self-maintaining as the *Enterprise*. Calmness flooded his thoughts, smothering any uncertainty. He'd been working too bloody hard, he had! Take some time to smell the lubricants. Relax, settle down, stand at ease. Engineering instrumentation would warn him if anything needed attention.

He was so tranquilized that he did not mind it at all when the four Perenoreans pushed past him and fanned out through the length and breadth of his engine room.

Spock saw the two Perenoreans coming toward him. As the order to restrict them to quarters had just gone out and had not yet had time to be fully implemented, he thought little of their presence. Somewhere along the corridor or wherever they were headed, they would run into one of the designated security teams who would take them in hand, politely explain the captain's decision to temporarily restrict them to quarters, and escort them back to their cabins.

Though Spock's reflexes were faster than those of a human, the Perenoreans' turned out to be faster. He was not able to react in time to prevent being doused with spray when one of the aliens unexpectedly stopped in front of him and squirted a fine mist into his face. Instinctively he drew back as he prepared to respond physically to the expected assault. But the two Perenoreans simply stepped back and eyed him curiously out of yellow-gold eyes while waiting to see what he would do next.

"It is a new multispecies fragrance we have been working on," the non-sprayer explained. "What do you think of it, Mister Spock?"

The science officer straightened and considered. Truthfully, the fine mist reminded him of the desert flowers his mother used to grow in boxes on the deck outside the family home. Kindled by the aromatic fog, the old memory was almost powerful enough to generate a mist of an entirely different kind.

"It is most interesting, but courtesy demands that before asking for an opinion it should be subjected to more detailed analysis so that I can . . . can . . ."

He sneezed. Loudly. And again. As he turned away, covered his mouth, and continued to violently expel air, the puzzled Perenoreans exchanged a glance. Seeing several crewmembers coming toward them, they abandoned the ship's science officer to what would surely be at most a transient respiratory reaction to the mist and headed purposefully up the corridor toward the as-yet-unsprayed humans. As they did so, one of the aliens withdrew a small pocket communicator from the folds of her clothing and whispered urgently into the pickup.

Spock's sneezing finally ceased just as he stepped out of the lift and back onto the bridge. The peculiar encounter with the two Perenoreans had left him wary and bemused. While insofar as he could tell, inhaling the cloud of mist had left him unaffected save for the uncharacteristic burst of sneezing (and the dredging up of old memories), it seemed a peculiarly atypical gesture on the part of the Perenoreans, their penchant for constant invention and improvisation notwithstanding.

On the bridge, everything seemed normal. Nothing had changed since he had last been on duty. Moving to his station, he said, "Ensign Marinsky, you are relieved."

"Hmm?" The younger officer's reply was barely audible. Seated before the science station, he appeared to be intent on contemplating nothing, his gaze locked on some unseen, distant speck.

"I said," Spock reiterated a bit more forcefully, "that you are relieved."

Blinking and shaking his head, Marinsky finally turned to look up at him. "Oh. Hi, Mister Spock. Relieved . . . ?" Incredibly, he seemed to be having trouble comprehending the simple directive. "Right—thanks. Good timing, sir. Because I think I'd like to lie down for a while." Rising, he shuffled glassy-eyed past his superior. A frowning Spock watched him head for the lift.

"I think perhaps you *need* to lie down, Ensign." Having voiced the admonition, Spock took his seat.

Odd, he thought. Perhaps Marinsky had missed a sleep cycle. His speech had been slow, slightly slurred, and his expression borderline vacant. Turning to the science console, Spock ran through the standard quick check of department operations. Everything was functioning normally. Only when he turned away from the console and back to his colleagues did it strike him that something was very wrong. It was quiet on the bridge.

Too quiet.

Normally there would be at least a little casual chatter. Human volubility was a trait that practically defined the species. Sulu should be discussing matters of tactics or navigation with Chekov. Or Chekov would be issuing periodic updates and casual status reports to Kirk. For his part, the captain would be requesting information on this or that matter of the ship's operation. Uhura would be . . .

Swiveling farther around in his seat and looking toward communications, he saw that Uhura was singing softly to herself. Unusual. Nyota had a beautiful voice, but she quite properly did not employ it for amusement while on duty. No one was commenting on her vocalizing.

His attention shifted to the captain's chair. Staring straight ahead, eyes half-closed, Kirk looked completely relaxed. That in itself was neither unusual nor unprecedented. What Spock found disturbing was that the captain also appeared utterly disconnected from his surroundings. That *was* unprecedented.

Something was very wrong.

Rising, he walked immediately over to stand to the side and in front of the commander of the *Enterprise*.

"Captain, I am troubled."

It took a moment for Kirk to react. Too long. His friend gazed up at him—and smiled. It was a wide, uncaring, contented, lazy smile. As the science officer had already surmised, disconnected.

"Hi, Spock." His smile widening even more, Kirk slid lower in the command chair.

"Captain . . . something is not right here." The science officer looked up and gestured at the rest of the bridge. "Everyone
here is acting abnormally. No one is talking to anyone else."

"Maybe . . ." A frowning Kirk struggled to find appropriate words. "Maybe—they've got nothing to say." His smile
returned, more fatuous than ever.

"Humans always have something to say, even if it is not
worth saying. It is a truism of human culture that the worth-
lessness of subject matter never prevents it from being voiced,
frequently to excess." Spock paused a moment. "To give just
one example, you *always* have something to say. What is going
on here?"

Maybe it was Spock's demanding tone, but Kirk sat up
a little straighter and looked around before returning his attention to the steely-eyed science officer. For the briefest of
instants, the captain seemed alert and himself.

Then he shrugged.

"Everything looks okay to me. Better than okay." He
smiled afresh. "You know, you worry too much, Spock. You
need to calm down. Take it easy. Lean back and smell the
Felaran roses." He slid down in the chair again.

Smell. Putting both hands on the arms of the command
chair, the science officer thrust his face toward Kirk's.

"The Perenoreans, Captain. They were to be confined to
quarters except under designated escort. I just encountered two
of them walking freely about the ship. They sprayed me with
something they called a perfume. Have any of them been here,
on the bridge?" He anxiously looked around. Sulu and Chekov

were still seated at their stations, working silently and grinning to themselves. Uhura was communicating with no one but her inner muse. The science officer returned his attention to Kirk.

"Did they spray you with something, Jim?"

"Spray? Me?" Kirk's expression twisted. Plainly he was struggling to remember. Finally he looked back up at his friend. "I don't recall any spray, Spock. 'Sprayspock'—that has a nice ring to it, doesn't it?" He looked around, once more blissfully happy. "Today everything has a nice ring to it."

"The Perenoreans," Spock persisted. "*Were they here?* Their movements should be *restricted.*"

Reaching up, Kirk tried to place the tip of his right index finger on the end of Spock's nose. The science officer drew back and Kirk sighed as he slumped back into the chair.

"Spock, Spock—always so tense, so controlled. You really do need to . . . lighten up. Enjoy life a little more." He spread his arms wide. "Why lock anybody up in their cabin? There's plenty of room on the ship, and our guests aren't gonna do anything. They're nice, friendly people. Today everybody's nice, friendly people. Even you, you pointy-eared old stick-in-the-mud." His eyelids fluttered and half shut again.

Spock stepped back, regarded the sleepy captain a moment longer, and then moved purposefully to communications. Taking Uhura by the shoulders, he swung her around in her seat, peered hard into her eyes, and shook her firmly.

"Nyota! What's wrong with everyone? What happened here? Did the Perenoreans come in and spray everyone with something? Tell me!"

Loose as a rag doll in his hands, when he released her she finally opened her eyes fully to meet his. Her expression brightened. "Spocky-honey! Where you been?" Her arms went around his shoulders and neck, and her eyes, like Kirk's, remained half-closed. "Slip us a little of that Vulcan sugar, won't you?"

Tenderly, worriedly, Spock disengaged himself. "Perhaps later."

He stepped away from the bridge and into the turbolift.

Who else but the Perenoreans could be responsible? While he still had no proof that their fragrant spray was responsible, the deliberateness with which he had been approached and doused in the corridor seemed to point toward the mist as a causative factor. Yet insofar as he could tell, he remained unaffected. His Vulcan respiratory system differed just enough from that of humans to make such an outcome conceivable.

He needed confirmation. And where physiological variants and their effects were concerned, there was one man on the ship who could provide a response as fast as any computer.

McCoy was in sickbay when Spock arrived.

"Doctor. Much as it pains me to have to say this, I need your advice."

As soon as McCoy turned from where he had been working, a sick feeling spread through the science officer's stomach. The doctor had that same contented, blissed-out, stupid-drowsy smile Spock had last seen on the faces of everyone on the bridge.

"Spock. Really nice to see you!"

If the science officer needed any further proof the doctor had been drugged, McCoy had just provided it. Nevertheless, he pressed on with his questions.

"Doctor, I think everyone on the ship—everyone except possibly myself—has been chemically impacted by an aromatic spray disbursed by the Perenoreans. Even the captain is displaying an inexplicable happiness."

McCoy drew himself up to his full height. His expression darkened, and for a moment Spock felt hopeful. The hope lasted only until the doctor's quasi-insulted response.

"Leave it to a Vulcan to think something must be wrong when everyone else is feeling good. There's no such thing as 'inexplicable happiness,' Spock. Like any other sensation, happiness has an explanation."

"Fine, Doctor," Spock responded. "Think! What could be the reason behind this outbreak of inexpli—of widespread happiness?"

As he leaned toward the science officer, McCoy's voice dropped to a conspiratorial whisper. "Well, I'll tell you, Spock. It's because . . . because . . ." Drawing back sharply, he broke out into a reprise of his earlier absurdly wide smile. "Because everyone is—happy!"

"That's what I thought, Doctor. And that's what I was afraid of." Leaving McCoy to his joy, Spock hurriedly exited the sickbay.

Back out in the corridor, the *Enterprise*'s science officer periodically passed other members of the crew. Without exception, each and every one of them wore the same sappy, self-satisfied smile. Insofar as he could tell, he was the only one on the ship who had not been affected by the Perenoreans' delightful-smelling but—he was now almost certain— ultimately insidious perfume spray. Cunningly, they had not taken control of the *Enterprise* so much as they had rendered its crew apathetic to their presence. In keeping with the Perenorean belief of gratitude, no one had been harmed. Sulu, Chekov, Uhura, even Kirk: all continued to carry on with their duties as usual, if a bit more slowly. The significant difference was that they had been rendered so content that they were now indifferent to the potential threat in their midst.

What, Spock wondered as he stalked the pleasant-smelling but narcotized levels of the *Enterprise*, would the Perenoreans do next? And what, if anything, could he do about it?

Assuming that they had begun logically from a tactical viewpoint, the Perenoreans had doubtless commenced their program of spraying with Kirk and the other senior officers on the bridge, intending thereafter to work their way gradually down the *Enterprise*'s chain of command. Very well. He could and would proceed with his own efforts in similar fashion.

Pivoting on one heel, he went looking for Leaderesque Taell.

15

As luck would have it, Spock nearly ran into the Perenorean commander. Taell was accompanied by his chief medical officer and two escorts. The leaderesque and the physician gripped modified atomizers. To the science officer's quiet dismay, their companions carried not spray bottles but phasers. Taken, no doubt, from stupefied crew who no longer felt the need to trouble themselves with such potentially mood-destroying devices.

The Perenoreans did not waste valuable seconds engaging in useless dialogue, time-consuming questions, or querulous looks. Without uttering a word, Taell and Founoh simultaneously sprayed the science officer right in the face.

The fine droplets of sweet-smelling mist enveloped him from bangs to chin. As he blinked away the liquid, he noted that the two Perenorean officers bringing up the rear had their phasers pointed in his direction.

Coughing hard, he bent double and clutched at his throat. The Perenoreans looked on compassionately.

"Too much went down his throat." Founoh was genuinely sympathetic. "It will take a moment to clear."

Taell gestured apologetically in the science officer's direction. "It could not be avoided. He came too close and . . ."

Reaching up and lunging forward, Spock got both hands around the Perenorean leaderesque's torso. Turning his captive parallel to the deck as he raised the lighter body into the air, the science officer threw the slender form with all his strength. Thrown backward, a startled Taell slammed into his two armed companions. All three landed in a jumbled heap on the deck as the surprised Founoh continued to frantically pump mist into the Vulcan's face. Unaffected by the spray, Spock whirled and fled back down the corridor. By the time the fallen Perenoreans managed to untangle themselves, the science officer was gone around the nearest bend and vanished from view.

Carefully straightening the traditional fabric that encircled his body, Taell gazed down the corridor where the science officer had disappeared.

"That was quite instructive. We thought we might encounter anatomical anomalies among some of the *Enterprise*'s crew. Mister Spock's apparent lack of susceptibility has confirmed at least one such."

"We naturally focused on human biochemistry, as humans comprise the bulk of the crew," Founoh replied. "Even though the records identify him as half-human, some Vulcan component in his physiology renders him immune to the mist." He whistled softly, the Perenorean equivalent of a resigned sigh. "While you secure the rest of the ship, I will return to our lab and make chemical adjustments to the spray. The next time we encounter Mister Spock, I do not believe there will be any further difficulty persuading him to join his human colleagues in carefree tranquillity."

It did not matter whom he encountered or yelled at. Despite Spock's most strenuous efforts to gather some allies among the crew, everyone responded to his increasingly anxious entreaties with the pleasant bemusement of those who have suddenly discovered nirvana only to learn that actual thinking was no longer required of them. They drifted about the ship, some wandering aimlessly while others stayed at their stations as if waiting to be told what to do next. The science officer could envision the Perenoreans would be giving the orders.

The Perenoreans had taken over the *Enterprise*—and without firing a shot.

Her stupefied crew could not have cared less. As far as they were concerned, everything was fine. Things were "peachy," according to one bemused but still on-duty officer. "Apple pie" in order, according to another. "Copacetic," in the words of an ambling and notably weaponless security team member who was one of the few Spock encountered who did not favor cheerful fruity analogies. The crew of the *Starship Enterprise* was utterly convinced that everything was operating just fine.

Moving swiftly and with resolve through the ship's corridors, its science officer felt decidedly different.

Flattening himself against a corridor wall while taking care to keep a wary eye on his immediate surroundings, Spock tried to think of what to do next. As thoughts swirled, he started sneezing again. But there wasn't a spray-wielding Perenorean in sight. A glance upward in the direction of a corridor vent supplied the explanation. Having taken full control of the *Enterprise*'s life-support systems, the Perenoreans were now pumping the disabling mist directly into the ship's atmosphere. The hope he had been holding on to that the effects of their addling vapor might start to wear off vanished under the wave of pleasing scents that came pouring out of the vent.

If they were smart, their next step would be to—

He cut the thought short. If it had ever been in doubt, the one thing that was no longer open to question was the extent of Perenorean intelligence. Recognizing that Spock was immune to their disorienting spray, they would surely by now have taken steps to secure his own cabin. That meant he had no ready access to a weapon. Even if he did manage to get ahold of a phaser and succeeded in surprising the Perenoreans anew, any threat he made could be met by a counterthreat to use the weapons they held against Kirk and other members of the crew. Perhaps even more importantly, they had to be modifying their spray to be used against him.

Ignoring the wall communicator, Spock flipped open a hand communicator, hailing Taell. The Perenorean leader responded immediately, as if he had impatiently been awaiting the call.

"Yes, Mister Spock. I am here."

The science officer knew there was nothing to be gained by trying to conceal his identity. They already knew he was the only one left on the *Enterprise* capable of engaging in coherent conversation.

"Leaderesque Taell, you must cease this interference with ship operations. Your actions are only delaying the inevitable. Once we reach the Sol system and prepare to dock, you will be taken into custody. You cannot introduce your disabling mist into an entire starbase. That is even assuming we can successfully complete the necessary docking maneuvers once we arrive in orbit. Two dozen of you cannot run an unfamiliar starship."

There was no hint of concern in the leaderesque's eerily confident reply. *"But the* Enterprise *is not strange to us anymore, Mister Spock. We have been passengers on it for a fair number of days now. In fact, we are sufficiently comfortable and familiar with its operation that we are even now in the process of introducing some improvements. To give one example, the ship's computer now recognizes us as legitimate users."*

Spock was taken aback. If what Taell was telling him was true, then the Perenoreans had managed to reprogram the security restrictions of the main computer. Such external intrusion into and interference with the most sensitive portion of the *Enterprise* was presumed to be impossible.

As Spock broke off the communication and headed back the way he had come, toward the lower cargo bays, there was no doubt in his mind that if they were given the opportunity to comment on the situation, the much maligned Dre'kalak would say they tried to warn the *Enterprise*.

Warn. An idea suddenly came to mind.

There were only two dozen Perenoreans, but given their extraordinary intelligence and unprecedented ability to coordinate their actions, there were more than enough of them to slowly force Spock into the recesses of the ship. Now armed with phasers, as well as modified sprayers, several of them had taken care to block all access to the shuttlebay.

All that was left were the escape pods. Settling himself into one, Spock prepared to blast free of the *Enterprise* despite the dangers of doing so while the ship was at warp. The vessel should be near enough now to Earth for a lifeboat's signal to be picked up. It took only a moment to prepare the little vehicle for departure.

"Prepare for emergency ejection," he calmly declared. "On my countdown to zero. Three, two, one . . ." He tensed slightly.

Zero came and went, but Spock did not.

He rechecked the controls. "Emergency ejection, priority override. On three, two, one . . ." Again, nothing. Spock considered for a long moment before speaking again. "Ejection failed. Explanation."

The pod's computer responded without delay. *"Ejection command override. Priority command reset."*

Absurd, Spock told himself. The whole point of an escape

pod's programming was intended to ensure that it could carry out its designed function *without* any outside interference: a necessity in the event the ship's main computer was damaged or inoperable. Denying such independence of action contradicted the very purpose of such a craft. He tried a third time.

It was following the fourth attempt that he noticed long, wide-eyed faces staring in at him. Their presence at the airlock meant that the seal around the escape pod was still secure.

His communicator was flashing for attention. Despite the internal tightness he was feeling, his response was as composed as ever.

"How did you reprogram the escape pod system?"

"Someday we will tell you." Half a dozen other Perenoreans assembled behind him, Taell was peering into the escape pod as he spoke into his communicator. *"It is a simple modification with other useful applications besides the present one."*

"I would not call the present modification either simple or useful."

"You speak from the unenviable vantage point of disappointment and discouragement. I am sorry for that, but it is necessary. Please come out. It has been stimulating, but there are more important and pressing matters to attend to. Once you emerge, you will find that all your concerns will be addressed in a satisfactory manner."

"Because you will drug me to the point where I do not care. I do not consider that to be addressing my concerns in a satisfactory manner."

Taell leaned forward until his face was almost pressing up

against the airlock to the immobilized escape pod. *"Well then, we will just have to settle for addressing your concerns in a manner that is satisfactory to us. Rest assured you will not be harmed, Mister Spock. Quite the contrary."* He managed to convey an unblemished feeling of pride. *"I myself have several useful ideas I badly wish to discuss with you."*

"Your dubious attempt at reassurance depends on how you choose to define 'harm.' My definition would include muted awareness, dimmed powers of cognition, and loss of full control of one's mental faculties."

There was no question in the science officer's mind that the leader of the Perenorean contingent was genuinely frustrated. *"We only want to help, Mister Spock. To help the Federation as we have helped others. As we have helped the SiBoronaans."*

Spock met the alien's gaze directly. "So you have 'helped' yourselves to control of the *Enterprise*?"

"It was not a course we would have taken, but we were given no choice. For no reason except for the venturing of several useful suggestions, it was decided that we should be confined to our cabins and held there until some unknown group of Starfleet scientists decided whether or not it would be 'safe' to allow us to continue with our visit. The notion that ignorance and indifference on the part of a few might prevent us from helping the many goes against everything our culture stands for."

Spock could not keep an accusatory tone from his voice. "You are determined against any and all resistance to 'help' even those who do not seek or want your help?"

"Every species to which we lend our advice and assistance

ends up better fed, healthier, and benefiting from all the improvements we provide. These gifts we give freely, expecting nothing in return."

"Except control," Spock quietly countered.

Taell could not contain his growing exasperation. *"We do not 'control' anything or anybody, Mister Spock! We merely give of ourselves when and where we see an opportunity to help. I would think that being the most logically inclined of all the crew, you would understand that."*

Within the escape pod, Spock straightened in his seat. "I understand that 'control' is a matter of reality as much as semantics. Return to your quarters, allow the crew to recover full control of their faculties. It may be that if you are properly supervised, you could visit Earth. Otherwise, you are in violation of at least two dozen Starfleet directives and appropriate steps must be taken."

"On that we are agreed, Mister Spock." Taell stepped back into the semicircle of atomizer- and phaser-wielding Perenoreans. *"Regrettably, steps must be taken."* Turning, he murmured to several of his colleagues. Three of them advanced to aim phasers directly at the airlock.

"You will please come out now, Mister Spock, or we will be compelled to extract you by force. Again, you will not be harmed. Do not attempt to resist. We are well aware, both from research as well as from our extensive personal contact with you, that Vulcans are on average three times stronger than humans. By the same token, I am sure that you are aware that while smaller than your kind, Perenoreans can move extremely quickly. If you attempt to

flee, you will be shot. Of course, care will be taken to inflict as little physical damage as possible."

Several moments passed with no response from the pod. This time it was Founoh who stepped forward.

"Please, Mister Spock. We have harmed no one on this ship. One could easily argue that at the present time, your crewmates are more content and more relaxed than at any time in the recent past. Once we have safely been transported to the surface of Earth and allowed to begin helping other humans, they will soon recover, albeit with memory loss of recent incidents. They will suffer no lingering damage from breathing our calming mist." His voice hardened ever so slightly. *"It would distress me personally if you were to be the first and only one to suffer injury from our need to assert our helpfulness."* Taking another couple of steps toward the pod, he leaned close just as Taell had done. *"I make one personal request of you, Mister Spock. Respond logically."* With that, he retreated to retake his place in the semicircle of waiting Perenoreans.

Another long moment passed in silence, which was then broken by a distinct mechanical click and a hum of machinery as the door to the pod rolled back. The phaser-wielding Perenoreans tensed slightly, but the Vulcan science officer made no sudden moves. It was impossible to tell if Spock was resigned; his expression had not changed. As he walked toward Taell, half a dozen phasers rose simultaneously to track his advance. He halted a safe distance away from the Perenorean leaderesque.

"As I can neither fight nor flee, logically the only thing for me to do is accede to your wishes."

Taell gestured his relief. "*Thank you*, Mister Spock. It would have upset me greatly to have been compelled to injure someone who has helped us so much." Turning, he gestured to his companions. Two of the spray-carrying Perenoreans stepped forward. Eyeing the innocuous containers, Spock did not flinch.

"Please relax, Mister Spock." Founoh did his best to sound reassuring. "It will only take a moment. Like the variant that has been used on your companions, the mist itself will have a most pleasant bouquet. As it takes effect, you will feel no change to your system, either physically or mentally." His round mouth flexed. "Except in a few moments, you will be a good deal more relaxed. Your concerns and your worries will vanish. And you will be able to function and perform all your usual duties normally."

Spock stiffened as the two atomizers were raised and pointed directly at his face. A double dose. They were taking no chances. As both Perenoreans were about to unleash the soothing mist, the leaderesque stepped between them one more time.

"Please, Mister Spock. You are very subtle about it, but I must insist that you stop holding your breath. I know that Vulcans can hold their breath for a very long time. You will please just comply."

Spock slumped. His posture said that there was nothing more to be done. A satisfied Founoh gestured, and in response two blasts of fine mist struck the science officer directly in the face. Closing his eyes, he inhaled. About one thing at least the Perenorean physician-in-chief had been telling the truth. The ill-omened fragrance was nothing short of enchanting. He exhaled.

"Again," Founoh ordered immediately. A second gush of vapor hit the science officer just as he was taking his next breath. For a moment, he stood blinking and swaying slightly. As he moved nearer, the leaderesque closely scrutinized the Vulcan's face. "How do you feel, Mister Spock?"

"Feel? I feel . . ." He sniffed. "I feel—quite well, thank you." As he looked past the leaderesque his gaze fell on the patient, alert arc of armed aliens. "I see weapons. Is there some sort of problem?"

Taell gestured at his armed associates. Sprays and weapons disappeared into bright folds of concealing clothing. "There is no problem, Mister Spock. Just a momentary uncertainty now resolved. Shouldn't you be at your station?"

Once more the science officer blinked. Memory of what he had just gone through appeared to vanish like a crumb flicked from a tabletop. "Yes. Yes, of course, you are right. I should be at . . . my station." He took in his surroundings and his brows drew together. Confusion underlined his question. "What am I doing here?"

"You were kind enough to give us a tour of this section of the *Enterprise*. We thank you. It has been very educational. You don't mind if a couple of my colleagues and I accompany you to the bridge, do you? Captain Kirk kindly agreed to let us monitor your daily operations."

"No—no, of course not. We would be glad of your company." Raising an arm, Spock gestured down the corridor in the appropriate direction.

And smiled.

For the first time since the plan to confine them to quarters had been discovered, Founoh allowed himself to relax.

As the *Enterprise* continued toward Earth, no one thought to remark on the frequent visits being paid by the Perenoreans to every corner of the ship. Why should they? It was well known that the aliens were highly inquisitive and no one on board saw any reason why their guests' courteous curiosity should have to go unsatisfied. Occasionally the word "security" found its way into the thoughts of this officer or that engineer, only to just as quickly fade away again. In fact, everything seemed to fade quickly in an atmosphere dominated by warm feelings, excessive politeness, general contentment, and the lingering fragrance of soporific mist.

In his brief sojourn as captain, Jim Kirk could not remember a time when managing his duties had been so stress free. Chekov was happy to leave navigation to the ship's computer. Sulu hoped that nothing hostile presented itself, as he was in no mood to fight anything. Uhura didn't even bother to monitor communications. Earth? Starfleet? There would be plenty of time for casual chitchat once they arrived. Why waste perfectly good relaxing time in repetitive communications checks? Spock . . .

Spock spent most of his time at the science station, doing as little as possible.

The laid-back attitude of the crew stood in sharp contrast to that of the Perenoreans. They were all over the starship, probing every corner and questioning the purpose of every instrument no matter how seemingly insignificant, asking questions, examining and recording readouts. Having acquired access to the main computer, they queried it constantly. Having gained the full cooperation of the crew, they peppered specific personnel with endless queries; none were ignored, and no access refused. Everyone got along just fine.

While replies to the Perenoreans' questions might have been lethargic, none of the responses the crew supplied to Starfleet upon entering Earth orbit were similarly sluggish. When they occasionally showed a tendency to slide toward incomprehensibility, there was always a Perenorean at hand to coax a clearer response from the bridge crew. Sulu had no difficulty docking the ship—not with computers to do most of the work and an attentive Perenorean by his side to correct his minor mistakes.

The presence of the Perenorean delegation on board was already known to Starfleet. All that remained was for them to be processed and then shuttled down to Earth. There they would be dispersed to scientific centers and learning centers scattered across the planet. Not only would they be able to ask any amount of questions, they could immediately begin to share their suggestions for improvements with their human hosts.

As for the crew, the Perenoreans believed any differences of opinion as to what might have happened in those final days prior to arriving at Earth would wither with time. None of the officers who had once been aware of the potential "danger" posed by letting Perenoreans run free on Earth would be able to dredge up an inkling of a memory of that supposed threat. Confused and uncertain as to the meaning of something they could not properly recall, they would choose not to dwell on it. Uncomfortable with a notion doomed to linger forever on the edge of understanding, they would set it aside. Left unchallenged, the aftereffects of the mind-deadening fragrance that had been circulated through the ship would prevent full recovery of relevant memories.

On the bridge, Taell put a seven-fingered hand on Kirk's shoulder. The main viewscreen showed a clearly visible Starfleet dock. Maintenance teams were already moving toward the starship.

"It is time to go, Captain."

"Go?" Still seated in the command chair, Kirk looked up at the Perenorean leaderesque. "Go where?"

"Official clearance. You, Doctor McCoy, and Mister Spock are to escort us. Once we have been passed through the last checkpoint, your responsibilities toward us will be considered fully discharged. Aren't you looking forward to going down to the surface for some much-needed and well-deserved rest and relaxation?"

Smiling beatifically, Kirk rose from the chair. "I don't see how I could get any more relaxed than I've been for the past—

how many days has it been since we left DiBor?" He shrugged. "Doesn't matter. It's been a pleasure having you on the *Enterprise*, Taell. All of you friendly little furry guys."

"We of the DiBor colony look forward to a long and mutually advantageous relationship."

Kirk put his arm around the Perenorean's narrow shoulders. "You need to come with me to Iowa. Great bars in Iowa. Lotta memories there." His expression twisted, as if the thought of memories was on the verge of conjuring up unsettling ones that had nothing to do with cornfields and alcohol. Then he inhaled again of the slightly cloying but soothing air of the bridge and his facial muscles relaxed.

Lilacs, he thought. *Always liked lilacs. Yesterday it had been hibiscus.*

They joined McCoy and Spock in the airlock. The science officer was smiling contentedly. For the second time that morning, Kirk found himself slightly disconcerted. Spock did not smile. But it wasn't as if he was frowning or angry, was it? If his mouth was going to take a break from its usual set, why not into a smile? Kirk beamed as broadly as he could manage. If the science officer wanted to engage in a grinning contest, he would not find James T. Kirk wanting.

McCoy was beaming, too. Not the Perenoreans. They couldn't smile. Not with those silly permanently puckered round mouths. But they seemed happy enough. This pleased Kirk. The *Enterprise* had arrived safely, they were home, and everyone should be happy.

With the Perenorean delegation chatting amiably in their

own language and clustering behind the three officers, the group left the *Enterprise* and ambled into the transfer corridor. Espying a barrier at the far end, Taell and Founoh moved up to stand beside Kirk.

"What is this obstacle before us?" Though calm as ever, there was a touch of uncertainty in the leaderesque's voice. "Have we not been granted preliminary clearance?"

"What, that?" Kirk gestured carelessly at the closed portal ahead of them. "Normal operations. While we wait here, the air in this corridor is being checked for possible contaminants we might have picked up on our journey even as it's being continuously refreshed. Standard hygienic procedure for anyone who's returning to Starfleet and Earth from outsystem." Leaning toward the leaderesque, he put one finger to the side of his nose and whispered conspiratorially. "Never know what kind of potentially dangerous pathogens a starship crew visiting a new system or two might inadvertently acquire."

McCoy nodded agreement from nearby. "Even though it's unlikely an alien pathogen could infect a human system, Starfleet will never take that chance."

Founoh spoke, but not to reply to the human doctor. "What he says makes sense, Leaderesque. As the captain says, the delay is doubtless part of their routine disembarking procedure. Returning to the *Eparthaa* from visiting another world, we would do the same."

Taell tried not to show his impatience. "We need to get off this orbiting station and down to the surface, where we can begin to irrevocably ingratiate ourselves to more important personages." He indicated their cylindrical surroundings. "Now that we are off the *Enterprise* and away from its enclosed recycled atmosphere, the effects of the mist will begin to wear off."

"Yes, yes." Founoh was unconcerned. "Their memories as to what occurred will remain compromised. Even if there is some partial recovery, we will be well established on their homeworld and will have made indispensable ourselves, our knowledge, and our suggestions."

"Helpfulness always," Taell concurred.

"Helpfulness first, last, and forever," Founoh added. "It is our destiny to provide assistance to those who, no matter how intelligent and well meaning, and through no fault of their own, simply do not see things as clearly or as quickly as the Perenoreans."

"Speaking of mist . . ." Mouth flexing, his ears going straight up, Taell sampled the air in the corridor through the olfactory organs located on the underside of his ears. "Do you not sense an increase in ambient moisture?"

Founoh took a cursory sniff. Behind them, an increasing number of their cohorts were doing the same, turning in several directions as they checked the air from different angles.

"Perhaps the humans and other occupants of this outpost prefer a higher humidity than they maintain on their ships?"

Taell sounded dubious. "Why should the moisture content of the air they breathe be different on a station than on a starship? One would expect consistency."

In response to the sudden rush of incoming damp air, the *Enterprise*'s officers blinked in rapid progression.

So did the Perenoreans.

Starting to sway, Taell eyed the science officer uncertainly. Then his eyes grew very wide indeed.

"But—but you were under the influence of the spray!"

Founoh had been forced to take a seat on the floor of the corridor. "The modified mist that was used on you was specifically tailored to target the Vulcan respiratory system."

"But—how . . . ?" Taell had also dropped to the floor. So had the majority of Perenoreans as one by one they were rapidly overcome. Behind the leaderesque, they had been joined by Kirk and McCoy.

Falling to his knees, Spock was also in the process of passing out. His unnatural smile had vanished, to be replaced by the familiar Vulcan expression of calm resolve.

"Perhaps," he murmured in a sly echo of something the leaderesque had said to him days ago, "someday I will explain."

Before he could continue, the level of anesthezine gas that had been injected silently into the corridor reached a concentration that barred consciousness as well as conversation.

16

No detail was overlooked to ensure that the Perenorean delegation would not be able to make or, more importantly,
implement any helpful suggestions while they were being
transported back home. The section of the *Enterprise* where
they were quartered had been sealed off from the rest of the
ship as completely as it was possible to do so. It was made very
clear that serious consequences would accrue to any member
of the crew who even tried to open a line of communication to
the secured area, even if only to say "hello."

After analyzing the basic chemistry of the sleep-inducing
mist that the Perenoreans had introduced into the atmosphere
of the *Enterprise*, a Perenorean-specific equivalent was swiftly
synthesized by Federation biochemists. This was then introduced into the air of their collective living quarters to ensure
that they would remain both docile and "suggestion-free" on

the journey back to the SiBor system. With Starfleet taking no chances, they were also relieved of their clothing and personal effects for the duration of the trip. Food and water was provided via an automated delivery system that itself was subject to military-level security.

Thus drugged, naked, and provided with the minimum requirements necessary to sustain life, from Leaderesque Taell on down, the Perenorean delegation offered neither suggestions nor trouble as the *Enterprise* sped through warp space on its way back to DiBor.

Confident that everything was secure and under control, his memories restored by the antidote concocted by Starfleet experts, Kirk finally asked his first officer: "How, Spock? How did you pull it off?"

"I knew it was only a matter of time until the Perenoreans manufactured a spray that would disable me. I was able to send a message to Starfleet. I reported our status and I suggested what should be employed upon the *Enterprise*'s arrival—what I believed would prevent violence and avoid any suspicion until the last possible moment."

Kirk's tone revealed his bemusement and impatience. "Spock, how was the message not detected by the Perenoreans?"

"It was their own narrow view of what has value that blinded them, Captain. The force field had already been dropped."

McCoy whistled softly. "Jim, the Voyager probe. They probably only saw it as junk."

"Correct, Doctor. I let the Perenoreans believe that they were cornering me in the cargo bays and I was forced into using an escape pod. However, I was able to access the probe and use its communication array to send the message. Starfleet—as the successor to Earth's ancient space programs—listens for any signal from the countless probes that have been launched."

"I was guilty of the same narrow view," Kirk confessed. "I didn't see any value in something so small and primitive."

"But you did have the good sense to listen to your doctor," Uhura observed. "So what happens now, Captain? To the Perenoreans, and to their relationship with the Federation?"

"And to SiBor," Chekov added. "Don't forget the SiBoronaans."

Kirk straightened slightly in the command chair. "Starfleet has decided that for the good of the Perenoreans, as well as for that of the SiBoronaans and the Federation, the Perenoreans are to be confined to their new home until such time as an appropriate means has been found to deal with their dependence-inducing and depression-causing 'helpfulness.'"

"In other words," McCoy chimed in, "they're gonna be quarantined on their new world, and not just on this ship."

Kirk nodded. "Representatives from Starfleet will replace the Perenoreans as advisors to the SiBoronaans, to help them understand their new technologies—without imposing feelings of inferiority on the recipients. No more shuttles, either from Federation worlds or from SiBor, will be permitted to land on DiBor. The Perenorean refugee ship, the *Eparthaa*, will be immobilized along with any shuttlecraft. As for the refugees, they'll be allowed to continue to develop their colony in peace and quiet—but *only* their colony." He turned thoughtful.

"Meanwhile, I think it would be useful for Starfleet to renew contact with the Dre'kalak to explain that we regret the circumstances of our earlier encounter, and that we would like to proceed to open diplomatic relations on the basis of a new understanding. Also," he added dryly, "to inquire if there are any other species who have been the recipients of Perenorean 'help' to whom we might render assistance."

McCoy dourly grunted. "Hopefully the Perenoreans won't manage to build a starship out of leftover settlement materials and any junk lying around until we've figured out a proper way to cope with them."

It was quiet on the bridge for several moments, each officer attending to their respective duties, until Spock spoke up. "Everything seems to be under control, Captain. There is only one thing that troubles me."

Kirk idly glanced up. "What is it, Mister Spock? Something we've overlooked in dealing with the Perenoreans?"

The first officer nodded in the direction of the main viewscreen. At that moment, it showed only a starfield ahead.

"No, Captain. Not the Perenoreans. I cannot help but wonder: What if one day, in the course of carrying out our explorations, we eventually encounter a new species that is a hundred times more . . . 'helpful' than them?"

Kirk said nothing. Neither did McCoy. But the attention of all was fixed on the vast starfield that lay in front of them.

ABOUT THE AUTHOR

#1 *New York Times*–bestselling author Alan Dean Foster's work to date includes excursions into the hard science-fiction, fantasy, horror, detective, and western genres, as well as historical and contemporary fiction. He has also written numerous nonfiction articles on film, science, and scuba diving, as well as the novelizations of many films, including such well-known productions as *Star Wars*, *Star Trek*, the first three *Alien* films, *Alien Nation*, and *The Chronicles of Riddick*. Other works include scripts for talking records, radio, computer games, and the story for *Star Trek: The Motion Picture*. His novel *Shadowkeep* was the first-ever book adaptation of an original computer game. His work has been translated into more than fifty languages and has won awards in Spain and Russia. His novel *Cyber Way* won the Southwest Book Award for Fiction in 1990, the first work of science fiction ever to do so. Foster's sometimes humorous, occasionally poignant, but always entertaining short fiction has appeared in all the major science-fiction magazines as well as in original anthologies and several "Best of the Year" compendiums. His published oeuvre includes more than 130 books.